CONTEMPORARY AMERICAN FICTION

THE GREATEST SLUMP OF ALL TIME

David Carkeet is the author of one earlier novel, *Double Negative*. His honors include the James D. Phelan Award from the San Francisco Foundation, an Edgar nomination from the Mystery Writers of America, an O. Henry Award, and a fellowship from the National Endowment for the Arts. He lives in St. Louis with his wife and two daughters.

The Greatest Slump of All Time

DAVID CARKEET

Penguin Books

PENGUIN BOOKS
Viking Penguin Inc., 40 West 23rd Street,
New York, New York 10010, U.S.A.
Penguin Books Ltd, Harmondsworth,
Middlesex, England
Penguin Books Australia Ltd, Ringwood,
Victoria, Australia
Penguin Books Canada Limited, 2801 John Street,
Markham, Ontario, Canada L3R 1B4
Penguin Books (N.Z.) Ltd, 182–190 Wairau Road,
Auckland 10, New Zealand

First published in the United States of America by
Harper & Row, Publishers, Inc., 1984
Published in Penguin Books by arrangement with
Harper & Row, Publishers, Inc., 1985

Copyright © David Carkeet, 1980, 1984
All rights reserved

A portion of this book first appeared in *Carolina Quarterly* and in *Prize Stories 1982: The O. Henry Awards*.

LIBRARY OF CONGRESS CATALOGING IN PUBLICATION DATA
Carkeet, David.
   The greatest slump of all time.
   I. Title.
[PS3553.A688G7   1985]   813'.54   84-26411
ISBN 0 14 00.7909 2

Printed in the United States of America by
R.R. Donnelley & Sons Company,
Harrisonburg, Virginia
Set in Caledonia

To Anne and Laurie

1

Frank Joiner first notices it when he goes to his right and makes backhand snags of ground balls hit hard down the line. The swift arrival of the ball unequivocally dooms the batter and creates a tiny void in the game. Frank pauses. This in itself is not bad. Every third baseman pauses at such a moment. But in Frank's case the devil seems to find some mischief for his idle hands. It is difficult to say what he thinks as he slowly comes out of his twist-and-crouch. That he is glad—though not surprised—to have stopped the ball so cleanly? That there is a minuscule 1.7 percent chance his throw could go wild? That in baseball whenever one has extra time one must fill it up? Whatever the thought, his brief possession of the ball brings forth a sagging of the spirit which must ultimately be incompatible with success. Significantly, though, his throws to E.T.A. at first base are as good as they have always been, measured by the exact (but incomplete) science of physics. His problem, at the moment, has no visible consequences.

John "Apples" Bagwell notices it during the playing of our national anthem. He stands on the mound, cap to chest, and faces the American flag high above the darkened centerfield bleachers, one of four players in a straight line pointing to the flag. Behind him is his pessimistic catcher, Narvel Adams; directly in front of him is cruel Bubba Phelps, who perches atop second base and flexes his already incredibly tight buttocks on the downbeat of every fourth or fifth measure; and beyond Bubba there is swift Eddie Johnson, the popular center fielder who likes to needle his teammates (but who, in his own words, "needles with love"). Apples mouths the words of the anthem and feels a sense of loss. He does not know why.

Here is why: as a young spectator at ball games, Apples used to pray during the playing of the anthem that nobody would be hurt in the contest. He now believes praying is silly and that that particular prayer was very silly indeed. Thus he feels vaguely ashamed of himself whenever he hears the national anthem. His self-esteem actually declines, though admittedly it is hard to measure these things. It is sad that Apples does not fully understand this simple association.

E.T.A. Whitaker, a myopically self-absorbed first baseman, initially notices it during disputes between Grammock and umpires. Grammock is quick to argue, to defend his "boys," and two or three times a game he pops out of the dugout and trots in little-girl steps into absurd conflict. E.T.A. watches the arguments with the twitching anguish of a youngster whose parents are suddenly screaming at each other over the breakfast table. He feels responsible for every such argument, even for those over plays occurring nowhere near first base.

It is not just Frank, Apples, and E.T.A. They are all sinking fast. In left field, Buford Ellenbogen is saddened by foul balls. Behind the plate, Narvel sees himself not as an accomplished major-league catcher but as a young man who squats for a living. Right fielder Jaime Jan Orguyo van der Pijpers fogs out on high pop flies, barely recovering in time to do something about them. Bubba's hatred of his fellow man has become truly all-consuming, for it now doubles back to consume even him. Rookie shortstop Scrappy Hawthorn remembers—more than remembers; in truth he thinks of little else—that Eddie once unlovingly called him "Dirtbrain." As for Eddie, he often wonders why, when his gliding, swiftly backtracking feet touch the warning track that gives notice of the perilous proximity øf the hard center-field wall, he feels an urge to accelerate and smear his mind on the 404-foot mark.

The truly smart money would not be on this team. The outlook is not brilliant for them. The good habits which have sustained them thus far must eventually buckle under the weight of their depression. Prostrate and ashamed, they will then crawl into the cellar, where they believe they belong for all time.

○ ○ ○

They have noticed it, but they do not understand it, and they cannot stop it. Like gentle territories occupied by repulsive conquerors, they watch their personalities being transformed into ugly, distorted versions of their originals. Apples becomes a champion mumbler and moper, polishing his flatness of affect beyond improvement. Between half-innings of sad but competent work, Grammock criticizes him, telling him to bear down, goddammit, and push off the be-Jesus mound. Apples, his once fiery cheeks now always pale as death, listens and feels each word adding measurable weight to his body. When he returns to the mound, his motion is even more ponderous than before.

3

Frank is different. He plays well at third and looks normal, but his mind is full of spiders. He thinks people are talking about him. On the road, he lurks just inside the door of his hotel room, listening to his teammates going down to breakfast, wondering why they haven't asked him to join them. He hears words that could be about him—words like "am" and "my"—and he aches for acceptance.

Narvel squats and sighs. Then he droops into the dugout and sighs some more as he plops down on the bench and searches for the energy to take off his ridiculous armor, which he once donned with pride. He unsnaps the buckles and he sighs. He just fills that dugout with those sighs. When he looks up, he appears to be watching the game. Actually, he is waiting to cry.

Bubba fears someone is going to break into his apartment on a dark night while he is in bed. The intruder will of course steal from him, but he will also abuse him with words. Bubba feels that the man will have every right to do this.

Eddie is full of surprises. After a good game in which he hits well, he jokes with his teammates on the bus to the airport; later, when the team's flight is delayed by a mechanical problem, he smashes two formica chairs in the airport lounge. He deserves to be watched closely.

Scrappy can't sleep. He awakens at four o'clock every morning as though called by God. He lies awake and stares, then lurches in bed as if having sex with the air. Then he stares some more. His daytime naps debilitate him further. The sleep he loses at night is unrecoverable.

E.T.A. can't concentrate. With each pitch, he must peek up at the scoreboard over the press box to see what the count is. When he fields a ground ball and hurries to first with it, he wonders if any runners are on base. When he showers, he can never remember if he drove to the park or rode with someone else.

Big, blond Buford, once featured in the hometown news-

4

paper for the way he ate six entrees in succession at a Denny's, has lost his appetite.

Jaime, whom Eddie dubbed "the Latino with libido" during spring training, simultaneously explores ancestral Caribbean impotence cures and modern American suicide techniques.

○ ○ ○

But good habits die hard, and good habits get them through April with a one-game lead in the division.

2

Many professional athletes still abstain from sexual intercourse for a day or two in advance of major contests. In some cases, an athlete will abstain for several days. In a handful of cases that are certainly complicated by other interesting factors, the abstinence can last for several weeks or months.

These facts do not comfort Apples in the least. Apples is a fireballer only on the mound. Thus far, his sexual experiences, excluding unassisted self-abuse, have been digressive and unclimactic: hours and hours of hugs and kisses; one or two self-conscious (and therefore rebuffed) forays down this garment and up that one; and, with partners whose passion matched his more closely (though still imperfectly), some fully clothed grinding that at fleeting moments felt like the real thing but more often seemed to him like the mating of two cinder blocks rubbing together.

He missed out. When his contemporaries were groping their way through their sexually instructive teens, Apples, a preacher's son raised in a small town in California's fertile Central Valley, was busy trying to speak in tongues. He would descend to the dark, cool shade under the front porch of the parsonage, and there, shielded by the lattice fence, he would inhale the local fragrance of canneries and cow pies and he would pray. He would pray for hours. He would pray and wait. Once, when his birthday happened to fall on Pentecost, he thought he came close. But later he had to admit to himself that he had forced it. According to the testimonies of his mom and dad and several others in the church, it came upon you with a flash. You didn't have to force it. But for him it never happened. Sometimes after such a failed outing, he would pray for the strength to accept God's will. More frequently, he would stretch his already gangly body out and furiously masturbate on the cool earth, finding the steady success of *those* efforts refreshing. Then he would pray for forgiveness afterward. Those were prayerful times.

Apples lost his faith for a number of reasons, none of them having to do with God: embarrassment over his father's dinky church; bored disgust with the pathetic congregation— worldly losers always waiting for Jesus to ride down on a cloud like Hopalong Cassidy; and bitter envy of his parents' sex life and resentment over the unfair edge held by his father, who preached with horror of sex outside marriage, preached with hot fervor of sex within marriage, and every night made the walls of the little parsonage shake in lawful, joyful copulation.

The loss of his faith was a mixed blessing for Apples. It was sad for him to lose a relationship with, as he had put it up until that time, "the most important Person in my life." At the same time, he could not help thinking, "Now I can get a piece of ass." It was no longer a sin. Nothing was a sin.

He felt such a sense of expectancy with his newfound atheism that every morning he was surprised to find that the sidewalk in front of the house was *not* crowded with females in heat. It struck Apples that when Paul said, "It is better to

7

marry than to burn," he had made it sound too easy, as if all you had to do was say to yourself, "Okay—enough burning, thanks. I'm ready." There was more to it. He would have to seek and find. That was when things became tricky. At nineteen, he felt painfully conscious of his ignorance. The kind of bumbling that is expected of one a few years younger he saw as unforgivable in a man his age. "Geez—where *you* been?" he imagined a potential partner saying as she shoved him away, gathered her things together in a huff, and stormed out the door.

With each passing year, his plight grew more hopeless. Now, at twenty-three, he sees himself as forever virginal. He does not avoid women. On the contrary—he likes their company and is sometimes charming and witty with them. He even engages in the most rudimentary of foreplay, in which the hug and the kiss dominate to a point of extreme mutual tedium, varied with an occasional bit of wistful scraping and grinding. He stops there, because that is all that he knows. He is trapped in his ignorance. He looks at the husbands and fathers on his team—Narvel, E.T.A., Frank, Buford, and Eddie—and wishes he knew all that they know. His self-concept: a man cruelly tricked out of life's full pleasure. His prognosis: more and more of the same, year after year, until the grave swallows him up and the earth chuckles at the amazing novelty of receiving, in this day and age, such a pure corpse.

○ ○ ○

Because he is thoroughly evil, Bubba has the highest on-base percentage in the big leagues. He sees all pitchers, even the ugly unknowns, as over-celebrated pretty boys. His hatred of them is the best hitting coach he has. He can hit any pitch anywhere, if not with power at least with passion, albeit of a negative sort. He can tease a walk out of a weary pitcher, and he knows how to crowd the plate and get nicked in the shirt. He is a classically pesky hitter—a pest, a "skeeter."

Once he is on base, he is no less a torment. He walks off an amazing distance toward second, then barely beats the pitcher's throw to first. Then he takes a tiny lead, stands stiff-legged and nonchalant, as if saying—as he often *does* say, in hotel elevators and airport restrooms, when some innocent happens to glance at him—"What de fuck you starin' at, muhfuck?" and then he flies to second with the pitch, sliding in a violent, last-second dip of his body that brings him popping up to his feet spoiling for a fight. With a runner on second ahead of him, he likes to dance back and forth to block the first baseman's view of the batter. And he would roll to Ogallala to bust up a double play.

Although the season is only a month old, Bubba has been involved in three unusual plays featuring deception, all of them occurring in a single series against Atlanta. In one of them, he managed to pull off a trick he had been considering for years. With the bases loaded in the ninth, the score tied at three-all, one out, and an ignorant-looking cracker reliever working on the mound for Atlanta, Bubba danced off third, filled with demonic purpose but biding his time to see if the count would reach three-and-two on E.T.A., a left-handed hitter. When it did, Bubba undertook to steal home. It was an unusual steal. Rather than delay his break until the last instant, he advertised his intention so clearly that when the pitcher was in mid-windup, he could easily see what was going on. Then Bubba pretended to fall down. The pitcher, all but grinning at this opportunity to get a sure out, completed his windup and threw a soft pitch two feet outside the plate, so that the catcher could take it for an easy tag of Bubba. But, caught up in his lust for the out, the pitcher had forgotten the count. When the ump called the pitch a ball, E.T.A. walked, automatically advancing all three runners, and Bubba's flagrant vulnerability to the tag gave way to instant immunity, *as he had intended from the outset*. He picked himself up and cockily trotted on home, leaping high in the air above home plate and coming down on it with both feet, while the pitcher, grim reality finally dawning on him, reddened and rebuked himself for a numbskull. Bubba's teammates, amused and excited by the play, cheered in celebration of the run. If they had liked Bubba at all, they would have congratulated him more than they did, which was precious little.

In the second game of the series, with one out, Narvel on third, and Bubba on second, Jaime lofted a high fly to left field, on which Narvel tagged and crossed the plate. Two outs, a run in, and Bubba still on second. But wait. Narvel left third base early, before the ball was caught. Everyone in the stadium saw it. The next few seconds would be utterly predictable, they thought. A leisurely throw would be made to third to appeal the call, and when the third baseman stepped on the bag, Narvel would be ruled out for his unconscious attempt to compensate for his slowness afoot. But wait! There goes Bubba, breaking for third as the relief pitcher—the same ignorant wretch of the night before—starts to throw to third. He won't be fooled, not this time. He knows that the ball is in play during an appeal. He knows a runner can try to steal. And Bubba falls down *again*. Finding it hilariously easy, the pitcher hustles over to Bubba and slams the ball between his shoulder blades as he ostensibly tries to scramble back to second. Three outs. The pitcher and the infielders chuckle sadistically as they trot off the field.

But *wait!* Look at them slowing down as soon as they have cleared the foul lines. Look at them turning to one another with anguished questions on their faces, then to their manager, who too late has leaped out of the dugout with vain, frantic instructions. Grim reality dawns again: if Bubba made the third out, then Narvel's run *counts*. After all, the appeal was never completed. Could Bubba possibly have foreseen all this? The players on both teams watch him grin and bug his eyes out as he dusts himself off and strolls over to take his position at second for the new inning. They ask themselves, "Where does he learn this stuff? What kind of wizard is he?"

"Qui?" Jaime says in the dugout.

"Forgit it, Jaime," Eddie says, chuckling as he reaches for his glove, then Bubba's. "You got to be a Ph.D. to understan' that one. Either that or a born criminal."

At bat the next day, after nearly losing his face to a high, inside fast ball, Bubba swung late, with fear, but still managed to get a hit—a grounder far to the left of the second baseman, who scampered after it and got off a throw that pulled the first baseman off the bag. The first baseman and the pitcher, who was in the area ready to cover if necessary, briefly argued the call and returned to their positions. Bubba, still dwelling on that terrifying brush-back pitch, took a short lead off first, eager for the pitcher to get on the rubber so that he could menace him with a longer lead and a hateful glare. But suddenly the first baseman punched him in the stomach with his glove, then fired the ball to the leering second baseman for a trip around the horn. It was the hidden-ball trick, a rare play in which the runner assumes what he has assumed in every serious game he has played thus far, namely that the pitcher and no one else—certainly not the first baseman—has the ball. The play is a deep insult to the runner, and for this reason Bubba hit the first baseman in the face. The benches cleared, but the rest of the fight came to nothing. The first baseman suffered a badly bruised cheek, while Bubba suffered ejection, a four-day suspension, and depression.

○ ○ ○

Big, blond Buford doesn't make decisions. Things happen, and then he decides if they are good or not. He didn't really decide to marry Ellie. He met her in the off-season two and a half years ago at the Tots-'N'-Kids Pre-School. It was sheer luck. E.T.A. was giving him a ride home and had to stop to pick up his son. Ellie, a wholesome, freckled woman and a passionate fan of the game, recognized Buford right away and asked him to a school picnic the next weekend. He went. At the picnic, she asked him to her apartment for dinner the next night. He went there too. She asked him what he would like to do next. He said he didn't know, so she said how about if they got engaged. He said fine. One day three months later, while he was scratching his big head, he suddenly realized that Ellie was going to be his wife. It seemed an okay idea. Ellie picked the wedding date when they couldn't arrive at one by talking about it. Four months after the wedding, it struck him that he was married. He looked around him and felt that all in all it was pretty good.

A year later, after many hours of fruitless discussion, Ellie said she thought they ought to have a baby. Buford said okay by him. In three months, she was pregnant. "Holy shit!" said Buford when it finally sank in. Only this time there wasn't that certain feeling it was good. He still didn't know. Besides, sympathetic nausea had been causing him to match Ellie moan for moan over the breakfast table, further clouding his judgment. Four months into the pregnancy, sonar revealed Ellie was carrying twins. "Holy jumpin' shit!" said Buford, and he said it right away, because he could see them kicking each other right there on the screen. The technician pointed one finger at the screen and one at Ellie's belly and said that this one here was this one here, and that one there was that one there, and Buford wanted him to turn off the machine because it must have been upsetting them, what with the way this one here kept kicking the hell out of that one there.

Ellie patted Buford's beefy hands, which lay inert on the examining table. "We'll manage," she said.

It is important to realize that Buford isn't dumb. He is quick to get a joke and once or twice a year comes up with one himself; he *is* ridiculously quiet, but that's just because he's usually sitting back feeling fat and happy to be a professional ballplayer and a husband to Ellie. Yet he does have trouble sorting out his feelings. Sometimes, he thinks he'll be a good father; he listens to Eddie talking about what he does with his daughter and thinks, "I can do that." Other times, he hates the kids for the way they will make a fool of him and turn Ellie against him.

Ellie's due date is August sixteenth, a little over three months away. She still works part-time at the pre-school, not because they need the money but because she likes to. Buford sometimes drops by for lunch, and to watch and see how things are done. But he usually ends up wolfing his food down and leaving fifteen minutes after he arrives, though it seems to him more as if he has been there for two weeks. One day not long ago, one of the teachers in the four-year-olds' room proudly introduced him to the class and asked him to say something about his work. He reddened with panic, then seized hold of the first topic that came to him: the importance of hitting the cut-off man, a feat he had bungled shamefully in back-to-back innings the night before. His talk, ill-focused to begin with and overly rich with detail born of his brooding memory, didn't go over very well. He could tell. Ellie gently said later that maybe it probably was perhaps a little too advanced. The next time he visited the four-year-olds, he took the basic equipment with him and started off simple. He said, "This is a ball. Say 'ball.' This is a bat. Say 'bat.'" The kids hooted and howled and had a great time imitating him, pretending to teach one another these obvious truths.

When he went to bed that night, his ears were still ringing. Beside him, Ellie slept. Inside her, the twins conspired through their placentas.

O O O

Frank is a thrice-divorced chatterbox. He is an astonishing bore. This is not his self-image, either. Objectively, he is a

13

bore. His ex-wives found him boring and fled him with their teeth rattling from his constant barrage of words. His teammates have learned to blink and nod and grunt at intervals when he speaks. They are bound by their contracts to endure him.

Frank is a stat man. He has a prodigious memory, and this is one part of his problem. On demand, he can cite all non-trivial baseball records but one: the largest number of teams any one player has played on. Thirty-six years old and well traveled, he has deliberately refused to look this one up, skipping passages in his books and magazines that threaten to touch on it. Last year, the guys on all three of the clubs he played for called him "Suitcase." The nickname is odious to him. Thus far, no one on this club seems to have heard of it or thought of it, but every time the word is mentioned with real suitcases as referents, he perks up in panic, fearful that someone is going to pick up on it and use it against him.

During spring training, Frank found it fairly easy to memorize the team's schedule of games for the entire season. Most of the guys were impressed but vaguely repulsed at the same time. "What's the point?" they wondered. He could see it in their faces. He could easily imagine them talking about it, making fun of him for it. But Eddie, the nearly undisputed team leader, picked him up—as he has picked up so many of his teammates in his career—just when he needed it. Eddie not only complimented him on the accomplishment, but went on to tell him not to worry about his upcoming birthday two days away. Sure, his playing days would probably end in the next few years, Eddie said, but with a mind like his, he could easily start an exciting new career and do well in it. It was the only compliment Frank received as a thirty-five-year-old. He was so overwhelmed that he got a bit carried away and figured the guys had arranged a surprise birthday party for him. It was all he could do not to talk about it and spoil the surprise. There was no party, of course. But there *was* a compliment.

The other part of Frank's problem is his absurd belief that he is interesting. He is ever alert for a chance to speak. He is a dreaded conversation-killer, a Frank Buck of the verbal savanna. In the clubhouse, Narvel and Apples might get together and quietly worry about an opposing batter's home-run total—and they are almost whispering, for they know that Frank is near—when he is suddenly upon them, his happy square face all aflame with agitation as he says they have nothing to fear because such-and-such a percentage of the homers came in so-and-so park, where the wind is this and the wall is that and the humidity is the other. Frank is always right, but he takes all the fun out of talking.

Of late, Frank has become a figure of special interest to E.T.A. Eyeglasses are rather rare in baseball. Consequently, players who wear them automatically look intelligent, not counting the few whose glasses make them look like psychopaths. E.T.A. is one of those who benefit from their eyewear. In addition, he is the most educated player on the team. But lately he has grown doubtful of his smarts. He watches other people a great deal, trying to see the mind behind their words, anxiously comparing their intelligence with his own, and Frank amazes him most of all. Watching him over a period of several weeks, E.T.A. becomes convinced that a memory like Frank's is the essential ingredient of a good mind in public performance—that and a gross insensitivity to the feelings of one's audience, which Frank possesses to absolute perfection.

○ ○ ○

Eddie watches television with his daughter, Tina, and listens to his wife on the telephone in the kitchen. She is talking to someone about her plans for the World Series money. It is May and already she is counting on the Series money. His resentment is like a cloak that warms him and darkens his life.

He pulls it around himself tighter and tighter. She has come to expect satisfaction. She is never surprised when they win. She will never see his achievement for what it is—not just a well-paying job, but a glorious, precarious moment of trembling balance. An injury, or a brief slump turning into a long one because he gives it too much thought—either of these could close it out and turn him into a regular guy with nothing more than a few years of interesting history behind him and absolutely nothing before him—just a bitch for a wife, to whom baseball means nothing more than lots of money for shopping her butt off.

He looks at Tina, who sucks her thumb as she watches the television. (Three years old—should she still be sucking her thumb? If he asks his wife, she won't know. She's got other things on her mind.) With her free hand, Tina fiddles with his fingers, stroking them almost as if she senses his unhappiness. He imagines her future, a product of his wife's unassisted bungling because he is on the road so much: knocked up with nine kids and no man; or maybe a good Christian who prays her bruises away while her man drinks and beats up on her; or maybe a political woman—a radical feminist who uses her dead father in her speeches as an example of persistent racism because in spite of his brains there was no room for him in baseball management after it came to an end for him in his fifth year because of an injury or a slump that he gave too much thought to.

○ ○ ○

They win a tough one against the Dodgers, 5–4.

After the game, E.T.A. sits alone amidst his teammates, paralyzed by the huge task before him: undressing, showering, and dressing. The individual steps in the process stretch out before his eyes and disappear, their number making it impossible for him to concentrate on the first one. Right now he is *particularly* gloomy because of an eighth-inning moment of personal shame. They were down by a run, and Eddie led off the inning with a double. Buford stuck out, and then E.T.A. sent a weak roller to short. Eddie broke for third and was caught in a run-down and tagged out by the third baseman. E.T.A. rounded first and almost tried for second, but the third baseman was wily and held him with a sharp glance. Besides, E.T.A. knew that switch-hitting Frank, who would bat next, had been pulling the ball well to right, and E.T.A. figured he could score from first on a ball into the corner. Better to be at first with two outs than to risk a try for second and make the third out, he figured. In the second or so available to him, he thought hard about it and merely faked a try for second before hurrying back to first.

Eddie's assessment of his strategy differed. After he was tagged out in a very messy play at third, and after he rose and brushed himself off, spitting dirt, he saw that E.T.A. was still at first and made a disgusted wave at him—a single downward, dismissing thrust of the open hand and the forearm. E.T.A. saw it, and his neck burned with humiliation.

As it turned out, Frank did pull the ball hard, almost for a double or triple. But the right fielder made a diving catch just inside the line to retire the side. In a sense, E.T.A.'s decision to stay at first lost all significance, for it had no effect on the score. Besides, they later went on to win the game. But significance takes many forms: all through the rest of the game, E.T.A. saw Eddie rising from the ground and spitting dirt at him.

Now he sits and studies his anger. When he imagines saying something to Eddie about it, his throat instantly contricts. Eventually he makes it to the showers, where he watches the water drain at his feet. Then Eddie is suddenly beside him, lathering his muscular black body and singing. He has just come in from a post-game radio interview—"The Star of the Game." He deserved it. He went four-for-five and won the game in the ninth with a bases-loaded, two-out single that scored Narvel from third and Bubba from second. He is happy, and his teammates make him happier with the kind of ribbing he would give them if they were the heroes of the night.

The words fly all around E.T.A. He goes through the motions of showering. He feels uncoordinated, and he thinks his awkwardness must be obvious to his teammates. Surely Eddie is watching him out of the corner of his eye. Meanwhile, his anger is beginning to make him light-headed. He *must* say something to Eddie. He surprises himself when he does, for he is not at all sure where he is going.

"You thought I flubbed it," he says.

He has chosen a bad time to speak. Eddie stands under the shower, the water bombarding his head, and he doesn't hear him. This gives E.T.A. a chance to withdraw and say nothing. He is tempted to, sorely tempted. But he regathers his courage and presses on.

"You thought I messed up," he says more loudly.

Eddie finally realizes E.T.A. is speaking to him. Still grinning and radiant with pride, he leans his head out of the spray and yells, "Say what?"

"You thought I flubbed it—not making it to second."

Eddie frowns through his smile, then lights up. "The run-down. Yeah. Forgit it, man. It he'p set up the glorious ninth fo' me."

E.T.A. is confused. Then he understands: Eddie evidently thinks he brought up the play in order to apologize. The injustice of it dazzles him.

"I meant . . . you were really upset," he says.

"Forgit it, E.T.A. We *won*, man. It don' matter none."

"I mean you *showed* it, Eddie," he says with passion, his voice cracking. "You showed me up!"

"Huh?" says Eddie. E.T.A. squints—his glasses are back

in his locker—and sees a hint of annoyance in Eddie's face. This makes him feel like a little buzzing insect.

"You did *this*." E.T.A. performs Eddie's hand-waving gesture and feels ridiculous as he does. And again a sense of injustice overpowers him. He should not feel ridiculous about this, he says to himself. The gesture had meaning for every player on the field and every sophisticated fan in the park.

Eddie pauses to think. He now seems to see that E.T.A. has an argument in mind and stops smiling. "Yeah," he says coolly. "You shoulda made it to second."

"It wasn't at all obvious that I could."

"It was a helluva long run-down. I seen to that. You coulda made it."

"That's not obvious. They were watching me too."

"Ain't no third baseman gon' worry 'bout you if it mean I can git to third. They was after *me*."

"They could have gotten both of us if I had tried for second. That would have been an extremely dispiriting double play for us. We might not have come back from that."

"You woulda made it. It's simple as that. It's no big deal, though—why you bringin' it up, anyway? I'm willin' to forgit it."

"Because you tried to shift the blame to me," E.T.A. says in a rapid-fire delivery. "You showed me up, and I refuse to let you escape the responsibility for that."

"You sure makin' a big *thang* out of it," Eddie says more loudly, waving his arm in a pallid imitation of the original gesture, divesting it of importance. E.T.A. hears a cruel guffaw from Bubba. He looks up, squints, and sees that a few others in the shower are listening as well.

"I just don't think it's fair for people to blame others."

"You don't, huh?"

"No, I don't. I just personally happen to think maybe you shouldn't have gotten caught in the run-down to begin with. I hit it to short. You don't try for third on a ground ball hit to short. Everyone knows that." E.T.A. is amazed at himself. He is really arguing. And with Eddie!

"I run 'cuz it was a pissy-weak roller."

"So why didn't you beat the throw?"

"Besides, you shouldn'ta hit it there. *You* the one we call 'Mr. Steady.' *You* the one we call 'Ice Man.' You shoulda scored me."

"You've never grounded out to short?" E.T.A. asks incredulously. Eddie's position is so unfair that he can hardly speak to it.

"Besides," continues Eddie, going on like a talking machine, in E.T.A.'s eyes amazingly detached from the dispute, "once I got caught, everything shifted to you—yeah, I *was* shiftin' the blame, if you wanna put it like that. Yo' job is to git to second. Sure, I made a mistake. But you shoulda pick' me up. We all 'pozed to pick each othuh up. We ain't goin' noplace but down if we don't."

"Yeah, but whose mistake was worse?"

"*Stu*pid fuckin' question."

E.T.A. flinches and loses momentum. The word "stupid" goes through him like a bullet.

Eddie suddenly laughs, his booming voice filling the shower. "Say, now—I'm glad to hear you callin' it a mistake. Befo', you was tryin' to defen' what you done. Less say they 'bout the same kinda mistake. Neither of 'em's worse than the othuh. Then all we gotta do is remember how we got where we was. I doubled. You hit a pissy-weak roller." He raises his hands toward E.T.A., palms up, presenting him with a very simple case.

E.T.A. falls silent. The argument has become too complicated for him, and his feelings are getting in the way. Eddie's nonchalance makes him feel like an hysteric. It does not occur to him to ridicule Eddie's last point by stating that his own batting average is twelve points higher than Eddie's. It does not occur to him to remind Eddie that Frank very nearly hit the ball in such a way that he would have scored from first as well as from second. It does not occur to him to tell Eddie that it was the swift, intelligent calculation of such a blow from Frank that contributed to his thoughtful decision to stay at first. All of these points will occur to E.T.A. later—unfortunately, not as support for his position but as evidence of his flimsiness as a debater. Why couldn't he have thought of them when it counted? he will ask himself. And Eddie was right to jump on him when he labeled his decision a mistake. Why did he betray his position like that? It was as if he didn't believe in himself at all.

○ ○ ○

In Scrappy's first hour, he tells the doctor more than he has ever told anyone before. He tells him about Gram', who had insisted shrilly, every day of their lives together, that she be buried on the south side of the town cemetery, so that she could face Licking Creek, a stream famous in Ozark folklore for its magical, life-renewing properties. Scrappy had seen to it too, dashing away from spring training just as he was getting his stroke down, arriving home just in time to bribe the caretaker to find room in the overcrowded south plot for Gram's body, which had come within twenty-four hours of ending up in a hole on the north-facing slope, far away from the creek. Gram', over whose grave he had wept in desperate hope that he had done the right thing for her at last. Gram', who had taken him in when he was nine months old, after his father had skipped town and his mother, Gram's daughter-in-law, had been killed at a train crossing. Gram', who gave him care and love and beat him with a yardstick at the end of a meal only if, under his chair, she was able to collect enough spilled food to fill her favorite baby spoon. Gram', who took him in even though she didn't have to, just because she was that

21

way, just because she loved kids. Why, she would babysit at a moment's notice, and how she liked to take those little ones in, little neighborhood babies she could pinch until they screamed so she could love 'em up and make them feel better. Gram', who always looked in on him before she went to bed, no matter how much she had drunk. If she woke him up and slapped him around, she probably had good reasons for it, the way he was always getting into trouble, never able to figure out what was right, so generally worthless. That was why she called him her little Scrappy. He was just a useless piece of scrap that someone threw away one day. And she didn't always wake him up. Sometimes she let him sleep right through the night.

○ ○ ○

Apples stands stripped to the waist before the long mirror on the inside of the hotel bathroom door. He is looking at his breasts. They suddenly seem to be unusually large. He first became interested in their size when he noticed that Buford's were pretty big. His own seem even bigger, though. He wonders if his teammates have noticed his breasts, and, if so, what meaning they see in them. To his way of thinking, their size is consistent with the fact that he has never made it with a woman. Perhaps his breasts are trying to tell him something. Maybe he was born into the wrong kind of body. Maybe what he *really* wants is to make it with a man. It's something for him to think about, and he sure will.

Actually, Apples is a very thin man with an average bosom. In breast size, he ranks in the bottom half of all starting pitchers in the National League. In other words, he is mistaken. It's a shame to see such a nice guy—his teammates all love him—suffering from such a delusion. But the more he looks at those breasts, the bigger they seem.

○ ○ ○

Narvel sighs and squats with mingled boredom and self-contempt. Repetition swirls about him like a dust storm around a blinded infielder. Catchers take a lot of punishment. Narvel takes more than most.

High and tight, low and away. One-and-one. Big deal. High and tight, low and away. Two-and-two. Who cares? Scroogie. Misses. Three-and-two. Snore. Heater. Oops. Double to the wall. But who gives a shit?

The second Astro batter of the game fouls off pitch after pitch into the stands, making Narvel squat and squat some more. It is a classic battle between pitcher and batter. Narvel stifles a yawn. Apples finally gets the hitter to pop up. Frank catches it, because Frank never misses pop-ups. And yet it is not an out until he catches it, so Narvel must watch until he does. The fans cheer. Narvel scowls through his mask at them.

Apples fusses with the dirt on the mound. Down the line, the Houston third-base coach goes through his signals as if he were important to the game, looking like a loony searching his body for a mislaid tobacco plug. Narvel wants to lob a grenade at him and blow him out of the stadium. The new batter gives the coach a long, mouth-open, Cro-Magnon stare, then steps into the batter's box. A pitch on the outside corner is called a strike, and the batter studies the air through which it passed, then backs out of the box, shakes his head a bit, presses his lips together, and steps back in. It is a crashing bore. A pitch hits the dirt and, sure enough, the batter asks the ump to examine the ball, and, sure enough, he does, and, sure enough, he puts it into his reject pocket (last time, he rolled it into the dugout—a real exciting variation), and then, rather than hand Narvel the new ball to throw to Apples, the ump steps out like a goddamn little schoolboy and wings it to the pitcher himself, and Apples naturally *must* wedge his glove under his arm, freeing his hands so that he can pinch the ball with his fingernails and rub it and rub it. And now Narvel himself must contribute, because the batter has almost gone around on a half-swing ruled a ball, and Narvel has to seek an independent judgment from the ump down the first-base line, who signals it was a ball, because it was, and of course the boring fans boo boringly.

The batter finally does something to advance the game. He grounds sharply to E.T.A., moving the runner to third, and E.T.A. rushes toward first, holding the ball in his out-stretched hand toward Apples, signaling that he can make the play himself, that Apples doesn't have to cover first. Narvel sighs. Of *course* you can make the play yourself, E.T.A. After all, you fielded the ball three steps from the bag. But you had to signal to Apples anyway, didn't you? Why didn't you do something interesting for a change? Why didn't you signal with the ball to Apples and sprint over to Bubba and stuff it in his pants?

The next batter hits a rising line drive to the right of second base. From his position behind the plate, Narvel can see that Bubba has jumped a bit too early for it. The runner at third will certainly score. Houston will take the lead, then the game as well—it is only the first inning, but Narvel can see it coming—which will bump them out of first place by, according to Frank's unsolicited pre-game calculations, seventy-four hundredths of a percentage point.

Instinctively, Narvel elevates himself a bit, trying to give Bubba extra lift. Bubba looks as if he knows he has left his feet too soon, and by sheer force of his vicious will he appears to linger up there for a while, fighting the earth's weighty pull on him with a convulsive wiggle. When he must eventually come back down, he has one half of the ball in the webbing of his glove, the other half sticking out above it, blazing white, yearning for the outfield, a disappointed satellite.

Narvel sighs with mixed relief and despair. As he slumps into the dugout, the earth seems to pull heavily on his feet. He feels sickened by the same thought about the game that he now has about life: he wonders what could have possessed him ever to have found it interesting.

But then he thinks about the way he tried to help Bubba catch that ball. Now, why did he do that?

In the dugout, Apples sits down on the bench next to Scrappy, and as they watch Bubba approach the plate in his typically silent, menacing way, he asks Scrappy to have a look at the mound when they take the field again. Scrappy is a dirt man—last year the unchallenged expert on minor-league infields and mounds, this year a budding professor of major-league slopes, dips, creases, and clods. He has caught on fast: in this season, he is still errorless after forty-two games.

Scrappy says, "Sure, Apples. I'll have a look at it. What's the problem?"

E.T.A., mired in futile reflection on the run-down play and his argument in the shower with Eddie, half-listens to them.

"I don't know," says Apples, stretching his long legs out. "Just doesn't feel right—sort of like my foot drops into a bucket with every pitch."

"Then goddammit, Apples," Grammock barks down the length of the dugout, making E.T.A. jump an inch above his seat, "tell me why in hell ya' didn't call the ground crew out there." Grammock doesn't miss much.

"It's okay," Apples says with a shrug.

"It's not okay if it's not okay, and you're sayin' it's not," says Grammock. "Jesus. Do I gotta do *all* the thinkin' on this team? If it bothers you, we'll fix it next inning."

"Whatever you say," Apples mumbles.

E.T.A. gives a final shudder. Then his thoughts mire again in memory of the run-down play, his argument with Eddie.

They watch Bubba tease the pitcher into a base on balls. Jaime advances him to third with a single. Eddie, after being moved off the plate by an inside pitch, booms an angry double against the wall, scoring Bubba while Jaime holds at third. Buford approaches the plate in his slow, bovine way, and just when half the crowd in the park is dropping off to sleep at the sight of him, he hits a patented Buford wallop deep into the left-field bleachers, making the score 4–0.

"Goddammit," screams Grammock. "Goddammit now." One of the ways Grammock registers his pleasure at the quality of ball he is watching is by swearing—a habit initially bewildering to rookies when they first come up, like Scrappy at the end of the previous season. Grammock also looks rather angry during these happy curses. An isolated film clip of him at such a moment would go nicely with a shot of a buttock with an ill-cast fishhook lodged in it. "Let's get some more now," he yells to his boys. "Let's put this one right outta reach."

But his next three boys go down in order. Scrappy, after making the third out on a ground ball, rounds first and pauses fondly at the mound to study its slope while Buford brings out his cap and glove.

"It's okay," Apples says as he steps to the rubber. "Forget it."

"It *is* a little steep," says Scrappy.

"I can live with it."

Scrappy shrugs and takes his position, continuing to cast an expert eye on the mound while Apples takes his warm-up throws and begins to work to the first hitter, which is why Scrappy is a bit more surprised than he should be by a hard-hit ground ball, which he bobbles and finally ends up just holding as the runner crosses first.

"Fuckin' E-6," mutters Grammock in the dugout. Then he shouts to the infield, "That's *one*"—not in praise of Scrappy's long perfect streak, but in scorn for his failure to sustain it.

Apples continues to struggle with his footing until the bases are loaded. Grammock trots out to the mound, his round belly preceding him.

"Why didn't ya' take care of this before?" he says with disbelief to Apples, kicking at the mound. "Why?"

Apples looks at him sheepishly. "I didn't want to impose."

Grammock curses and calls the ump out, who studies the ground doubtfully and shakes his head. Grammock points his finger downward and remonstrates, like an Arkansas water witch trying to convince an urban skeptic. The ump finally calls for the ground crew, who appear instantly with their incongruous farm implements. Apples is embarrassed. He feels like a grown man in need of diapering. Narvel kicks at the chalk behind the plate and wonders if anything could be more boring than his life at this precise moment.

Scrappy is the only one who likes this part of the game. His feet involuntarily go to work, kicking into place the dirt freshly delivered by the ground crew, who do not know quite what to make of his assistance. When Grammock and the ump and the crew leave, Scrappy is still there, only now he is on his knees, working with the dirt closely, molding it into place with his hands. He is in a world of his own, back in the Missouri Ozarks, working with the county road crew, discovering dirt—one of the few good things that ever happened to him back home.

"That ought to do it, Scrappy," says Apples, his arm now as cold as a watermelon. Scrappy reluctantly rises and returns to his position, his knees boyishly smudged. Apples takes some warm-up throws. The new dirt is slippery and is packed too high. It feels as if he is stepping up onto the platform of a

27

withdrawing caboose. He nods to the ump that it is just fine. His first pitch is hit for a grand slam, tying the score at four-all.

Scrappy sees what the problem is and rushes forward to correct it with his cleats. After he is done, Apples is surprised to find his footing is now perfect, and he retires the next three batters easily. Scrappy returns to the dugout with a little strut of pride. Grammock, his stomach boiling over the grand slam, for which he has decided to blame Scrappy, makes a point of walking over to him and telling him that he will always be assured of a job in the majors, and as Scrappy frowns in initial pleasure and then mounting confusion and dismay, Grammock roars with laughter and walks back to his end of the dugout.

The next five innings are goose eggs for both sides. Apples has found his rhythm. At the bottom of every inning, the Houston pitcher kicks extra dirt up on the mound, not so much because he likes it that way but because he is a jerk and knows Apples doesn't. Scrappy corrects it for Apples each time they take the field. For Narvel, the repetition of it all brings a familiar taste of nausea to the back of his mouth. But then he realizes it would be even more boring—pointlessness heaped upon pointlessness—if they were in last place instead of first place.

Meanwhile, in the dugout, Grammock watches the progress of the game, looking for hidden meanings. Profoundly superstitious, he is regularly able to find them in unlikely places: his clothes, his breakfast, or the way he can recombine the words he hears on the radio when he drives to the park. Today he thinks about the field. He thinks about how Eddie blew up just before the game when he learned of Grammock's plans to have a part of center field leveled and evened out during their next road trip, removing a nastily subtle, gradual dip where a drain used to be. Eddie stormed into his office and said that was *his* territory, *his* real estate, *his* dip. He had grown used to it, he said. He knew it was there and dealt with it better than the opposing center fielders, who knew about it as well but didn't play here often enough to have fully mastered it. Eddie could point to specific plays that only he could make, precisely because of that dip. So Grammock agreed to leave the field as it was and chased Eddie out of his office with a few shouts to let him know who was really the boss. Now surely, he thinks, it can't be a coincidence that another physical feature (the mound) loomed so important in the first inning. The key is there, somewhere. He has to find the key—he hasn't yet, but there are two innings left—and once he does, all he needs is to find something to unlock with it.

Perhaps Grammock wouldn't be driven to reflection on paranormal phenomena if his standard efforts to get his boys back into the game hadn't failed, as they always seemed to. The flurry of hits in the first inning, or maybe the tedious mound repair in the second, seemed to make them all incurably logy. In the third, when Eddie hit another double and the pitcher was obviously toying with the idea of making a pick-off throw to the shortstop, Grammock yelled to his players on the bench to watch for the sign that would set it up, because he likes to teach his boys whenever he can. That's part of his job. But when he glanced at them to see that they were paying attention—Jesus, it was like looking at a row of laid-off undertakers on the unemployment line. He saw that same expression in the top of the fourth when he charged out to argue a close call at first, not because it was all that close but just to inspire his boys and kind of goose them; when he sneaked a look at E.T.A. to see if he was getting riled up from the argument like he wanted him to be—Jesus! He was as pale as a four-eyed, blood-shitting albino. And Buford—his best boy—when he struck out in the fifth and came back to the dugout and should have been thinking about how he'd gotten fooled by the three-and-two curve ball, what does he do but start pawing through a book full of horrible pictures of unborn babies, his big jaw hanging down nearly all the way to the bench? Jesus—it was all he could do to keep himself from putting a curse on Buford's twins coming down the pike. As he thinks about it, he wishes he had. You can't let up on these guys.

In the eighth, with the score still tied, Narvel reaches on a bleeder through the infield.

"Sacrifice, Apples," Grammock says to him as Apples removes his jacket in the on-deck circle. And then, remembering that Apples is the son of a preacher, and seeing a way to loosen him up, he enthusiastically adds, "Like Christ! Just like our Lord, Jesus Christ!"

Apples, saddened by this reference to his chaste and embarrassing past, fouls off three consecutive pitches in his attempt to bunt, dribbling them ineffectually into the dirt behind the plate. It is a totally inglorious at-bat. As he shuffles back to the dugout, Grammock bellows for all to hear, "If Christ botched it like that, I'm a Mohametan!"

Bubba follows Apples with a grounder to deep short, which forces a sluggish Narvel at second. Jaime hits a comebacker to the pitcher, who throws him out at first.

"Funny game," says Frank to no one in particular as he reaches for his glove. "No fly-outs. Every single one of our outs has been a strikeout or a ground-out."

"What'd you say?" Grammock says with excitement.

Frank grins, delighted to have an audience. He sits down on the top of the dugout in front of Grammock. "It's an interesting situation, Skip. Every—"

"I heard ya'," Grammock snaps. "Take the field."

Frank rises to his feet with a sad frown and hurries out to third base, where he completes his lengthy thought in private.

In the top of the ninth, Apples walks the lead-off man. Grammock comes out of the dugout and begins a slow walk to the mound, lifting his eyes from the ground just once as if to survey his bullpen. In truth, his mind is not on the bullpen at all. He is still looking for the key. There was a repair to the field that he thought needed to be made when there was no need, and there was a repair he *didn't* know needed to be made when there *was* a need. He nibbles at his lip in thought as he crosses the foul line, lengthening his stride so as not to step on it, looking like a portly former broad-jumper caught in a moment of nostalgia. Repair. Field. Dip. Dirt. Mound. The ground. The earth. This ugly, rotten, spinning world. The key is there . . . somewhere.

When he reaches Apples, he moves in close and puts an arm around him. It is such an intimate moment that Apples thinks Grammock has come out not to talk about his pitching but just to touch him. Maybe next he is going to fondle his breasts.

"How ya' feelin'?" Grammock asks.

Apples sighs. "Kind of low."

Grammock frowns. "The front of the mound's too low now?"

Apples shakes his head. "I feel kind of down."

"Down? Down?"

"You know—discouraged."

Grammock snorts and points to the Astro dugout. "They ain't here on this earth to encourage ya'. Neither am I. You wanna work? You wanna show me what you're made of?"

Apples shrugs. "I don't care much. Either way's okay."

Grammock gives a slow blink and looks at Apples. Never in his managing career has he heard such a lifeless remark from a pitcher. The average guy can be watching his earned-run average soar out of sight and he'll say he can get the next guy, never mind that the next guy has been eating him for lunch all day. If it was anybody but Apples, he would yank him, besides which his bullpen stinks so bad he can smell them over the phone.

"Go get 'em, kid," he says.

Apples watches Grammock return to the dugout, shrugs, sighs, rubs up the ball, goes into his stretch, sighs again, and balks, advancing the runner to second. While Grammock goes crazy in the dugout, Narvel hurries out to the mound.

"Hi ya'," says Apples.

"I've been thinking," says Narvel.

"Yeah?"

"I've been thinking during this whole lousy game."

"Yeah?"

"The thing is, what I decided is, I don't wanna lose."

"Yeah?"

"I mean, all of a sudden I really don't wanna lose."

Apples rubs the ball and looks at him.

"Sometimes when things are getting you down," Narvel continues, "you don't want more troubles on top of . . . you know, on top of everything. You know what I mean? I just really . . . don't want . . . *to lose.*"

"The ump's coming out," Apples says sadly. "They never give us time to talk."

Narvel sighs, searching for words. "Just bear down, okay, Apples? Okay?" He turns around and goes back to the plate.

Apples steps off the mound, facing second base, wondering what on earth Narvel was talking about as he rubs up the ball. His mind lingers on Narvel only for an instant, then settles back on the same thoughts he has been lugging around for a month: he is on a first-place team and has been ever since he won the season-opening game against Cincinnati; he does not belong on a first-place team, given who he is; there is heavy pressure on the front-runner, mainly taking the form of written and spoken doubts about worthiness—he doesn't need that right now; if they drop out of first, he will be free to worry about his problems without being seriously distracted by his job; but if they drop out of first, he will be on a second-place team, then a third-place team, and finally a last-place team. He needs that even less than he needs the other. Now that they are this close to losing their hold on first, he can sense how awful it would be for him. He can smell it—the foul breath of failure stalking him. He can feel it—the clutch of hands rising up to pull him down, down. He looks at the runner on second and thinks, "Why, this asshole here wants to score and depress me."

Apples calls out a coded word of encouragement to Scrappy, who responds in kind and then distracts the runner by asking him what he thinks of the slope of the mound. Apples returns to the rubber, looks in to Narvel for the sign, and nods deeply, beginning his private count with his nod. Grammock senses that the pick-off is on and gets mullygrubs. This isn't the right time for it, he thinks. Apples, still in his stretch, silently counts "two," and on "three" he whirls and fires the ball to the place where Scrappy is supposed to be on "four"—and where he *is*, it turns out. Scrappy has counted with him and has dived for second, just like the flailing baserunner, who dives too late and is messed up a bit by Scrappy's glove and ball, slammed as a sort of surprise package into his face.

Having restored the bases to a pure, perfect, unoccupied state, Apples works quickly now, keeping the ball low, and Narvel helps him, squatting so far down to the earth that he is almost prone. The next two batters ground out weakly. As Apples walks to the dugout, he feels a new surge of strength. He knows what he wants.

Grammock's mind races. Ground balls. Repairs involving center field and the pitching mound. So the key play will involve a ground ball, a center fielder, and a pitcher. Okay, but which team's center fielder and pitcher? Eddie is due to lead off. Okay, so it's Eddie and the Houston pitcher. Okay, but how? And what can he do to help fate along? He bites his lip, slips his hands under his shirt, and strokes his globe-like belly. Maybe there is nothing he can do. Maybe it is enough that he has seen the pattern. Sure. That must be it.

Eddie hits the first pitch right back at the pitcher, low, the ball hugging the earth. It just misses shearing off the pitcher's left anklebone, and the first object it strikes is the rubber of the pitching mound. It rebounds vertically, as if launched from a silo hidden under the rubber, and by the time it drops back into the pitcher's glove, Eddie is safe with a single.

"Goddammit," yells Grammock as if angry with the world. "Goddammit now." Then he cackles strangely, and the players sitting nearest him slide away down the bench a bit.

Buford comes to bat and deals Grammock's world view a severe blow of contradiction when he grounds into a double play that erases Eddie and effectively strips his base hit of all meaning. Grammock is so confounded by this turn of events that he barely sees E.T.A. single, Frank walk, and Scrappy, after a pitching change, reach on an infield hit. The bases are loaded for Narvel, who concentrates as if his life depends on it, for in a real sense it does, and he strokes the second pitch into right-center.

It hangs up. Grammock yells at the ball, forcing it down, and he yells at the earth, forcing it up, while the Houston center fielder loses a half-step in Eddie's special dip in a desperate attempt to catch the ball on the fly. It drops inches in front of his glove while E.T.A. dances home from third to score the winning run.

The dugout explodes with a cheer and the players rush out to slap Narvel around with their congratulations. Grammock stands transfixed, his limbs tingling, his lips moving soundlessly as they form the words, "I seen it comin'. I seen it comin'."

Apples shouts to Narvel amid the tumult of celebration, "I didn't want to lose it either, Narv'. Way to *be*, babe."

Apples and Narvel have independently discovered a new formula for success, one that will keep them on top much longer than good habits alone could have. Some of their teammates have already discovered it. Others will discover it very soon. The formula: profound fear of failure.

3

"Hey, boys, ya' remember my story of the Ozark blacksmith with two tallywhackers? Well, I got another one for ya'. There was this preacher fellow, skinny as a plucked chicken an' hung like a bull, an' he always preached that if'n the good Lord give us gifts, we should oughta use 'em, an' you can bet he practiced what he preached. An' there was this farmer's wife lived down the road that he had the hots for, an' . . . Eddie? Hey, Eddie, you got a question?"

"No, Skip. I was jis' askin' E.T.A. here 'bout one of the signs we jis' went over—the suicide squeeze."

"Damn it, Eddie. I'm in the middle a . . . All right, all right. Indicator. Then belly rub. Batter acknowledges with slap to left buttock. Coach at third says to runner, 'Don't fuck up.' Runner acknowledges with 'I'm hip'—that part oughta come easy to you, Eddie. Okay? No more interruptions now. So, anyway, this preacher fellow, skinny as a plucked chicken, he's got the hots in a real mournful way for this farmer's wife.

But the farmer, he's a mean 'un, an' he's always on the lookout for other studs makin' eyes at his woman, an' top a that, he don't like that skinny preacher a-tall. He don't take no stock in religion, if ya' don't mind me sayin' so, Apples. He don't go to church none an' don't say grace neither, not even when he's pullin' a chair up to his all-time most favorite meal, which is cornmeal mush. Now then, this preacher . . . Scrappy, what the hell you doin'?"

"Jist cleanin' the old dirt from outta my cleats, Skip."

"Well, you're makin' a helluva mess there, besides which you're distractin' me. Hell, you oughta enjoy this, Scrappy, bein' a peckerwood boy like me. Jist settle down now."

"Okay, Skip."

"Well, this preacher, he's a quick 'un, an' he plans things real careful. He knows that on the first a every month the farmer goes into town an' gits blind-drunk, an' he figgers that'll give him his chanst. He picks a date for when he's gonna make his big move, an' then weeks ahead of time he sets to work on gittin' that woman heated up. He courts her real subtle-like, so's the farmer nor nobody else'll notice. You're probly all askin' yourselves how he done it. Well, relax, 'cuz I'm gonna tell ya' how he done it. He done it with his preachin'. You fellows know the Song a Solomon? Hell, Apples, I'm sure *you* do. Horniest book in the Bible, ain't it? Well, all that month he preaches outta the Song a Solomon, jist whippin' up that farmer's wife into a lather, not to mention the rest a the congregation. Why, nine months later the population a that county jist plumb exploded. So, comes the first a the month, he sneaks outta the parsonage . . . Frank? *Frank?* What's eatin' ya'?"

Frank looks up from the floor, blinking rapidly. "What, Skip?"

"Your lips is movin'. What're ya' jabberin' to yourself about?"

Frank's square face splits with a foolish grin. "I was just figuring up my batting average beyond three points."

"Jesus H., Frank. Gimme some respect, will ya'?"

"Sorry, Skip."

"So, comes the first a the month, this spindle-assed preacher fellow sneaks outta the parsonage, peeks in the bar, sees the farmer in there burpin' up cornmeal mush 'n' goin' blind with drink, an' rides outta town with his heart an' his tallywhacker a-thumpin'. An' when he gits to the farm, he don't have to worry none 'bout none a that foreplay shit. That woman, she's *primed*. They whip their clothes off in the kitchen an' scamper into the bedroom, an' in no time a-tall that preacher's got his tallywhacker—"

"Skip," a flunky coach calls from his office. "Telephone."

"Tell 'em to fuck off," Grammock barks over his shoulder.

"Front office," says the coach.

"Ah . . . *shit*," says Grammock. "Don't you boys go 'way. I'll be right back."

As soon as his office door closes behind him, the ball-players steal out of the locker room, carrying their baseball shoes with them, padding silently in their socks.

○ ○ ○

Since his argument with Eddie in the shower, E.T.A. has decided that a Frank-like memory is not what distinguishes good minds. The important thing is mental flexibility. Someone like Eddie can roll with the blows of a debate and come back confidently just when he seems to be decked out for good. Eddie can see new ways of looking at things right in the middle of a fight, right when everything is on the line. That's what most amazes E.T.A. When the pressure is on him, how can Eddie think about anything but the pressure?

There also remains the original point of dispute—the

quality of E.T.A.'s base-running. Sometimes E.T.A. gives the impression that that one play is all he has to worry about. He tediously discusses it with his teammates—one at a time, aside—and with sportswriters, replaying it for them, milking them for support. He also resents Eddie for the way he has made him suffer. At the same time, with precisely equal conviction, he knows the fault is partly his own, for being such a social misfit when it comes to the freewheeling exchange of ideas.

O O O

Bubba studies the rule book—something he knows few ballplayers do—looking for new ways to deceive the enemy. He learns that it is legal, though pointless, for a batter who has struck out to run to first base even if the catcher holds the ball—that is, makes a clean catch of it. If the defense responds with panic, that is their problem; they should know if he is out or not. He sees interesting possibilities. He reviews what he knows about the catchers on the other teams. He goes to his annual baseball guide for more data on them.

Two weeks later, against Montreal, with Narvel on third, one out, and an 0–2 count on him, Bubba decides to try it. He swings weakly at the next pitch, missing it by a foot, and the freckle-faced catcher—the greenest, most anxiously eager catcher in the league—holds the ball. Bubba sprints for first. Behind him, the catcher quickly plumbs his soul. He wonders if he dropped the ball, decides he is certain he did not, wonders why in that case Bubba is running, worries there is something he has somehow overlooked, figures the safest thing is to throw to first just to be sure, hesitates because there is a runner at third, decides to go ahead and throw it anyway, and concludes with his release of the ball that he is making a very big mistake.

Propelled by the catcher's anguished mental energy, the

ball soars into the right-field bullpen. Narvel hurries home from third. Bubba rounds first and grins all the way back into the dugout, where his teammates cheer and despise him. Though thankful for the run, their sympathy is with the freckle-faced catcher, on whose behalf the opposing manager is now arguing vociferously with the ump, though to no avail.

That night, back in his den, E.T.A. writes a brief note of condolence and encouragement to the catcher.

○ ○ ○

Narvel calls home. His wife, a graduate student in economics, has driven off to the library, and he is alone. Only when he is alone will he call home, for he is certain he sounds like an idiot whenever he does. He must look up the number even though he has dialed it once a week for the past two years. Narvel was raised in a dry little town in the Imperial Valley, but his parents now live in San Diego, where Narvel has set them up in a retirement community. His father, a man tiny in both stature and achievement, a beastly failure at everything he touched, a contagious dud who could cause a heavily occupied office building to implode just by opening the front door, *loves* San Diego—not for the climate, not for the zoo, but only for the security he enjoys from living in the midst of its armada of retired naval officers.

His mother, a behemoth of a woman, all breast and husband-dwarfing torso, answers the phone and calls with powerful elderly enthusiasm to his father, who picks up the extension.

"How are you, boy?"

"Fine, Pop."

"Help me be a believer, boy. Help me."

Narvel frowns.

"Sure, you've been quick out of the chute. Sure, you've

39

ridden out some tough bucks and kicks and stayed on top. But I'm not a believer. Help me, Narvel. Talk to me, boy."

Narvel blinks heavily. His father lives for the game, not out of love of it but because Narvel's paycheck is *his* paycheck. His mother, though likewise dependent on the quality of Narvel's daily play, refuses to inform herself about the game. She still doesn't know what a hit is. If Narvel flies out four times in a game, she will say he got four hits. She takes a radio to the games when Narvel's team is in San Diego to play the Padres. She needs it to tell her who is winning, because Narvel's father refuses to.

"I don't know, Pop. Gotta take 'em one at a time, I guess. How's everything with you folks?" He winces at his words. He knows his conversation is lifeless. He never could talk, he thinks. Not well, anyway.

"Us?" his father says loudly. "Fine, fine. Not bad for a couple of old fogies who could easily drop dead at any moment. Your mom's back is giving her some trouble, but what else is new, you know what I mean?"

"I'm sorry—"

"It's nothing," his mother bellows in her high-pitched voice. "Narvel, do you remember Mrs. Webster?"

Narvel blinks. The conversation seems to dart like a startled rabbit. "No, I—"

"The Sunday School teacher? She lived on Escondido Street?"

"I don't remember her, Mom." He hears his father's pipe banging into an ashtray. It makes an angry sound, as if he detests his wife's speech and wants to drown it out.

"The house with the teeny fountain in the back?"

"He was too damn young, Ruth," his father says impatiently.

"She passed away," says his mother, ending the tale.

"Hunh," says Narvel.

"Narvel," his father says, "you sure you guys aren't playing over your heads—you know, playing better than you really are?"

"I don't know, Pop. Anything's possible, I guess. Listen, the reason I called—I mean, *one* reason I called, is—"

"I worry about it, Narvel. I don't want to be disappointed. I've been disappointed too many times."

"I know, Pop."

"Whaddya' mean, ya' know?"

"The *team*," he says quickly, his face going blank with fear. "We've let you down before."

"Yeah," says his father, giving the word a suspicious edge. "Ruth, you got something cooking? I smell something burning."

"Not that I know of."

"Not that you *know of*?" He laughs derisively. "Ya' think maybe ya' can figure it out?"

Narvel closes his eyes tightly and clenches the receiver. He wonders if he should hang up. Maybe they would rather just yell at each other over their phones.

"Narvel," says his mother, "do you remember old Dr. Watkins?"

Geez, he thinks. Another corpse. He can't stand it. "No, I don't, Mom," he says. "Listen, do you remember an old diary I kept when I was little?"

"No," his father says curtly.

"Of course," says his mother.

"I wrote in it when I was about ten or eleven, I think."

"Nah," says his father.

His mother says, "Ha-ha for you, Herb. I happen to know right where it is. It's in the trunk in the basement." Her voice is chipper and sing-songy.

"Can you send it to me?"

"I'll do it first thing this afternoon," she chirps.

"Gettin' sentimental, boy?" his father says suspiciously. "Seems to me you ought to be thinking of the future, not the

41

past. Like tomorrow's game with the Pirates. Those guys'll eat you for lunch if you let 'em."

"Yes, sir," he says, feeling reprimanded. His throat tightens and his voice thins out. "It's just that I've been thinking about my childhood and all, and I keep on wondering if it was, well, you know, what it was like and all, and I thought maybe the diary would help, because lately—"

"Of course, dear," says his mother. "I'll put it in the mail right away."

Narvel laughs incongruously.

"The future is for the living, Narvel," his father says sententiously. "You guys have been looking pretty drab for front-runners."

"Maybe it's our TV reception, Herb. Ever since they built that high-rise—"

"I know drabness when I see it," his father insists. "Do you hear me, Narvel? Talk to me."

"Funny," says his mother. "I smell something burning too." Her receiver clatters on the table as she dashes away.

Narvel listens in silence.

"Narvel? Narvel?" his father shouts.

Narvel listens.

"Ruth? Ruth? Christ Almighty, he musta hung up."

Narvel listens. He hears his father's receiver rattle into its cradle. He imagines his father walking from his den into the kitchen, timing it. Then, just as he expected, he hears their loud voices over his mother's abandoned extension. They are oblivious of his presence, as always, their aimless, angry voices clashing in eternal dispute.

A grim little smile begins to play at his lips. It is just like when he was a boy.

○ ○ ○

"Bein' a daddy ain't that bad, Bufe."

Buford sighs, his large face sagging down toward his lap.

42

It is a stormy evening. The game has been called two hours before it was to have begun, and Eddie is giving him a ride home. But first they must stop at a church daycare center to pick up Tina. Eddie's wife leaves her there, he has explained, so that she can go out with his paycheck and buy herself more clothes for her skinny body. Buford is uncomfortable with Eddie's public scorn of his wife. He is also sadly reminded of the time E.T.A. took him by the Tots-'N'-Kids Pre-School on a similar errand, the day he met Ellie. On that day, they began their special life together—special until the enemies arrive on August sixteenth.

"I don't know, Eddie," he says, staring at the rain pelting the windshield. "Looking ahead, it's like I'm driving into a wall of fog."

"Don' look ahead, man. With kids, you got to go with the flow. They need this now, you give 'em this now. Tomorrow they need *that*, you give 'em *that*. They be changin' all the time, an' you gon' find you can keep up with 'em." He adds with a laugh, "Jis' *barely*."

Buford shakes his head. "It's foreign country. Ellie was talking about buying some bumpers yesterday. I don't even know what bumpers are, Eddie."

Eddie laughs. He pulls to a stop at a red light and looks at Buford. "You gon' do all right, Bufe. You got that gentle touch, man. No shit, I mean it. An' you got you a real wife there. Ellie's gon' be a real he'p to you."

"A help to me?" Buford says in a panic. "I always figured—"

"You gon' have any more? I mean after the twins?"

He sighs. "I don't know. Ellie wants to, I think."

Eddie nods his head as if he is not surprised. "*My* bitch don't. She done had herse'f all froze up inside when Tina was born. She say that gon' make Tina feel like a special girl. I say *bullshit*. It jis' gon' make Tina feel like a lonely li'l mistake." The light changes and he drives on, silent for a moment. Then a smile brightens his face. "Listen to this, Bufe. Tina, she be

43

on this spooky kick, you know. She be askin' me for a scary story, then another one, then another, an', *man*, it wear me out like nothin' else. I tell her one an' she say, real slow-like, 'That not very spooky.' I out with another an' she say, 'That not very spooky.' I wanna say, '*Shit*, girl. I bus' my ass thinkin' up these stories, with greazy monsters an' people chewin' on each other an' they eyes poppin' out an' shit, an' all you got to say is they ain't spooky 'nough.' It useta jis' burn me up, Bufe. Then I got to thinkin'. You always got to be thinkin' with a kid. I thought, '*Shit*, Eddie—you a growed-up man with a big career an' good stats. How the fuck a three-year-ol' li'l girl gon' hurt you? Look at it from where *she* sittin'.' So I done it, an' right away I seen it. She was proud—plain an' simple. Thas all. She wannit to show me, an' maybe herse'f too, that she could deal with any ugly ol' story I could dream up. Thas all. Now when she say that, I jis' laugh an' say, 'No, babe? I 'uz pretty scared tellin' it. You *sure* you wasn't scared?' An' we bofe laugh an' laugh."

Buford stares ahead at the rain while Eddie pulls over to the curb in front of the church annex. Eddie gets out and dashes through the rain into the building. Buford sits, stares, and mopes. When Eddie comes out, Tina is with him, crying hysterically. She cries all the way to the car, and seeing Buford doesn't cheer her up. Eddie calmly helps her into the back and buckles her into her car seat. Buford watches her fight and squirm. The lower part of her face is a glistening mass of tears and mucus.

"You ready to tell me now?" shouts Eddie, leaning in her door, the rain splattering his back.

She bellows.

"*What?*"

She shrieks.

Eddie shuts the door, hurries around the car, and slips in behind the wheel. "Somethin's botherin' her," he yells over the din to Buford, who sits facing forward, immobile. "She too crazy-mad to tell me what."

She yells. To Buford it is nothing but moist vowels.

"Froot Loops?" Eddie calls back over his shoulder. He looks at her. "Oh—your necklace? Not enough on it, huh? It's okay, babe. We don' got no Froot Loops at home, but we can finish it up with Cheerios."

It is suddenly quiet in the car. Buford, thinking Tina must surely be stricken dead with a heart attack, whirls around. She sits calmly and fingers a necklace of colored string, beaded with several (but not enough!) Froot Loops. He looks into her miserable, wet face. Just as he wonders if he has a handkerchief, Eddie is there with a fistful of tissues apparently plucked from the air, reaching them behind him with one hand while he wheels smoothly into the stream of evening traffic with the other. Tina takes them and wipes her face.

Buford turns back around and watches the rain on the windshield. He shakes his big blond head, then gently slaps the side of it once. "Finish it up with Cheerios," he says softly. "Who would have thought of that? *I* never would have. Never in a million years."

○ ○ ○

Frank takes advantage of an off-day to do some chores around the house. He didn't plan on doing this. His two sons were to spend the day with him, a day he had worked out in detail: zoo, amusement park, and, before the hot-dog cookout in the back yard, a little batting practice in the lot across the street, with Dad naturally giving them tips on the grip, stance, stride, and swing. But at the last minute his first ex-wife called to tell him the boys had changed their minds and adamantly refused to do anything but accompany her to the beauty shop—something Frank hadn't known they enjoyed doing.

He shuffles down to the basement for his toolbox. As he reaches for it, he barks his knuckles on the wooden shelf just above it. He repeats the gesture and his hand arrives smoothly at the toolbox without injury. So why did he reach out so spastically the first time? As he studies his knuckles—two are scraped, a third bleeds—he thinks about similar clumsy mishaps over the past months. His limbs sometimes seem drawn into little catastrophes as if by a magnet, bumping into door jambs, slamming into table corners. He wonders why.

Out in the street, he moves his car a little ways away from the curb and drives the front wheels up onto two wooden blocks. He sets the brake, scoots under the car, and applies his Vise Grip to the oil-pan cap. As he unscrews the cap, he remembers introducing the Vise Grip—its structure and functions—to his first wife, then to his second wife, but not to his third wife, who filed divorce papers before he had the chance, and then to his sons and people up and down the street. He wonders if his neighbors are watching him now and asking themselves why a well-paid ballplayer would change his own oil. If they come up and ask him, as he fervently wishes they would, he will have an interesting explanation handy. The words multiply exponentially in his head, filling it and pouring out to his lips, which begin to flutter as he addresses his oil pan in rapid, soundless rehearsal.

A quarter-turn before the cap will be free, he realizes he has forgotten a pan for the oil. His forgetfulness makes him chuckle good-naturedly, much as a mentally healthy man would do, and he eases out from under the car and looks up the sidewalk for someone he can share his near-oversight with. He is in luck. The friendly (though busy, always in a hurry) pharmacist from next door comes out onto his porch and heads across his lawn toward the sidewalk, toward Frank. But when he sees Frank, he snaps his fingers, spins around on his heel, and hurries back into the house—clearly a man who has forgotten something. Frank sighs and looks after him, blinking in the early-morning sunlight. A metallic *thunk* on the hood of his car makes him jump. A large stick clatters off the hood to the street below. Frank looks up. High in the branches directly overhead, a squirrel is building a nest, sending occasional bits of debris down upon his car. Frank watches the leaves and twigs dripping down and is not fully aware of how distressed he is until he hears himself moaning softly. He stops doing that and looks around. The words. The words are what make him sad. He needs to get them out. Far down the sidewalk, two neighborhood children on their way to school slowly approach. Frank wets his lips, which still flutter. The boys look up toward him and angle across the street to the opposite sidewalk.

Frank goes into the basement again, his sad face leading the way. He finds the old plastic dishtub he uses for oil changes and goes back outside, wondering how he is going to get through the long day alone. The words rattle around, filling him up, threatening to tear him apart as he does one thing, then the next, then the next—draining the oil, replacing the filter, and taking five quarts of recently purchased oil from the trunk of his car. He pauses before pouring in the new oil, checking the hole in the valve cover to make sure he will be pouring it in the right place. He is a careful worker, fearful of failure, these days especially, and in this nervous moment of checking and checking again, another stick crashes on the raised hood over his head, rattling to rest against the windshield. The squirrel continues to tease him as he works. By the time he has emptied four quarts, he is thoroughly shell-shocked.

He stares at the reading on the dipstick. It is dry, free of oil. He frowns, then understands. With a despair so well honed that it almost gives him pleasure, he looks at the gutter and sees an abundance of oil mingling with the leaves and sticks—a disgusting, polluted log-jam. He forgot to screw in the oil-pan cap. He will have to buy more oil. He will have to walk four blocks to the gas station. He will have to carry it back and pour it in. And the mess—what about the mess?

Thunk. The squirrel, busy building a nest that will last, chucks more stuff down on his car. Frank feels his face tighten strangely. He looks up and sees another schoolboy far down the sidewalk, slowly approaching, his head bent down in concentration over a tin can, which he kicks before him. Frank panics with the thought that the boy will see the large mess he has made of things, so he scurries under the car, clutching his Vise Grip desperately to his breast. He nudges the overflowing tub aside, spilling more oil, and begins to screw in the cap.

The boy approaches. Frank hears the can. The squirrel's clattering debris. The can—it clanks and rattles down the sidewalk toward him, making a noise like the sound of *can* repeated several times: *cancancancancan* . . . Silence. *Cancancancancan* . . . Frank lies flat on his back, his lips fluttering futilely up at his car's undercarriage, while the can comes near, pauses for a long while at his car, and finally moves on, now calling out his own name. *Frank!* it says. *Frankfrankfrankfrankfrank* . . . Silence. *Frankfrankfrankfrankfrank* . . .

○ ○ ○

By the end of his sixth week of treatment, Scrappy is willing to agree that Gram' was inconsistent in the way she raised him. She probably gave him a few more lickings than he deserved, and maybe sometimes when she was mad and he was the handiest thing to hit, she would give him a couple cracks just on the grounds of his general availability. Scrappy is willing to agree that this was probably not good for him. Maybe, too, on that day in spring when she discovered he'd been visiting Miss Eula down the road, Gram' really shouldn't have cut off his hair and strewn it all over the yard for the

48

birds, in the superstitious belief that if they wove it into their new nests, it would drive him insane. And he knows a case can be made that she shouldn't have whipped him for singing "Hippity Hop to the Barber Shop" in the bathroom. How was he to know that singing while urinating was bad luck? He feels the same way about her sending him to his room for two or three days at a time when he was bad—say, when she found a smudge on a window he had forgotten to clean that day. She was nuts about those windows, because she believed the sunshine kept her alive.

But Scrappy is quick to defend her when he thinks of other times—like when she let him have a taste of her green-tomato pie, or when she let him pinch and love up a neighborhood baby, or, best of all, when she twisted his ears in her fists and called him her little "muggins." Scrappy gets a lump in his throat when he remembers those ear-twistings and that word "muggins." He figures she called him that because even though he was ornery as heck, he still had a cute little mug that she loved him for.

○ ○ ○

It is no accident that Jaime has thus far played a small role in these events, almost as if he has been forgotten. It is Jaime's nature to be forgotten. The last of fourteen children born on a tiny Caribbean island to a preoccupied Dutch petroleum dealer and his generally unfocused black wife, Jaime was forgotten at the market and at home. He was forgotten on the beaches, on the landing grounds, in the fields, and in the streets. He was forgotten in the mountaintops, in the dell, upon the hillside, and upon the flat. His father forgot him on the dock when they moved to Caracas, and, after a long moment of wild vacillation, he finally tendered the boat captain twenty Bolivars to induce him to turn around and go back for his last-born.

Jaime's teammates forget him too. His English is awful: weird, rasping consonants; nasal eruptions; impenetrable proverbs; a tattered lexicon of baseball clichés; and not an auxiliary verb to his name. On radio and television, he says things like "Eesa masha goo baw cub" and "Me posetu heet mas batatas." Once, when asked to give his opinion about two consecutive losses by Apples, he howled, "We no pay masha goo behine eem." It was his last interview.

Unfortunately, Jaime's Spanish is only trivially better than his English. He grew up speaking an Iberian-based creole quite different from the Spanish of Caracas, his home after his tenth birthday. His attempt to learn conventional New World Spanish was foiled by the heavy nasality and useless Dutch vocabulary of his native tongue, which also began to deteriorate through disuse and the family-wide deaf ear he was given, making him a wretch inarticulate in three languages. His Anglo teammates speak to him only when calling for a fly ball; to his Latin teammates raised in Mexico, Puerto Rico, and the Dominican Republic, his Spanish sounds devil-possessed; and his parents and siblings, vague on his exact whereabouts, no longer communicate with him at all.

For solace, Jaime got in the habit of buying sex. He knows prostitutes in every National League city. "Masha bunita," he would always say to them, or, when he saw an especially fetching one, "Masha masha bunita." This led the whores to think he liked the name *Marsha*, so they would always give him a Marsha or pretend to give him a Marsha if no real ones were in the house. This in turn led Jaime, who is easily confused, to believe that the English word for whore is "marsha." In spite of his confusion, Jaime is always very polite, and after every outing he likes to thank his marsha in his native tongue, with the Dutch-derived "dankee," which in turn led the whores to believe his name was "Donkey," which used to puzzle him quite a bit.

"Used to," because he doesn't say "dankee" anymore.

He doesn't see his marshas anymore, not since three consecutive mysteriously soft attempts. Instead, he stays in his hotel room and tries to talk to himself.

Jaime is also more than a little confused about Grammock. To Jaime, he is not even Grammock, but rather "Gruñón," which is Spanish for "grouch"—a nickname given him by the normal Spanish speakers on the bench, people with a firm enough grasp on reality to know it is only a nickname. But Jaime, who spends more time trying to figure out their conversations than he does trying to figure out those of the Anglos, hears only "Gruñón" and thinks this is Grammock's name.

But Jaime's confusion on *this* point is perhaps understandable. Who *is* Grammock, after all?

To E.T.A., he is a rhetorical genius, magically capable of humiliating umps up to a point just short of getting himself chased. He is a master of periphrasis when he is wrong and a bulldog with lockjaw when he is right.

To Frank, Grammock is like all the managers he has played under—pitifully weak in his grasp of the statistics necessary to run a ballclub to best advantage.

To Eddie and Bubba, he is an Arkansas redneck. To Eddie, this means Grammock will occasionally commit social atrocities which simply have to be overlooked for the good of the club. To Bubba, it means Grammock should be stuck like a pig in the guts with a knife.

To Narvel, Grammock is not special in any way at all. He is as boring an example of humanity as everybody else Narvel knows.

To Apples, Grammock is an intriguing physical specimen. In terms of their attractiveness, Apples privately ranks his teammates this way: Eddie (massive upper-body strength atop a thirty-two-inch waist and doe-like legs), then E.T.A. (very clean, wears glasses well), Bubba (an ass that simply will not quit), Jaime (dark and cute), Frank (bouncy, curly hair;

red, square face), Buford (a blond Wisconsin cow-lifter), Narvel (bland, potato-faced), and Scrappy (the all-time bad head). Grammock falls near the bottom, between Narvel and Scrappy, what with his Marine's haircut, soft, sagging breasts, and a perfect half-basketball of a belly so distinct from his otherwise average frame that it looks surgically attached. Grammock oddly seems to want to call attention to his belly: by often going topless; or by rolling his shirt up and tucking it into the deep fold between his breasts and its round top, the better to stroke it with his hands circling in quiet rhythm; or, when he slouches on the bench during a game, his fingers laced behind his head, by balancing a full coffee cup atop its northern pole. Grammock has another habit that interests Apples. His pants, like those of his players, lack front pockets, so when he tires of sitting on the bench, he likes to lean against the water cooler at the end of the dugout and slip the fingers of both hands down under his elastic waistband and fiddle with the tippy-tops of his pubic hair, right there in full view of thousands of spectators. He's got a woman's voice too, and he clears his throat all the time, as if hoping to make it deeper, especially over the phone. The guys always know when someone on the phone has taken him for a woman, because he'll make them take extra batting practice, or lay down rigid new rules governing clubhouse behavior. The woman in Grammock gives Apples lots to think about.

To Buford, Grammock is a wellspring of love. Buford thinks Grammock must love him as a person. Actually, Buford swings the bat with such power, especially in the clutch, that Grammock, a mediocre loser as a player decades ago and single-mindedly desirous of begetting winners now, loves Buford precisely as a failed, selfish adult loves offspring who may yet redeem him. That is, there is reason to doubt that he loves him at all.

To Scrappy, Grammock is a figure whose respect he is sure he will one day earn, if only he does the right thing.

Scrappy knows he's not worth an awful lot, being a chinless, lonely kid with a .230 average on its way to .220, but he hopes that if he just hangs in there, Grammock will recognize his pluck and one day say something nice to him. Scrappy doesn't ask for much. Hell, he doesn't mind that Grammock giggled all the way to his office the day the guys in the bullpen nailed Scrappy's shoes to the floor, but he wonders if it was right for Grammock to give those guys a bonus for doing it. Or the time they were losing a laugher to St. Louis on a hot, muggy day and Scrappy wanted to get a drink of water in the dugout, but Grammock was leaning against the water cooler and told him to go into the locker room because he didn't feel like moving just then. Scrappy was embarrassed and kind of shrugged and sat down, wondering if maybe Grammock thought he shouldn't be drinking water, and if so, why, but then a minute later Buford came over for a drink and Grammock stepped away from the cooler and walked to the other end of the dugout as if he had some important business there. Scrappy wouldn't have minded it so much if Grammock hadn't looked back at him with a sick smile, just to let him know what he was doing. Scrappy doesn't ask for much. Hell, Grammock could go ahead and do stuff like that if he wanted to. But he didn't have to give him that awful smile.

○ ○ ○

A conference on the mound. It is the rubber game of a series with the second-place Dodgers, who, just three games behind them in the standings, have been knocking on the door for two weeks. Apples has pitched a three-hitter into the ninth. The score is knotted at 1–1. It has been a beautiful ball game so far. Brilliant pitching and defense on both sides. Peppy, savvy base-running and close plays at the plate. Grammock watches with nervous reverence from the dugout, encouraging the action on the field with happy curses. The sportswriters in the press box are itching for it to be over so that they can put it all into writing. The umps keep getting chills.

The conference originates strangely. As Narvel takes his position behind the plate in the bottom of the ninth, he gets a cramp in his leg and jumps up to shake it out, groaning. The entire infield reacts as one man. They think Narvel has jumped out to go to the mound, and Frank, Scrappy, Bubba, and E.T.A. all draw toward Apples. Narvel looks up and is a bit surprised that a conference is being held with not a pitch yet thrown by Apples in this inning, but he too walks out to the mound.

Apples is rubbing the ball. As the men move in on him, he feels a rush of love for the way they play behind him. He feels a warmth, a sense of being protected. His thoughts linger tenderly on the standard word for the defense behind a pitcher: "support." What a lovely word, he thinks.

Frank looks across the mound at the approaching E.T.A. and suddenly sees him as his mirror-image. They're both smart. They both play at a corner. They both have to contend with eyeblink-fast one-hoppers, with nasty little bunts, and with ribbing from the opposition dugout. He feels a keen sense of balance and brotherhood as he and E.T.A. arrive at the mound.

Although he normally fears him and never speaks to him, at the moment Scrappy is having good feelings about Bubba. Perhaps it is the three double plays they have executed, two of them 6–4–3's, one a 4–6–3.

Narvel is suddenly aware that Apples hasn't shaken off one of his signals thus far in the game. Apples doesn't even nod anymore. He just looks in, winds, and deals.

When they are all together, there is silence. Frank finally breaks it, saying, "Let's play tight, men. Let's play very tight. Let's play very, very tight."

There is a pause. Narvel says, "How do you want to pitch to this guy, Apples?"

Apples says, "Let's try and get him out."

Scrappy, puzzled because the conference seems to lack an agenda, says, "Exactly what's the point of us bein' here?"

E.T.A. looks him straight in the eye. "I ask myself that question every day."

This has a curtain-thudding snap to it, so they return to their positions. Apples goes to work, but he seems distracted. He walks the batter, a base-stealing threat, on four pitches. He goes into his stretch and peeks at first base over his left shoulder. E.T.A. crouches at the bag, glove open. The runner dances off first and swings his arms like a happy chimpanzee. Apples takes his back foot off the rubber and the runner hurriedly returns to first. Apples walks behind the mound, sticks his glove under his arm, rubs the ball, removes his cap, wipes his forehead on the sleeve of his shirt, replaces his cap, and looks back over at E.T.A. He presses his lips together, then signals with a short jerk of his head that he wants E.T.A. to come to the mound. E.T.A. calls for a time-out, and in the most dramatic development of the inning thus far, the first-base ump throws his fanny back and his arms up and shouts, "*Time!*"

Apples gazes out to center field and continues to rub the ball as E.T.A. comes to his side. Without looking at him, he says, "E.T.A., what did you mean by what you said just now?"

E.T.A. hangs his head. "I'm sorry, Apples. You're under a lot of pressure and I shouldn't say half-assed stuff like that. It was stupid of me."

"No, no," says Apples, turning to look closely at him. "Don't back down. You've been doing too much of that lately."

"They're workin' on their pick-off," Grammock says under his breath in the dugout. "I hope Apples don't throw it away."

"I just . . ." E.T.A. hesitates, sighs, and then opens up. "Sometimes it all just doesn't seem worth it anymore."

Apples cocks his head to one side. "Kind of like there's no point? Like you don't care about anything?"

"Exactly. I'd sooner sit at home and stare into space than do anything else."

"Sad? You been sad?"

"Oh, Apples," he moans. "My best friend dies every day."

"They jist better not git too goddamn cute throwin' that goddamn ball around," mutters Grammock.

"Did you know I've been feeling the same way?" says Apples, his throat catching on the confession.

E.T.A.'s mouth opens slightly. "But what about your record? This is the best season you've ever had."

"What about your batting average?" Apples fires back at him.

E.T.A. can't handle forceful contradiction like this, and he begins to feel troubled. But he fights the feeling and searches for the point behind the contradiction. He finds it. He even sees in it the acknowledgment of his hitting skill. Then he catches sight of the ump stepping out from behind the plate. "We'll talk after the game, Apples," he says.

"Definitely."

Apples goes into his stretch again and peeks at first. He makes a soft throw and the runner gets back easily. He makes a hard throw and the runner gets back easily again. He makes another hard throw and the runner gets back with difficulty. Then he makes a pitch. It is low and outside. The runner stays at first.

He goes into the stretch and peeks. He steps off and beckons E.T.A. again.

The Dodger third-base coach says to Frank, "You guys hopin' for rain? This is southern California." Frank responds with three dense paragraphs.

"E.T.A.," Apples says with a strangely nervous twitch at

the corner of his mouth, "we'll just keep it between us, okay? It'll be our little secret."

E.T.A. smiles weakly. "I was standing there shaking with worry about the same thing." He hurries back to first base.

The next pitch is a hanging curve which the batter lines to deep left-center. Eddie backhands it on one hop and rifles it to Bubba at second, behind the runner, who has taken a wide turn in hopes of a bobble. The throw screams in at Bubba's shoetops and the runner dives back to the base, safe by inches. The crowd gasps at the throw, Grammock swears in anger at the call, and Bubba removes his stinging hand from his glove and says with awe, "Sumbitch."

Apples rubs the ball behind the mound while the crowd settles down. He looks to E.T.A. and resists the temptation to call him over again. He desperately wants to talk some more, but he doesn't want to impose on E.T.A. Suddenly E.T.A. trots over to him on his own initiative, and Apples receives him with a grin.

"I was wondering," says E.T.A. "You think Eddie might have a problem too?"

Apples' eyes widen, then narrow.

"That throw got me thinking. It was just like the way he explodes all of a sudden, and I've caught myself almost losing my temper too. I think that's part of it. And his wife—the way he goes on and on about her."

"Let's check it out," says Apples. "We've got nothing to lose." He raises his hand and waves Eddie in. Eddie takes an uncertain few steps forward.

"What the hell?" says Grammock in the dugout. "Apples is in charge of positioning the defense now?"

Apples waves his arm in a big sweep, and Eddie begins to trot to the mound.

"You gonna tell him to sneak up on me for a pick-off?" the runner at second says tauntingly. "That's *real* clever."

Eddie pulls up to the mound. "Wha's happ'nin'?"

"Eddie," says E.T.A. "I'm going to ask it straight out." And he does.

"What the fuck you talkin' about?" Eddie says with automatic outrage. "You fuckin' crazy, or what?" Then, in an unplanned burst of frankness, he liberates himself. "*Shit*, E.T.A. I been blue since the season begun." He looks from E.T.A. to Apples. "How'd . . . Man, I been afraid this'd happen. Do it show *that* much?"

E.T.A. shakes his head. "Relax, Eddie. It just takes one to know one."

The ump is suddenly upon them. "Hey, Apples, you keep gettin' sad and lonely out here? Come on, let's play ball."

Before he turns to head back to his position, Eddie exchanges a last glance with E.T.A. and Apples. The runner at second grins and calls to Eddie as he passes by, "You gonna sneak up on me for a pick-off? That's *real* clever." The runner is obviously a dumb cluck, and Eddie would normally have told him to get the lint out of his head. But Eddie is thinking. His mind races as he takes his position. He doesn't even see the next pitch, which is fouled deep down the third-base line. He watches the ball land in the crowd, and his eyes come to rest on Buford, who also watches it—with distinctly slumped shoulders. He remembers Buford voicing his fear of fatherhood, and he sees that fear in a wholly new light. He looks in and sees that Apples and E.T.A. are having yet another conference on the mound, this time with Narvel. He takes advantage of the lull to jog over to Buford, who is still gazing mournfully into the stands.

They talk—the two in left field, the three on the mound.

"Jesus," says Grammock, frowning and looking out at the mound. "How in the hell is Apples gonna find his rhythm if they keep jawin' out there?"

"Johnson and Ellenbogen have also gotten together in

left field to discuss where to play the hitter," says the play-by-play radio announcer, who, having already had the opportunity to give all of the scores and highlights of the other major-league games completed that day or still in progress, wonders what to say next. "This is obviously a crucial moment in an all-important game. Now here comes the home-plate umpire out to speed things up again."

Apples' next two pitches are just outside the strike zone. Then the hitter lofts a foul ball deep behind third base. Frank, Scrappy, and Buford converge on it. Running at full speed, Buford and Scrappy collide and drop to the ground. Frank, the sole survivor, takes two more steps and dives to rescue the ball on the fly. He bounces twice on his chest, pops up, and wheels the ball down the foul line to third, where Apples, covering, takes his throw—which, in Frank's necessary haste to get it off, is slightly to Apples' left. The runner tagging from second slides in safely under Apples' tag. Apples jumps up and cocks his arm to try for the other runner, who has tagged up at first, but he is already pulling easily into second.

Buford is unhurt, but Scrappy remains on the ground. Buford bends down to him, then waves the trainer out from the dugout. Most of the team gathers in left field. The trainer spends several minutes with Scrappy.

"Jesus H. Christ," mutters Grammock. "The kid's only a .225 hitter, but behind him I got nothin' but junk." He turns and looks at his back-up infielders on the bench and he wants to be sick.

Eddie takes Bubba by the arm and walks him away from the others gathered around Scrappy, so that they can talk alone. Finally, Scrappy gets a modest hand from the crowd in the stands when he rises to his feet and puts his glove back on. As the rest of the players return to their positions, Apples notices that Buford spends some extra time with Scrappy in shallow left field. And he hears Eddie say to Bubba, just before he turns to go back to center field, "Maybe it ain't no big thang now, but it sure growin'."

The trainer gives Grammock a report: Scrappy, though shaken, is not injured. Also, he adds by way of a footnote, Scrappy was *crying* when he got to him. Grammock laughs and says, "Hell, I'd probly cry too. I'd sooner run into a train than Buford."

Apples works the next batter to a full count, then gets him on a hard slider for the second out. To the infielders, who are dying to get back together, the duel seems to last for hours. They rush to the mound with the third strike—all of them but Frank, who remains at third. Grammock swears and puts his foot on the first step of the dugout. Then he forces himself to stay there. He wants to save his trips for when they are absolutely necessary. In the broadcast booth, the play-by-play announcer has begun to give the history of the dimensions of the baseball diamond over the decades.

" . . . kind of like a grayness in the center of your head," Apples is saying. "A big, gray cloudbank in there."

"Yeah," says Scrappy.

"And you always feel like a failure, right?" E.T.A. says to the group. "Even after a good game, a game where you really contribute. You'll think of some way that you're rotten and worthless—like you'll think of games where you *didn't* contribute, games you tell yourself we lost because you didn't. You'll just deliberately bring yourself down, right?"

"Yeah," Scrappy says enthusiastically. "I wake up thinkin' about stuff like that along about four a.m. every mornin'."

"I feel so down on myself I feel guilty about winning," Apples says. "The way I see it, I don't *deserve* to win."

"I don't deserve to *live*," says Scrappy with a little laugh.

Narvel looks at him and says, with the fatalistic gravity of a depressed mad scientist, "There are people dying every day, Scrappy. People you don't even know."

Scrappy ponders this proposition.

"You guys," Frank says tentatively, stepping up to a point just outside their circle. "Hey, you guys, you talking about me? About my throw to Apples? I was a little off balance. I'm really sorry."

"Another one!" E.T.A. calls out. "Come on, Frank. Join the club."

Apples puts his arm around his third baseman. "That was a hell of a catch you made, Frank."

"A better throw would have nailed the runner," Frank insists.

"Only God could have both made the catch and gotten the runner," says E.T.A.

Apples wants to tell E.T.A. that references to God remind him of his adolescence and depress him. He wants to get into his symptoms in a big way. But Grammock is suddenly intruding among them, red-faced, out of control.

"Don't you bums know the difference between spring training and the real thing?" He waves his arm around the ballpark. "*This* is the real thing. *This* is Dodger Stadium. *This* is the big time. You want drills, I'll give ya' drills. You want strategy talk, I'll give ya' strategy talk. But you guys are worryin' this game right into the lost column."

"Hey, Skip, you depressed too?" Scrappy naïvely asks. Apples winces for him.

Grammock becomes a squeaking, fat tornado, his head whirling on his neck in disbelief at the question. "What the hell kind of smart-ass remark is *that*, Mr. Crybaby?" he snaps. "Now you guys shape up an' show me what you're made of." He spins around and heads for the dugout.

The epithet has taken the air out of their lungs. "It's okay, Scrappy," Apples says to him. "We've all been crying, I'll bet. We're all in this, and deep."

"Come on," says Narvel. "Let's put an end to this shit."

As they watch him go back behind home plate, they

61

realize he is talking only of the game, not of anything bigger. With sighs of relief and despair, they take their positions, struggling to remember where the game is: two out, bottom of the ninth, runners on second and third, the score at 1–1. They are able, all of them, to get back into the game this much and to ready themselves. Even Scrappy.

Apples winds and delivers.

A ground ball is sometimes described as "eating up" an infielder. A ball so described is invariably hit hard, usually right at the fielder, and it strikes the ground in front of him at a point such that guesswork and fear play a key dual role in determining his glove placement. It "eats him up" when it neatly avoids or glances off his glove and proceeds to gnaw at several parts of his body. For a brief moment, the fielder looks as though he is wrestling with a ghost. Once the fielder has retrieved the ball, if he does at all, he has neither time nor spirit to get a throw off. With two out, a runner at third would take off for home at the crack of the bat. He would score, unless suddenly immobilized by depression on the way home—an unlikely possibility.

The official scorer calls it a single.

Grammock disagrees. "Fuckin' E-6 in my book," he snarls in the dugout. He heaves up a huge load of bitter spit. Then he mutters, "Look at that. They're runnin' to him like he's the hero instead a the goat. Jesus H. I don't savvy this team a-*tall*."

Scrappy is overwhelmed by the support he gets. At first he turns away to hide his tears from the players around him, but then he turns back around, unashamed. They all huddle in the infield for some time, continuing to talk. The happy Los Angeles fans pause at the exits and cast curious glances back at them before finally shrugging with indifference and going on their way.

4

Their world is chock-full of raw material which, carefully misconstrued, nourishes their sickness. When E.T.A. speaks with mildly arrogant pride of his six-year-old son's progress in learning how to read, Scrappy thinks of the many clauses in his contract that mean nothing to him and wonders if E.T.A.'s boy has surpassed him in reading skill. Bubba, irate from a bout with a group of young autograph seekers, complains that the children of today have no manners, so Buford imagines his present fetuses as husky male teenagers morally misshapen from his ignorant, passive rearing: "Hey, Dad, ya' fat pushover, hand over the car keys before we belt ya' one."

In addition, they see themselves as *intentionally* implied by such remarks. At the same time, they know that not every utterance is as loaded as they think it could be. But how can they tell which ones are and which ones aren't?

Ideally, something like this would happen: After some time had passed, the speaker—in the first case, E.T.A.—

would think, "Gee, I sure hope Scrappy didn't take that the wrong way." Likewise, Bubba would think, "Wow, gentle Buford's gon' think I 'uz messin' with his mind." The speaker would take the injured depressive aside and spend the better part of an afternoon detailing how the depressive's situation differed dramatically from the instant case. The speaker's recognition of the potential for misconstruing the utterance is crucial. Why? It is evidence that the depressive is not crazy for the way he hears things.

Thus there are two parts to these events: the inference of an insult and the effective erasure of the insult, accompanied by warm praise. The first part is secret, isolated, anti-social, negative; the second part is open, sharing, socially binding, life-affirming. For this team, the second part hasn't happened. Of *course* it hasn't happened. How could it? How could anybody—especially a depressive with problems of his own—be sensitive enough to enter someone else's mind to this extent?

But, one wants to protest, *they have talked about it! It is out in the open!* This much is true. And they continue to talk about it. But talking about it doesn't stop it.

On an unseasonably cool day in early July, they sit in the dugout and watch the rhythm of the opposition's pre-game workout.

"Ain't it a bitch the way it takes aholt of you?" Scrappy says, addressing no one in particular.

"Right out of the blue," says Apples.

"Like a thief in the night," says E.T.A.

"I look in the mirror and, *man*—it's like I'm lookin' at another dude wearin' my face," says Eddie. "An' I miss my bad ol' se'f."

E.T.A. nods knowingly. "I feel the same way about *my*self, Eddie. I can feel myself mourning for a lost personality."

Eddie studies E.T.A. for a moment. "When we gon' git it

64

back?" he asks him. He turns to his teammates. "I mean, do folks git over this shit, or what?"

They all look from Eddie to E.T.A. They are waiting for an answer. E.T.A. is staggered by their attention, their evident respect. He questions it, doubts it, suspects it must be something other than what it appears to be. But, try as he will, he cannot change it. He cannot turn it against himself. "Sure," he says to Eddie. "I mean, some do."

"If not one way," says Narvel, "then the other." He makes a fist below his chin, extends his thumb back toward one side of his neck, and, with a quick *tsst*-sound, slices it across his neck.

"I'm hip to *that*," Eddie says with enthusiasm.

"No!" Scrappy says. "You got to *fight* it. You got to fight *back*. You . . ." He is suddenly conscious of their stares, of the beginning of what might be a mocking smile from E.T.A. "I dunno . . ."

"I agree," says Buford, picking him up. "You've got to hang in there, Narv'. We all do. There's always tomorrow, and it might bring something good for you."

Narvel shrugs. "Yeah?" he drawls skeptically. "Just don't you guys be surprised if someday I signal for Apples' fast ball and take my face mask off. You'll know where I want it, Apples." He taps his forehead. "Right in my crazy wheelhouse."

"What if the batter hits the ball?" asks Frank.

"I'll call for it on three-and-oh," says Narvel.

"What if—"

"I'll make sure he's a weak hitter. One who wouldn't have the green light."

"I think there's a rule to the effect that a catcher must always wear a face mask when the pitch is thrown," Frank persists, making a mental note to check this important point later. "Speaking of rules . . ."

The others resentfully fall silent as Frank continues to tread upon the corpse of their discussion. By the time he finishes, or rather, begins to sound as though he will finish fairly soon, Grammock is upon them, rubbing his hands and grinning.

"Say," he says, cutting Frank short, "where'd I leave off the other day? I got the farmer into the bar, right? Burpin' up cornmeal mush an' goin' blind with liquor? An' I got the skinny preacher plowin' the wife's twitchet, okay? So . . . listen up, Frank. Don't look so disappointed. The season's still young, an' the boys all know you won't forgit what you was sayin'. So, the preacher, he's banged her five, six times, an' while they're takin' a little break she says she's gotta go to the toilet, which a course in them days was a outhouse in back. So she gits outta bed and trots out the back door, leavin' the preacher layin' there givin' thanks to the Lord for what a lovely evenin' he's been havin'.

"But all of a sudden he hears the farmer a-stumblin' up the porch steps, so he leaps outta bed an' beelines it to the kitchen, where his clothes is layin' all over the table. He grabs 'em in a pile an' heads for the back door. In case you're wonderin', hell, a *course* he knew 'bout the superstition against men callers leavin' a house by a different door than the one they come in, else the woman of the house'll git pregnant, but he warn't gonna be fussy on that point jist then. Besides, one more of his woods colts litterin' the countryside wouldn't hardly git noticed, he figgers. So he's aimin' for the back door, only he's all turned around, on accounta it's dark an' he's in a strange house an' all, so he winds up back in the bedroom, with the farmer hot on his tail. He heads for the winder, but the farmer's in there afore he can git it open.

"The farmer, he flops down on the bed an' says, 'Maw'— he always calls his wife 'Maw,' like maybe he's fond a reminiscin' 'bout good times in the sack with his real mama— 'Maw,' he says, 'stop lollygaggin' 'round that winder an' git

66

your pud over here.' Well, the preacher, he don't know whether to shit or go blind."

"Skip," Eddie says, pointing to the field. "Our turn for B.P."

"Aw," Grammock moans. "Goddammit anyway. Well, git your butts out there, then, 'cuz you sure need it."

As the players flee the dugout, Grammock's eyes fall on the deaf, cud-chewing equipment manager, and his face brightens a moment, then falls into a disappointed scowl. "Nah," he says to himself. Then he spies the bat boy at the end of the dugout. "Hey, kid," he yells. "Come 'ere. Sit down."

The boy approaches and perches timidly on the bench.

"Now, then. There was this preacher fellow, skinny as a plucked chicken . . ."

○ ○ ○

Bubba has the hots for Eddie's wife. She's a high-yellow: light-brown skin of silken smoothness, ochered cheeks, eyes so painted up they make him dizzy, and legs that could wrap around him twice with some extra slack left over. The bitch in her that Eddie always talks about appeals to him. He sees himself matching it, destroying her with a power he feels Eddie doesn't bring to her.

But in another sense, Eddie is a force to be reckoned with. He's a big man who is given to fits, and though he always speaks of his wife with hatred, if he knew anything was going on between Bubba and her, he would probably hurt him just on general principles. So far, not a lot is going on. Bubba is not great with words, and he knows he couldn't get her that way. But he knows she's seen him looking at her in his special way when she's around the ballpark—it's the same look he gives pitchers he's about to attempt a steal against— and she has responded in a way that tells him all he has to do is come knockin'. Of course, there *was* that one time outside the locker room, when he was all showered and slicked up and she was waiting for Eddie, and his little move on her was greeted with a shove and a cry of "Gitcha meat off me, mud," but he knows that was just for show, because of the other wives who were there.

The real problem is that Eddie is always in town when Bubba is. And there's that damn kid too, the one Eddie is always going on about. He'll just have to wait to make his move. Lay low. And, above all, not give Eddie a hint of his feelings about her. That thought scares the hell out of him.

In fact, for such an aggressive young man, Bubba has surprisingly grown fearful of just about everything. He is sure that some sort of attack is imminent. Lying in bed at night, he watches the shadows in his bedroom and listens to the noises in his apartment, and to the significant silences between them. And whenever his bathroom door sticks when he tries to open it from inside, he imagines some fiend on the other side of it, devilishly holding the doorknob for sheer sport before pouncing on him.

In the daylight, where life should be less threatening, he is conscious of the footsteps of pedestrians behind him on the sidewalk, hearing these above all other city noises. Sometimes when they are close and loud, or appear to be speeding up, he imagines he will be jumped from the rear, and he quickly darts aside, sometimes bumping sharply into other pedestrians. When he sees that he has escaped attack, he purges himself of torment—temporarily, at least—by turning on these pedestrians, by following them closely for long distances and intermittently slapping his feet down noisily on the pavement, just to see if he can make them as frightened as he was.

O O O

Narvel's boyhood diary arrives from San Diego after a delay of more than a month: his mother miswrote the address and his father carried the unmailed package around in his coat pocket for two weeks, because mailing things demands a tenacity that is foreign to him. Narvel waits until his wife has left for the library, then skims the diary quickly, surprised to see that there are almost as many numbers as words in it. Then he goes back to the beginning and carefully reads it all in one sitting.

The words are simple. Rather than describing average boyhood pleasures, they focus on his parents, telling of a sad succession of failed small businesses and of mounting stacks of unread *Wall Street Journals*, overflowing from his parents' bedroom into Narvel's and out onto the back porch. The words tell of bitter fights at home between his parents, his mother's grasp of the world being just sufficient to have enabled her to ask nagging questions about the way her husband managed their finances—questions that were more penetrating than she could have appreciated, sprung as they were out of ignorance—and that his father, mortified by them, tried to turn against her by proclaiming he would be able to "bounce back," he would be able to "turn the corner" and "see daylight," if only he had a wife who believed in him. The words don't say all of this. They speak instead of apparent incidentals: canceled vacation trips, mysteriously disappearing automobiles, birthdays ruined by his parents' screaming, and incredibly shrinking houses as the three of them hurtled down the social ladder. The words form an imperfect record, but they inspire Narvel's memory, which does the rest.

The numbers are initially less clear. He sees that there are two sets, one with numbers that increase by one each year, the other having to do with money. He understands the meaning of the first set when he reads the plaintive words, "Why did they wait so long?" The numbers are running totals of his parents' years on earth, a record he apparently kept out of amazement at the distance between his and theirs (forty-one years in his mother's case, forty-eight in his father's). The ages are given with those of his classmates and their parents—data he remembers having gathered for a melancholy class report on the subject.

As he looks at two pie-like drawings, one of which is labeled "Where Your Dollar Comes From," the other of which is labeled "Where Your Dollar Goes," the meaning of the second set of numbers comes to him in a flash, and he bursts out in dark, sadistic laughter. He studied economics, briefly and superficially, in the sixth or seventh grade, and he was evidently so taken with the revenues-and-expenditures pies he studied that he drew one of each to express the monetary complexities of his life. The expenditures were typical for a boy his age: "Candy, $.25," "Gum, $.15," "Movies, $.45," and "Other Recreation, $.15." The sources of the income were probably a bit less standard: "Pop's Dresser, $.10," "Pop's Pants, $.05," "Pop's Easy Chair, $.45," "Mom's Kitchen Piggy Bank, $.10," "Mom's Purse, $.05," "Mom's Underwear Drawer, $.25." The grisly facts are there. He stole loose change from them over a period of several years. By the time he was in the eighth grade and stopped keeping the diary, he had stolen a sum easily determinable from the very last entry: "Grand Total of Revenues, $1,212.00. Grand Total of Expenditures, $1,212.00." The absence of a deficit put his father's finances to shame.

He closes the diary with a small sense of shame, which he is surprised to find quickly giving way to bitter regret that he did not manage to steal more than $1,212.00 from them.

○ ○ ○

E.T.A. has a new theory about "quality" in a mind. A Frank-like memory is somewhat important, as is Eddie-like mental agility. But the *sine qua non* is insincerity. Bubba is his latest intellectual model. For several weeks, Bubba had been subtly obstructing runners trying to go from first to third on a base hit. To slow them, he would stand in the base path and move away at the last instant, or stand out of the base path and then suddenly move as if to place himself in the runner's path without actually doing so—practices as illegal as physical obstruction, but less obvious to runner and umpire alike. E.T.A., however, with the depressive's hypersensitivity to bad vibrations, noticed it early on and studied Bubba's execution of the maneuver. Someone must have tipped off the umpiring crew before the New York series, because Bubba was called for it twice, and Grammock finally told him to knock it off. Now what E.T.A. finds remarkable as he obsessively dwells on the two incidents is that on both occasions Bubba charged the ump and argued the call as vehemently as Joan of Arc asserting her virginity. Yet it was a correct call. Bubba must have known that. The trick, E.T.A. decides, is not to be over-involved in your position—maybe even to know it is false.

○ ○ ○

The guys in the bullpen are assholes. They really are. They aren't the least bit depressed and know nothing of Apples' problems or those of the eight regulars. At rare moments of peak sensitivity, they'll sense someone needs a lift, so they will play a practical joke. Depressives don't need practical jokes. They really don't.

Apples, for example. Apples has a new theory about himself, with emphasis on his penis. He thinks it is small. But he is as mistaken about this as he is about the size of his breasts. He doesn't realize that every male's penis looks small when viewed from above, just as the Empire State Building doesn't look as tall as it really is when viewed from an airplane twenty-five thousand feet directly overhead. This visual distortion is exaggerated in Apples' case because of his extreme height. He looks down the length of his torso and thinks,

"How can such a man deserve to pitch in the All-Star Game?" Apples copes by hiding his parts from his teammates as religiously as he hides the fact of his sexual innocence from them. The home clubhouse man provides him with extra-long towels, and when Apples walks to and from the showers, he drapes a towel over his neck, pressing one fold of it against his loins with apparent casualness, hiding himself like a shy artist's model. He is actually glad when women reporters are in the clubhouse, for then several of the guys with regular penises wear a towel around their waists, and he simply pretends to be one of them. One Sunday evening, two of the bullpen guys were in his hotel room drinking stingers while he dressed, his back to them, preparing to go out with them. When the bullpen guys got their heads together and agreed that Apples needed some support for his tough loss that afternoon, and promptly pantsed him and threw him naked out into the hall, where he languished for ten minutes, they made a mistake. When they laughed at his tearful plea to be let back in, they made another mistake. And when they finally opened the door and heartily joked that they couldn't see that he had much to hide, they made yet another mistake and showed once and for all what assholes they are.

Buford too. A couple of southpaws from the bullpen planted two identical baby dolls, naked, on the top shelf of his locker, their painted pink mouths smeared with human feces. Big joke. When Buford found them, he was so saddened he couldn't get mad. And he couldn't pretend to laugh, either. He just took them down and quietly dropped them into the wastebasket. The guys who had done it laughed and laughed, as if Buford's reaction were the ideal one, the very one they had hoped for. Buford knew what it was all about. They must have heard him talking with Eddie about babies' bowel habits. They must have heard him ask Eddie if Tina had ever eaten her feces—not at all an idle question, because Ellie had told him just a few days before of toddlers left alone too long sometimes exploring their bodily products in this way. How do you deal with that? he had silently wondered, afraid to share his fears with her. How do you cope? Where do you begin? Eddie had said he didn't think Tina had ever eaten hers—unless, he added, his dumb-ass wife fed her some one night when she didn't feel like cooking. So Buford was heartened. At least the practice wasn't universal. And the other fathers, E.T.A. and Frank, took his question as seriously as Eddie had and reported no such ingestion. Things were looking up, and he was handling the problem pretty well.

But then this grim reminder. Who needed it? What assholes.

○ ○ ○

"I dunno, I can't seem to git that man offa my mind, even in here."

"Mm-hmm."

"It's like he's out to git me, ya' know? Am I crazy for thinkin' that?"

"Not necessarily."

"Like when he asks me about my chin. He's always askin' me when I'm gonna start growin' one. Hell, I can't help the way I look. What's the point a him harpin' on that anyway? Or like the time he told me about the batting order. Ya' see, I bat seventh. Behind me is Narvel—he's our catcher—and then the pitcher. Narv's got a better average 'n me, but I figured Grammock appreciated somethin' about my hittin' to put me in the seventh position, maybe because a the way I can slap the ball to the opposite field sometimes, or maybe because I can hang tough against righties. But it was somethin' I was proud of, and Narv'—he's a funny guy, always complainin', an' I wanna git to know him better someday, if he'll let me— one thing he never complained about was followin' me in the order, so all in all I felt pretty good about it. Then one day

Grammock comes over to me, right smack in the middle of a game, an' he sits down and says he wants me to understand somethin'. I say, sure, Skip, go ahead. He says he's got a kinda unique way a lookin' at the seventh an' eighth positions in the line-up. He says the eighth guy has to be good enough a hitter to git on base a lot when there's two outs, so's the pitcher will make the last out an' won't be leadin' off in the next inning. He says his way a thinkin' is the number-eight hitter hasta be better 'n the number-seven hitter. So he always has the crummiest hitter bat seventh. He says he jist wanted to be sure I understood that. Then he gits up and leaves me sittin' there studyin' myself. I'm thinkin', hey, thanks a lot, Gram'. Thanks for goin' out of your way to tell me I'm a crumb-bum. It was like he was afraid I'd go an' have a good thought about myself. You know what I'm sayin'? You understand?"

"Mm-hmm."

○ ○ ○

Like an incompetent committee with a vague charge and incomplete data, E.T.A. is still working on the same problem. He rejects his earlier view of the crucial role of insincerity as a cynical *ignis fatuus* kindled by his despondent mind. In fact, now he is absolutely certain of the opposite: what one needs to argue well is true belief in one's position. Bubba's violent confidence in his recent arguments with the umps does not contradict this view. Rather, it illustrates it, when correctly understood. Bubba must have actually believed he was justified in cheating because, having a criminal mind, he does not recognize traditional values. E.T.A.'s problem, as he sees it, is that he has a depressive's lack of real interest in life, and his apathy saps his opinions of their strength. Memory assumes a new importance here. Without strong feelings, one may well think through an issue and form a solid opinion, but if it lacks force and if, in addition, one's memory is not outstanding, *poof*—no opinion three weeks later. One begins to feel like, and is maybe thought to be, an intellectual lightweight— "despite his education," he hears them saying.

Clearly, E.T.A. thinks too much. He is really pretty tiresome, and he is mistaken in his belief that thought alone can save him—not friends, not a sympathetic spouse, not medication, not professional help, but thought. For all his mental energy, he is making no more progress than a Ferris wheel run amok.

The other guys are thinking too, if not more accurately than E.T.A., at least with a bit more panache.

Narvel likes to think in terms of doom. His innate pessimism finds rich nourishment in his father's history of failure. In spite of his wife's daily supportive arguments against the idea, he is convinced he is doomed to follow in his father's bumbling footsteps. Just as the houses of his childhood shrank before his eyes, confining and stifling him, his present work environment—chokingly defined by the batter, home plate, and the ump crawling up his back—seems to box him in and take his breath away. How he envies the other fielders' freedom to vary their positions, Apples' liberty to roam the mound between pitches. His favorite call is for the pitchout, which allows him to burst out of his shackles and leap, tall and free, into the open air.

Apples think he knows why he feels especially down during the playing of the national anthem. He believes it is because of his fascination with Bubba's buttocks, which hover beckoningly over second base. But Apples isn't really a homosexual. He is not really attracted to Bubba's buttocks. They are just visually interesting. Any man on the mound would drop his eyes from Old Glory and take a peek. Even the ump behind home plate is interested in them. Apples is really off the mark in his thinking.

Similarly, Eddie, having gone two months denying to

75

himself that he was depressed, now takes refuge in the view that *all* men are depressed: the sighing bellhop who carried his bags for him in Houston, the sad-eyed bartender down the street from his house, the gentle grown-ups who speak so kindly to Tina on public television—blue as hell, all of them. Of course, his theory is not totally preposterous. There *are* others out there, after all. (The freckle-faced Montreal catcher whom Bubba cruelly flummoxed last month, for example: he is slipping fast now, having taken E.T.A.'s note of condolence as viciously sarcastic.) They all hide it, some better than others. One symptom, perhaps the single unifying one for such men, is the desire to keep it a secret.

Who chews on this team, and who doesn't? The question is relevant to Jaime's thinking, which unfortunately is no more successful than his speech. Who does: Narvel and Scrappy. Who doesn't: Apples, E.T.A., Bubba, and Eddie. Special cases: Frank, Buford, and Jaime. Frank follows the trend of whatever team happens to be afflicted with him. While with Cincinnati at the end of the preceding season, he chewed his ass off, but, following the lead of this relatively clean-toothed club, he gave it up in spring training. His spit, while still excessive, is now lily-white. Buford has cut way down. The habit is at odds with Ellie's wholesomeness. And the kids—he imagines their questions about it embarrassing him; he sees himself slobbering his way through parent-teacher conferences. He has cut way down. And then there is Jaime. He knows about food. You chew it and swallow it. Gum: you chew it and swallow your sweetened saliva. Tobacco: ? He hasn't mastered the intermittent spit. He chews and chews, his mouth becoming a liquid toxic-waste dump-site, and then he finally erupts like a Caribbean volcano, clearing the bench on both sides of him. One day Bubba, in a rare burst of speech, took him aside and snarled to him that bloods don't chew. Jaime was confused. Bubba pantomimed chewing and shook a no-no with his head and finger. Jaime got it! Bubba was trying to tell him not to chew tobacco, because tobacco was what was making him sad. Of course! He was so overwhelmed with joy that he hugged Bubba, thanked him, and called him a name he'd been wanting to call him for months. "Bubba" sounds much like "Bobo," a word familiar to Jaime from days of yore, and he had always taken Bubba's name for a nickname, albeit an odd one. But if it *was* a nickname, he thought, why not call him by the English word for it? Wouldn't that be more courteous? So, overcome with misplaced gratitude for a message he misunderstood in the first place, he hugged Bubba and cried out, "Dankee, *Stupid!*" Bubba, repelled and terrified, backed off hastily and added Jaime's name to his enemies list.

Finally, one day in a game against the Pirates, E.T.A. has some insights worth recording—not for their validity, but for what will one day prove to be their ultimate consequence. They come to him on the heels of a superbly aggressive defensive play. With a man on third and one out, he takes a hard two-bouncer and sees the runner break for home. E.T.A. freezes him with a cocked arm, then runs right at him, full of purpose, as if this is the climax of a pursuit of long duration. He shades slightly toward home, and the runner, after too long a delay, finally tries to go back to third. E.T.A.'s momentum makes it no race at all, and he slams the ball hard against the back of the runner's neck and then guns it to Bubba at second for a neat tag on the batter trying to tiptoe in.

How can he think so quickly and act so confidently on the field and then turn into a Jaime in conversation? He works on the problem in the dugout. He begins to see that quick thought on the field isn't really thought so much as it is identification of a recurring pattern, followed by action that he performs confidently because he has performed it before. But surely, he thinks, such patterns occur in the world of ideas as well—undistributed middles, illicit minors, *ad hominem* arguments, not to mention those nasty fallacies *a dicto secun-*

dum quid ad dictum simpliciter. Why, back in the shower in May, Eddie thrashed him with a paltry *tu quoque*. All he has to do is identify these patterns in the future. Confidence will then come with successful verbal ventures, and he will be invincible.

And he must get used to being aggressive, as aggressive as he was on that tag he made. He shouldn't fear being successful in argument, the way Apples seems to fear winning too many games. That could be the sum total of the problem for all of them, he thinks breathlessly: their continuing success. After all, their spirits have declined as steadily as their lead in the division has increased. He sees two lines on a wall graph, congruent in April, then parting sharply, one heading for great heights, the other for the cellar.

With barely controlled mania, he shares his theories with Apples in the dugout. Apples isn't working that day, so E.T.A. doesn't have to worry about taking his mind off the game. He chronicles the course of his thought on the subject over the past weeks, taking and keeping the floor for a period of time approaching Frank's average, and Apples listens attentively, especially when E.T.A. gets to the part about Apples' tendency to lose his stuff in the late innings, just when victory is in sight—evidence, says E.T.A., that Apples fears and is depressed by the prospect of success.

But Apples sees things as simpler than this. Basically, he just wants a piece of ass—male, female, you name it, as long as he finds out who he is. Though a psychosexual basket case, Apples is really a good guy, and he tries to respond with enthusiasm to what E.T.A. says. But he doesn't believe a word of it, and E.T.A. can see that he doesn't. Formerly, this would have depressed E.T.A. Now, in the full flush of confidence, he sees it as an example of rather predictable resistance to the truth—a recurring pattern in discussions that he will have to be on the lookout for in the future. He resolves to work on Apples more, later. He is going to work on the entire team. He will save them with his mind.

○ ○ ○

Apples sits in his dentist's waiting room, reading about his "mysteriously uncatchable" team in *Sports Illustrated*, trying not to think about the well-muscled young man sitting across from him. Their eyes met and locked briefly as Apples came in, then again after Apples gave his name to the receptionist, picked a magazine from the stand, and sat down. Apples is not sexually aroused, though. He is merely uncomfortable because he suspects the young man is a homosexual who desires him. But Apples has managed to mistake his discomfort for repressed arousal. (Also, the man isn't a homosexual at all. He's just a fan who has recognized Apples and is tremendously excited about it.) When Apples' name is called before the young man's, Apples mistakes his slight embarrassment at being called first though having arrived last for keen disappointment at parting from such an attractive potential mate. He wonders if the young man will be there when he comes out, and he mistakes his idle curiosity on this point for a passionate wish that he *will* be there. By the time Apples is seated in the dentist's chair, he is so depressed by his sexual identity that he wouldn't protest much if he were to be treated to an oral examination, dental prophylaxis, and then castration.

As the dental assistant causes his seat to recline and rise, she says off-handedly, "You certainly are a long man." He hardly hears her. Then, at some point toward the end of the X-rays, he becomes aware of her fingers in his mouth. When she begins picking at his teeth, he feels her cool, strangely pure breath on his cheek and the pressure of her starched breasts on his arm. The tingling in his gums from the slippery, gristly, rubber-tipped drill bit works slowly down his spine. By the time she is struggling with the dental floss between his closely packed lower teeth, he is deliriously horny. As she puts the equipment away, he notices with joyful panic that she is young *and* pretty *and* wears no wedding band. Unless she must take it off to do her work? No, because here comes the dentist with *his* wedding band flashing, and he greets Apples enthusiastically, makes some small talk, and begins to examine him, dictating notes to the assistant—much more brusquely than Apples would, for she deserves better, he thinks. Apples races through his mind for something to say to her. But, alas, the dentist is through with him and she is gone. But wait—she is back, telling him to make an appointment for six months from now for another checkup. He nods, thinking, "Six months—a lifetime!" He must say something. But what?

She walks him to the receptionist and says in a quick, self-conscious burst of speech, "I hope to see you wearing a World Series ring in January, Apples." Then she is gone, leaving a smile behind her. His knees buckle and he steadies himself against the receptionist's counter. "Oh," he thinks, "if I am, I will give it to you to wear on a golden chain around your neck."

Crushing a remnant of pumice between his teeth, he doesn't even think to look for the young man on his way out of the office. He is busy thinking about the game schedule, wondering when they will be back home from the upcoming road trip, and wishing his teeth were all rotten.

○ ○ ○

"Howcome I always feel like a dumb shit in here?"

"You tell me."

"Look at those books. Howcome ya' got so many books in here?"

"I ran out of room at home."

"Jesus. Ya' got more there too?" He shakes his head. "I can't make heads nor tails outta some a them titles. I'm a pretty fair reader, though, generally. 'Member Miss Eula? That retired schoolteacher? I told ya' about her, didn't I?"

"Yes. I remember."

"She's the one taught me readin'. Gram'—hell, she told the school she was gonna teach me at home, but I didn't learn diddly-shit from her. A course she did teach me how to git unwitched if someone put a spell on me, but I ain't never found that too useful, somehow. She thought Miss Eula was a witch. Can ya' believe that? All on accounta Miss Eula let a redbud tree grow in her front yard. Ya' see, back home they say Judas hung hisself from a redbud tree. She made the *best* applesauce, though, an' there's another sayin' back home that ya' gotta be a good woman to make good applesauce. She'd fill me full a that stuff while learnin' me to read. Then she'd play her piano an' sing songs for me—ya' know, real gentle, peaceful songs about peace an' good feelin's an' people gittin' along with each other.

"Hell, I been tellin' ya' all this shit. Sometimes I go home an' I can't believe what I said here. An' you don't say a helluva lot, and that makes me nervous, like you're thinkin' about me. Yeah, I know, you're sup*posed* to think about me. And at least you say *some*thin'. Narvel—he's our catcher—he's always sayin' how he went to a guy that didn't say diddly-shit. He quit goin' to him."

"I say diddly-shit, at least."

"Yeah. But those books. Man. An' more at home too."

"Don't worry about it. We all do different things. I doubt if I could hit the curve ball."

Scrappy nods, taking him seriously. "The curve ball *is* a toughie. Grammock always gits on me when I git beat by it. Calls me names. I been called lotsa names by him. An' by Gram' too, come to think of it. But there was one that she saved for special times, when she was feelin' kinda taken with me, I guess. She'd call me a 'muggins,' 'cuz she thought I had a cute little mug, I guess. You ever heard that word before?"

"Just from you."

Scrappy frowns. "I guess I told you about this already, huh?"

"Mm-hmm."

"Well, you ever heard the word before ya' heard it from me?"

"No, I haven't."

"You think that's what she meant?"

"I don't know."

Scrappy shrugs. "I guess it ain't important. I don't know why I talk about it so much."

○ ○ ○

Apples is so madly in love with the dental assistant that he doesn't care about his sexual inexperience. He trusts her. They will learn together. Or, if she is experienced, he will catch up. He's a fast learner. It took him only a week to learn how to throw a slider.

But his teeth are perfect, and January is impossibly far away. If he pretends to have a toothache, the dentist will find nothing wrong and she will think him a pansy. He has toyed with the idea of deliberately injuring a tooth—say, with a hammer and screwdriver—but this idea depresses him more than anything he can think of, more even than his memory of watching full-immersion baptisms. He is not so far gone to want to hurt himself. He knows that is a possibility with his illness, and he is terrified of it.

It's a shame that Apples innocently thinks he has to make some small talk at the dentist's office before he can call this woman and ask her out. It's a shame he doesn't think enough of himself to see that her opening and parting words to him were a clear come-on, as clear a come-on as someone as sweet as she is can give. She *is* sweet, too. Just right for Apples.

○ ○ ○

The possibility occurs to most of them when Frank, whose lateral movement at third is as quick as his speech, ends the third inning with a catch far to his left two inches above the ground. Most of them are thinking about it as they trot into the dugout to begin the fourth inning. Those that aren't already have—Apples, for example. He thought about it after he retired the first three Phillies he faced. He feels good and is keeping the ball down. His teammates have staked him to a 3–0 lead. All the signs are right. But in the dugout no one talks about it. It is forbidden.

In the next three innings, the Philadelphia fans begin to stir. Each out brings a host of new believers. And Apples is getting the breaks he needs for such a game. A drive past E.T.A. is foul by inches. A ball deflected by Apples' glove bounces to Bubba, who whips the ball to E.T.A. and gets the runner by the length of his cleats. After six innings, no opposing runner has reached base. They don't say a word about it. In the dugout, they avoid Apples as if he has embarrassed them in some way. He sits alone and wipes his face with a towel, wondering if it can go on for three more innings.

In the bottom of the seventh, he works the lead-off batter to three-and-one, then three-and-two; then he fans him, allowing himself an uncharacteristic little surge of anger at the bum for making him throw all those pitches. The other two batters fly out, first to Eddie, then to Jaime. In the top of the eighth, Apples' teammates score four more runs, aided by a sacrifice bunt by him. It is a long at-bat for them, with two pitching changes by the Phils, and everyone worries that Apples' arm will grow cold and tighten up. When he finally has taken the mound and has thrown the eight warm-up

83

pitches to which he is entitled, the home-plate ump is down the line sharing some crucial message with the third-base ump, so Apples shrugs and takes three more warm-up throws before signaling to Narvel to throw it down to second. No one notices, except the home-plate ump, who deliberately absented himself from the plate just for that purpose.

But there are problems. Narvel, his equipment squeezing his lungs, has gone completely claustrophobic. He pants, reaching for air, his thoughts flying outward while his body feels doomed to a frog-like posture of perpetual squat.

"Whatsa matter, Narv'?" the ump asks during a lull after Apples' first pitch of the eighth, while an attendant chases a balloon that has drifted down from the stands into shallow right field.

"Whaddya mean?"

"You're all antsy lately."

"Whaddya mean?"

"Narv', the whole crew really loves ya' for not jabberin' all the time, and for the way you lay down and give us a good look at the pitch. You know that. But now you're groanin' and moanin' and bobbin' around all the time like a yo-yo. Whatsa matter?"

"You're crowding me. Give me some room."

"I'm standin' where I been standin' all my life."

"No you're not. You've been leaning into me all day. Back off."

"You got plenty a room, Narv'."

"You're touching me. You're always feeling me."

"No, Narv'. Honest. Nothin's changed."

"*Some*thing's changed."

"No, honest."

"You're letting the hitters stand too deep, then."

"I'm keepin' 'em in the box, Narv', just like always."

"The box is too long, then. It isn't drawn right."

"I'll measure it if ya' like, Narv'. Really, I'll be happy to measure it for ya'."

Narvel looks at the rectangle, the batter's rear foot digging into the chalk. He sighs in despair. "Nah. Don't measure it."

There is also a bit of trouble at third base. Frank's arm is an ice block. He gave a little too much attention to his warm-up tosses, and E.T.A. had to work to get all three, especially the last one. Frank shakes his arm, paces between pitches, tries to joke with the third-base coach, and wonders why his arm weighs so much. All he needs is to get off one good throw to pull himself out of it, he thinks. It's really an inaccurate way of thinking, after all. Look at all the perfect throws he has made across the diamond in his career—thousands of them. Just one good throw, that's all he needs now. He toys with the idea of asking Apples for the ball so that he can throw it back to him, but he fears this might disturb Apples' concentration. Then Apples would despise him even more than he already does. No. Wait. He identifies the dysfunctional thought and chases it away. There is no firm evidence at all that Apples despises him. "Hum, babe," he calls to Apples encouragingly. "Hum, babe." All the while he thinks, "Don't let him hit it to me."

Suddenly it is there, as big as a grapefruit, coming right at him on the fly, and he bends his knees just slightly and takes it chest-high. One out—and a chance to throw! He cocks his arm to whip the ball to Scrappy to celebrate the out, but the ball seems to spring out of his hand into right-center field, so far from Scrappy that he doesn't even try for it. In fact, some think he was trying to throw to Jaime, who comes in and picks up the ball in deep confusion and flips it to Bubba. Bubba then throws it right to Apples. No point in sending it on around the horn after a screw-up like that, Bubba thinks, as do E.T.A., Narvel, and most of the other players—in fact, all but generous-minded Apples, who, it must be said, is unique among his teammates in that he does not dislike Frank intensely. Thus Frank's earlier thought is right, in a ridiculously narrow sense.

The next batter is a right-handed pull hitter who has already grounded out to Frank twice in the game. The first pitch is a ball, the second a swing-and-a-miss, and the third a sharp foul to the right of Frank, who chatters nervously as he watches Buford pick it up and flip it to a stadium guard at the edge of the stands. The next pitch is also hit foul to Frank's right—a screamer that flies into the stands like an assassin's bullet. Somebody is hit. Stadium attendants rush to the scene. A woman is crying. Was she hit? No, they see it now. A small boy, hit in the head. He must be her son. Someone hurries down the aisle with a stretcher, and he is carried out.

Buford is close to the scene, watching in horror and imagining his own forthcoming kids at a game. He sees a ball that is hit hard—maybe by him!—wiping both of them out at once, catching one in the forehead and glancing off to get the other one just above the ear. He will forbid them from ever entering a baseball stadium. That's the only solution. Hockey too, with its hard puck. That's out. What about basketball? He sees a diving seven-foot center landing in his daughter's lap, crushing her pelvis. Football? Icy roads to the stadium. Indoor track? The roof caves in.

Again and again he sees the boy in the stands stretched out, the mother crying. His eyes fill. The stadium jumps with his every blink.

Unaware that the far left side of the field is virtually unmanned, Apples fires a high, inside fast ball. The batter, himself distracted by the injury in the stands, swings and misses, striking out. Narvel leaps up and whips the ball down to Frank, who does a weird and fancy dance toward Scrappy and squirts it to him underhand. Scrappy, surprised and repulsed, takes it on the second bounce and throws it on to

Bubba, who fires it angrily back to Frank, who delivers it shakily by hand to Apples.

The next batter also strikes out, but a squirming Narvel drops the third strike at his feet. As the spectators jump up, Narvel, his elbows swinging wildly to clear the air of the demons surrounding him, bolts out in front of the plate and, though dizzily hyperventilated, gets off a hard, true one to E.T.A. at first to end the eighth.

In the dugout, Apples is a pariah. Scrappy begins to worry that Apples might misinterpret their behavior, which has nothing to do with Apples nor, for a change, with their depression. It is just a traditional superstition. But Scrappy fears that in his excitement over the game Apples may have forgotten about the superstition. Maybe he feels snubbed and unappreciated. Maybe they're bringing him down. So Scrappy slides down the bench to him and says, "It's too bad we can't talk about the perfect game ya' got goin'."

E.T.A. gasps.

Bubba mutters, "Dumb shit."

Jaime crosses himself.

Grammock barks, "Scrappy, shuddup an' don't be such a goddamn muggins."

Scrappy slides away from Apples just as he slid toward him, with exactly the same kind of moves. But he is a different man. He doesn't hear Apples say, "Lay off him, Skip. I don't mind." He doesn't hear anything but the rushing and hissing noises of his past. That word. Grammock said it with hatred, not love. So what did Gram' mean by it all those years? It can't possibly be true that those few moments of tenderness he recalls were merely another form of torture. It can't.

Buford flies out to deep left, but Scrappy doesn't see it. E.T.A. grounds out to second, but he doesn't see it. Frank stands in, and Scrappy has worked up the courage to ask the question that haunts him. He rises.

Grammock is watching the game and sucking his teeth.

Scrappy walks to him, inhales deeply, and says, "Skip, what is a muggins?"

Grammock grimaces. The ump is complaining about something from home plate. "A muggins is what *you* are for not bein' in the on-deck circle. Now git your butt up there."

Scrappy reddens and hurriedly finds his bat and helmet. "But what *is* it?" he calls back, pausing on the steps of the dugout.

"A muggins is a goddamn fool, that's what it is," Grammock screams. "You're a muggins and a numbskull, Scrapheap, and if your battin' average slips two points lower, I'm benchin' ya'."

In perfect misery, Scrappy kneels in the on-deck circle, his hands aimlessly smearing each other with the pine-tar rag.

Frank gets a hit, his first of the day. There is scattered applause from his dugout, but they are all really thinking how like Frank it is to be a jerk and prolong their at-bat when they have a seven-run lead and the only real excitement is what's going to happen when they take the field. Frank prolongs the game further by taking a long lead at first and drawing some throws. They would really like to kill him.

Scrappy never takes the bat off his shoulder and is called out on strikes. He begins to walk back to the dugout, where he has left his glove, and he sees Buford running out with it. He is surprised Buford still thinks enough of him to do this for him. He is willing to get his own glove from now on. They shouldn't treat him as an equal anymore. They should stop pretending that he is. Maybe they have stopped already, he thinks. Maybe Buford is making some kind of sick joke by bringing his glove out.

When Scrappy takes his position, he turns his back on the infield during the warm-up, and E.T.A., about to throw him the ball, double-pumps and goes to Frank instead. Frank fields the ball with a hopeful flourish and fires a bullet into the dirt eight feet in front of E.T.A. Frank's shoulders slump. It is hopeless. E.T.A. seems so very far away now. Such a tiny speck. On his next practice throw, Frank lobs an eephus pitch to E.T.A., a big, arcing lollipop. Grammock sees it and mutters, "What now?"

When play resumes, Scrappy watches and crouches from habit, taking his customary half-step forward with the pitch. But he has no intention of fielding the ball. He will let it hit him wherever it wants to. He will enjoy the full wrath he deserves—Grammock's, Apples', everybody's.

Narvel signals for a pitchout when the count reaches two-and-two on the first Philly to bat in the ninth—an unorthodox call, given that no one is on base. Apples frowns and shakes it off. Narvel calls for it again. Apples steps off the rubber and beckons to Narvel, who runs out to him.

"I think we're a little mixed up in our signals, Narv'."

"Nah. I wanted to confuse him. Throw him off balance."

"I never heard of that strategy before. We better not."

"Okay, Apples." He slowly returns to his position, squats, and calls for a fast ball on the outside corner.

Meanwhile, E.T.A.'s mind has run off the rails again. Intellectually aggressive to a fault, he has decided to do Apples' thinking for him. He has just concluded that if Apples succeeds in pitching this perfect game, after the initial moment of superficial elation Apples will plunge to ugly new depths of self-recrimination. E.T.A. is so certain of this that he has committed himself to preventing it. If he is involved in a play—a certainty on any fielded ground ball—he will muff it. Oh, there's bound to be some disappointment at first, but in the long run Apples will be grateful. As Eddie once said, they're supposed to pick each other up. Well, this way he'll be picking Apples up.

The pitch is drilled to E.T.A.'s right. He lunges for it, striving to err, but it gets by him. A hit! he thinks. Better yet, Apples won't even get a no-hitter! But then he is discouraged to see Bubba take it deep in the hole and fire to Apples, hurrying to cover the bag. Apples does a quick rat-a-tat step and just beats the runner.

One out.

Apples rubs up the ball and sighs. The Philadelphia fans wiggle in their seats, most of them now wanting their own team to lose. What's a single game in the season? But to see a perfect game—that's something else. Out in left field, Buford's mind is with a small boy in an imaginary hospital emergency room. Fear has soiled Frank's underwear, boa constrictors are squeezing the life out of Narvel, Scrappy is immobile with funk, and E.T.A. is sworn to sabotage. Apples gets the hitter to fly out to Jaime, who in absolute fairness should probably receive more credit than he is ever going to get for not playing deranged ball today.

Two outs.

Apples rubs up the ball. E.T.A. is in a state. His only hope is to rattle Apples. He can't count on being involved in the last play. He bites his lip, searching for the right words to put the whammy on him. He calls out, "Lotta pressure, kid. Don't choke up and blow it now."

Apples smiles, his perfect teeth shining in the sunlight. It was just what he needed. E.T.A.'s a hell of a smart guy, he thinks, and a hell of a good friend to be able to see the need for a tension-reducing, ironic, half-assed remark like that.

He smiles and fires, feeling really good about E.T.A., but unfortunately not thinking quite enough about the pitch, and the ball explodes off the bat and comes right back at him.

The hitter in question is a good fellow, a rare, decent sort, and while he wants desperately to spoil the perfect game, he would rather make the last out than seriously injure Apples, whom he rather likes, though not in a physical way. He sees the flight of the ball and in the same instant wishes with all his might for Apples' glove to get up in front of his head in self-defense before the ball reaches him. The hitter sees a flash of white, a blur of brown, and Apples is down. He takes off for first, just in case.

The players in the infield rush to the mound. Apples is lying on his back, the ball wedged in the upper webbing of his glove, which in turn is crammed into his mouth, which bleeds. He lies rigid, demonstrating his control of the ball, and the four umps who have gathered at the mound bend over his body and simultaneously signal with four upraised thumbs that this miserable young man has just pitched a perfect game.

Apples rolls over and spits equipment from his mouth. Two teeth lie on his tongue like Chiclets. He reaches a hand in and takes them out. His teammates watch, horror-struck. Apples, still on his knees and groping in the dirt, looks up and smiles boyishly through the blood.

"Akhtah Ohah," he slurs toothlessly. "Akhtah Ohah."

He is telling them the name of his dentist.

5

The dental assistant is really something. There is nothing she does not know about the human body. She teaches Apples about his in the first week, then about hers in the second, dedicating her entire annual vacation time to the task. She works on him just as she worked on his teeth, moving deftly from part to part, silent, all business, her cool breath all over him as she cleans him out and makes him fresh and new. Because she knows so much, she is not surprised to find he knows so little. In her experience, most men know little.

Apples is amazed. Drugged against the pain in his gums and passive in the first week, he awakes at the beginning of the second week to find himself a Bacchanalian fireballer. Each day thereafter, he discovers a new technique. Hot and impetuous at first, he must go with his fast ball. But then he masters the change-up, slowing the clock and exquisitely drawing out the afternoon. Then the scroogie, the fork ball, the palm ball, and the split-fingered fast ball. The dental assistant goes down and calls for them, and he rears back and deals. Short, compact, smooth and white in the grasp of his browned hands, she cheers as he rolls her and rubs her up, wrapping his long, bony frame all around her.

Grammock tracks him down in her apartment, and his persistent phone calls interrupt their workouts and finally bring Apples back into the world. When he walks down the street now, he is slack-jawed and loosey-goosey. And, for the first time in his life, he sees women from the waist down.

○ ○ ○

On the day of Apples' return to the club, Buford catches the flu. At least, he thinks it's the flu. He is tired and feverish. He can play, but his timing is a little off and he gets pooped just running out to take his position. After a few days, he notices a sharp pain in his side when he inhales deeply. Every morning, he expects his fever to have broken, but every morning it is still with him, a low-grade heat that dulls him and puts him to sleep. When he is in a crowd of two or three people, they all seem to be on the move, making a big commotion. He feels terribly old.

At the suggestion of the trainer, he goes to the team physician's office for a blood test. It shows that he has mononucleosis. The doctor tells him it could last for three or four more weeks. He shouldn't run. The most he can do is pinch hit, and, even at that, not with his accustomed power. Grammock swears loudly at the news and considers putting Buford on the disabled list. But he likes Buford's stick. With enough sleep, he might be able to get back his timing, he thinks.

"Buford," Grammock says to him when he reports to the clubhouse, "you're one of my good boys. I got a couch in my office you're welcome to use. You feel the need a sleep, you jist come on in an' stretch out. If I'm talkin' on the phone or shufflin' papers, I'll talk quiet an' shuffle 'em quiet."

"That's swell, Skip," Buford says at sixteen RPM.

"Now git out there an' suit up."

Buford goes to his locker. Ten minutes later, his shoes are finally off. His head feels heavy and he is already tempted to return to Grammock's office. But he forces himself to stick with it and goes to work on removing one of his socks.

"Hey, Bufe," Eddie yells across the room. "Don' you worry none 'bout this mono you got. We'll pick you up. An' I don' want it to keep you an' Ellie away from a li'l barbecue party I'm plannin'. I wanna be sure everyone sees my bitch up close, so's you'll know what I got to put up with at home."

Buford looks up to respond, but he is too slow. Eddie is speaking again.

"Don' they call what you got 'The Kissin' Disease,' Bufe? Uh-oh—if your li'l wife don' got it, we all gon' know you been playin' in a different playground—one that ain't closed fo' expansion." There is much laughter at this. Fifteen minutes later, Buford gets the joke and speaks to it, even though most of the team is already out on the field warming up.

"Actually, Eddie," he says, "to our surprise, Ellie and I have found that up until very recently we have been able to enjoy normal relations."

"Say *what?*" yells Eddie, for he has had a dozen other conversations in the interim.

By the time his uniform is on, Buford is almost sleep-walking. He heads for Grammock's office, knocks, and opens the door when he hears Grammock speak.

" . . . you talk about a trade like that an' you're talkin' about guttin' the team," Grammock barks into the phone. He looks up and snarls at Buford, "Git the hell out."

Buford points lamely to the couch. "I thought maybe I'd—"

"Git the hell out."

Buford backtracks and closes the door. He shuffles to the aisle between the lockers, stands indecisively for a minute and feels his knees weakening, and then slowly lines up seven locker stools in the aisle. He lies face down on them, balancing with difficulty. As he relaxes, his hands and knees drop to the floor and drag to a stop, straddling the line of stools. With the legs of the stools spread out below him, he looks like some barnyard creature giving suck to her litter. The hard wood of the frontmost stool shoves the lower side of his face forward so that his lips pucker like a duck's. He drools into a deep sleep.

Ten minutes before game time, Grammock hurries out of his office and stops in his tracks when he sees Buford's mass balanced on the stools. He walks over to him. He stands beside him, then bends down close to his face. He takes a handkerchief from his rear pocket and wipes a film of perspiration from Buford's forehead. Then he gently pats his huge back, saying—softly, so as not to wake him—"My big boy. My big boy."

○ ○ ○

Come One,
Come All.
Come See

THE GREATEST BITCH ON EARTH

WHEN: Thursday, August ninth (off day), 5:00 p.m.
WHERE: Eddie's back yard
WHY: To see the bitch
EATS: Soul—you rednecks need a education in eating
DRINKS: You bet
ENTERTAINMENT PROVIDED BY: The bitch

Join the following for this special event—

APPLES	A Pentecostal redneck
NARVEL	A southern California redneck
E.T.A.	A northern Abolitionist redneck
BUBBA	A blood—'nough said
FRANK	I can't think of nothing funny to say about Frank that wouldn't hurt his feelings
SCRAPPY	A Missouri redneck
BUFORD	A breeder of rednecks
JAIME	A blood—leastways, he *looks* like one
GRAMMOCK	A Arkansas redneck

CATERED (You don't think the bitch can cook, do you?)
Bring wives, chicks, and such like, even if you hate them.

They find the above invitation, elegantly engraved, stuck inside their baseball shoes in their lockers. And they come.

First, Frank, with his two sons, each of whom keeps taking a crisp new fifty-dollar bill out of his wallet to examine it. Never before has their father been so generous. It really wasn't necessary. They would probably have agreed to come for a twenty apiece, maximum.

Then Buford and Ellie, her round belly looking surprisingly like Grammock's as she walks like a duck and pants from chair to chair. Buford sticks close to her, looking for signs. But not as close as Apples sticks to his dental assistant, who fondly watches him stretch out on a reclining lawn chair and pours herself into him.

Narvel and his wife, Mavis, come. So do E.T.A., his son, and Edith, his wife, whom the guys all call "E.T.D." even though the rest of her initials don't justify it and her personality (quakingly shy) can barely support the meager humor of it. Bubba, Scrappy, and Grammock each arrive alone. Jaime is a no-show. He spends the afternoon and evening hassling with a non-comprehending cabbie and searching the streets on the wrong side of town.

They don't know quite what to expect. Eddie puts them at ease by energetically getting up a game of Whiffleball. Evidently the special entertainment he has in mind will develop under its own strength. The only signs that something is in the air are his raucous animation as he hauls out the equipment and sets up the bases, and his frequent nervous glances around the yard to assure himself that the bitch, whose Christian name is Jacqui, is mingling and making his guests feel comfortable.

An old black woman clad in an ill-fitting white uniform begins bringing hors d'oeuvres out from the kitchen. She wears, to no clear purpose, a dingy turban, and she sports heavy, black-framed glasses cocked at a crazy angle across her face. She moves slowly and methodically back and forth from the kitchen to the back yard, bringing out one small load at a time, giving the impression that she could go on doing this forever, even if all other life were wiped off the face of the earth.

"Look! There's the pool!" one of Frank's sons calls to the other. "Come on." They race across the lawn and climb up the stairs to the deck surrounding the small, above-ground pool. E.T.A.'s young son follows timidly after them. Frank also takes a few steps in that direction, then stops uncertainly, thinking they would probably prefer to be without him. His eyes survey the yard, moving from the pool to the swing set, the sandbox, and the heavy-timbered climber, all spread along the periphery of the yard, leaving a large, grassy play area in the middle. A child's heaven. He looks back to the pool.

"You boys want me to build you one of those?" he calls across the yard to them, but they are busy evaluating the pool and scrutinizing the air mattresses and toys stacked up on the deck.

"It's a li'l biddy ol' thing, Frank," says Eddie as he paces off the distance between second and third base. "I'm gon' have a regulation-size one dug fo' mah Tina when she gits bigger."

"Me too!" Frank says impulsively. Eddie's frown makes him redden and look away. His glance falls on a beast in the yard next to Eddie's—a huge, repulsively spotted Great Dane, which paces along a gravel run on the other side of a high cyclone fence, studying the ballplayers and their families as if they were items on a menu.

"Apples," Eddie calls out, "grab that yellow plastic bat. I mon' show you some pitchin'."

"I'm pretty comfortable, Eddie," Apples says.

"Yeah. I can see maybe you are at that. Buford? Nah, forgit it, Bufe. You too damn sleepy to see the ball. Besides, you got you a nice woman to keep you busy too. You jis' stretch out on the grass there like a dead man, Bufe. We ain't gon' step on ya'. Scrappy? Hell, you only a .210 hitter. I want someone I can take pleasure in whiffin'. Frank? Git yo' ass in there."

"Hot dog!" says Frank, scurrying to pick up the bat. "Watch your old dad, boys." But his boys have disappeared inside to change into their swimming suits.

"Bubba, you play the field," says Eddie. "Narvel—"

"I refuse to catch. I flat refuse."

Eddie laughs. "Ya' hear that, Skip? An' I always thought Narv' was a team player."

"I heard it," Grammock says from the hors-d'oeuvres table through a mouthful of something breaded and fried, which he smacks around in his mouth a moment before spitting it back up into a napkin. "You guys be careful, now. No foolishness. Anybody gits injured today gits fined, ya' hear me?" He turns back to the table and surveys it with suspicion.

"That's the spirit, Skip," says Eddie. "Okay, Narv'. You be on Frank's team. Scrappy, quit messin' aroun' in that sand-box an' git behind the plate. An', E.T.A., you bat with Frank an' Narv'." He goes on to lay down the ground rules in an imperious fashion that leaves them dazed and ready to follow his every command.

The wives gather at the picnic table near the climber and exchange stories and household hints for coping with their husbands' complex eating and sleeping schedules. Then, at Mavis's subtle urging, they begin to trade progress reports on their husbands. Ellie says that Buford has temporarily stopped taking his anti-depressant medication because of his mononucleosis, but he seems to be holding his own. Mavis reports that Narvel refuses to talk about it, with her or with anyone. After one failed session with a psychiatrist, he distrusts the entire profession. Edith says nothing. She is afraid of misrepresenting E.T.A. and incurring his wrath. He is so changeable that she honestly doesn't know what to think about him. Jacqui says that Eddie is having private problems.

"What do you mean, Jacqui?" Mavis asks.

"It's kind of private," she says softly.

"You mean you don't know what it is?"

99

Jacqui sneaks a glance at Eddie, who is demonstrating a grip of the Whiffleball to Bubba. "I *know*, all right," she says. "You see, he doesn't seem interested in me. He doesn't want me." She gestures vaguely with her hands.

"Oh, what a shame," Ellie says.

"Does he talk about it?" asks Mavis.

Jacqui presses her lips together and gives a quick shake of her head.

"How long has it been?" asks Mavis.

"Three months."

"Oh, how awful," says Ellie. "I'll give you the name of Buford's doctor. He might be able to help him, Jacqui."

"That's sweet of you, Ellie. But . . . I'd prefer if Buford could give it to him. Eddie don't seem to want to talk to me much."

Ellie reaches a hand across the table and rests it on Jacqui's. "I'll talk to Buford about it tonight."

Mavis emits a little spurt of anger through her lips. "Doesn't it really get you how they seem to find it easier to talk to each other than to us?"

As Jacqui and Edith nod, Ellie says, "I wouldn't say that's true of my Buford, Mavis."

"Maybe not," she says. "You and Buford have something special going." Ellie's sudden blush makes her add, "I mean it, Ellie. It's wonderful. And Buford's so sweet. He's going to be a wonderful father."

A crack of the bat shakes Buford awake and he gazes up into the green leaves, wondering where Ellie is. As Frank scampers gleefully and noisily around the miniature base path and Bubba chases the ball, which has lodged in some bushes beside the pool deck, Buford rolls over onto his belly and heaves himself to his knees. He sees Ellie at the table with the other wives and begins a slow rise to his feet to join her.

"Lucky hit," Eddie yells. "Come on, Bubba. Git that damn ball back in here."

"Look at them," says Mavis. "They can't get enough of each other. Do you think they care about the chance to mix with us, to get to know their teammates' wives? Of course they don't. Half of them don't even know their own wives."

"Ain't that the truth," says Jacqui.

"What do you think, Edith?" says Mavis.

Edith blanches and sneaks a look at E.T.A. "I'm listening, Mavis. I'm listening."

"I think we have to join together in some way," Mavis continues. "We ought to meet regularly, and not just at the ballpark. We need to talk more. We need support. Lord knows I do."

"Me too," says Jacqui. "My Eddie an' me, we—"

"That's a wonderful husband you got there, Jacqui," says Buford as he lumbers up to the group and squeezes in between Ellie and Edith. "A wonderful guy."

"I know, Buford," she says with a sad smile.

"I wonder if you *do* know," he says. "I mean, I see him in ways that maybe you don't." He pauses and runs a huge hand through his blond hair, choosing his words carefully. "I see sides to Eddie that maybe you aren't aware of. The way he handles pressure. The way he helps us all out. And I don't mean just on the field either, though that counts for a lot too. I mean the way he picks us up when we're down, like he's done for me, lots of times."

"I know how good he can be," she says.

"Every team has a leader, Jacqui. Or at least most teams do, and those that don't, well, you can tell how much they need one. The funny thing is, no team *elects* a leader. He just kind of grows out of the team, and one day everyone knows who the leader is without having to talk about it. You ask the guys here today and every single one of 'em will back me up. Eddie's our leader, that's what they'll tell you. And you don't get to be a leader without being loved in the first place." He circles an arm around Ellie, who bats her eyes at him. She has never heard him speak so beautifully before. She can see the preparation that must have gone into his speech. But she feels his arm begin to slip from her shoulder and sees his head begin to droop toward the table.

"Buford, why don't you take a nice nap?" she says. "You've gone and worn yourself out." The wives break into light, relieved laughter. "Jacqui—"

"Sure. Buford, you go right up to our bedroom and stretch out. It's at the top of the stairs, on the right."

"I don't wanna be unsociable."

"Don't you worry about that. Come on. I'll take you up. I got to check on Tina anyway. She should be waking up soon."

The bat cracks resoundingly again, and Narvel chugs around the bases while the ball sails over the wooden fence surrounding the pool and rattles on the deck before plopping into the water.

"God *damn* it!" yells Eddie.

"Dad," one of Frank's sons calls from the back porch of the house. "Someone's crying in there."

Frank, yuk-yukking over his and Narvel's back-to-back homers, turns around with a huge grin and says, "Huh?"

"Ooh," says Jacqui, and she rises and hurries up the stairs to the porch and into the house.

"Git yo' ass in there, woman," Eddie yells after the screen door has banged closed behind her. "Leavin' the poor li'l kid all alone like that . . . Bubba, git that goddamn ball back in here."

Buford gives Ellie a parting kiss atop her wavy brown hair and excuses himself from the table. As he passes by the hors-d'oeuvres table, Grammock says, "Hey, Buford, ya' wanna taste somethin' that'll bring your stomach right up to your mouth?"

"No thanks, Skip," he says, and he climbs the stairs and labors into the house.

Scrappy says, "Eddie, ya' wanna take some cuts? I'll be happy to pitch to ya'."

"Nah. Git in there, E.T.A. I'm gon' melt yo' eyeglasses with mah numbah-one." Eddie lunges at the ball that Bubba has retrieved and lobbed to him, but instead of catching it, he accidentally swats it away. It rolls to the table, where Mavis picks it up and hefts it.

"Now, isn't this all pretty pathetic?" she says softly to Ellie and Edith. Then she tosses it to Eddie.

Eddie is about to wind up when Jacqui and Tina appear on the porch. He smiles broadly. "Tina, git up on that climber an' root fo' yo' daddy. I need some luck. You watch me turn ol' E.T.A.'s head aroun'. He ain't as smart as he thinks."

Tina scampers down the steps and runs to the climber.

"Thas mah li'l girl," Eddie says as he watches her climb up and perch on the top platform. He turns and faces E.T.A. and glares at him with mock menace. "How'm I doin', Apples?"

"Not too good, Eddie."

"I mean mah *moves*, man. Mah style. Thas what counts."

"You're over-involved. You've got to be loosey-goosey out there."

Eddie gives him a weak smile. "Easier said than done, Apples. Now I can really 'preciate what you be goin' through when you in a jam." He gives him a closer look. "Seem to me you makin' some pretty good moves right now yo'se'f."

The dental assistant giggles and shouts, "Come on, Eddie. Quit stalling."

"Yeah, Eddie," shouts Frank, his square face aglow with a sense of good fellowship. "Quit stalling." He follows this with some more yuk-yuks.

"What a creep!" the dental assistant whispers to Apples.

"*Shhh.*" Apples looks nervously at Frank. "He's got rabbit ears."

Eddie looks in to Scrappy for the sign and delivers. E.T.A. fouls off a crazily curving fast ball.

"I got yo' measure, E.T.A.," says Eddie while Scrappy chases after the ball.

Grammock abandons the hors d'oeuvres in disgust and wanders over to the picnic table, feeling a bit lonely and rejected because he wasn't picked to play on either team. He sits down, and Jacqui sits beside him. As he scoots away from her a bit, he says, "How are you lovely ladies today?"

Jacqui, Ellie, and Edith say they are just fine, couldn't be better, such a lovely day and all. Mavis looks squarely at him and says, "Do you know what this team is going through?"

He laughs. "Jist between us sittin' here, they're goin' through the best season of my career. Only I ain't gonna tell 'em how proud I am of it, no ma'am. I got to ride 'em an' ride 'em some more."

"I didn't think you knew," she says.

"Mavis," says Edith, sensing conflict, "maybe you shouldn't—"

"They're *depressed*," says Mavis. "That's what they're going through. What do you think of *that?*"

"Depressed? Why, we're on a tear now. Six out in front, goin' on seven."

She shakes her head. "They're suffering from depression. They're all quite sick. I can't believe you haven't seen it."

"Depression?" He guffaws. "That's a old woman's disease. Naw, my boys . . . Wait, I *do* know of one guy who was depressed once." He chuckles. "Yeah, he was depressed all right. A skinny preacher fellow back home." He clears his throat and scoots forward on the bench.

Mavis's jaw goes hard and tight. "We're faced with a very serious situation here."

"Now, now," he says. "Jist you listen to my story. It'll do ya' good, Mavis. You look like you could use some lightenin' up. Ya' see, there was this preacher fellow, skinny as a plucked chicken . . ."

Eddie continues to work to E.T.A., who has fouled off two more balls and taken three pitches ruled out of the strike zone by Scrappy, over Eddie's violent protests. E.T.A., bitterly motivated in ways that are obscure to him, muscles into the next pitch and sends it flying over the cyclone fence running along the side of the yard, into the Great Dane's running track. The dog heaves his frame over to the ball and sniffs at it.

While E.T.A. rounds the bases, his fist held high, Frank starts yuk-yukking again.

"Fuck off, Frank," Eddie snaps at him. "Bubba, git that goddamn ball back in here."

But Bubba's experience with dogs—slobbering street mongrels, junkyard jackals—makes him freeze in his tracks.

Cursing, Eddie stalks over to the fence. The dog curls a lip and growls. Eddie yells at him and reaches his hand under the fence for the ball. The dog goes after him and he pulls it out just in time, cutting his wrist on a jagged, projecting edge of the fence.

"Sonofa*bitch!* Scrappy, bring me that bat."

"Listen, Eddie, let's forget it."

Eddie storms across the lawn and grabs the bat. He returns to the fence and sticks the bat beneath it, reaching for the ball. The dog goes after the bat, pawing at it and worrying it with his teeth, while Eddie fights to hold on to it. The dog, in his struggle, kicks the ball with a hind leg and it rolls hopelessly far away from the fence. Eddie, breathing heavily now, withdraws the bat, clutches the fence with his left hand, and swings the bat over the fence at the dog's head, missing. The dog backs off a step, bristling, then lunges forward at the bat, snarling at it and boxing it with his forepaws.

Apples and the dental assistant sit up in the lawn chair.

Scrappy and E.T.A. take a few steps toward Eddie, then stop uncertainly.

"*Eddie!*" screams Jacqui, rising from the bench.

"Now, don't you pay him no never mind," says Grammock. "That's jist Eddie lettin' off a little smoke. Set back down. Now then, the preacher, he all of a sudden hears the farmer a-stumblin' up the porch steps, so he leaps outta bed an' beelines it to the kitchen, where his clothes is layin' all over the kitchen table . . ."

The dog finally seizes the bat in his teeth and wrests it from Eddie. He chews at the bat and fights it a while, then turns and faces Eddie. He lunges at the fence, barking viciously. Eddie drops to his knees in a face-off with the animal, matching the barks with wild, inhuman cries of his own. He finally spits at the dog, then pushes himself to his feet and wipes his mouth dry on his sleeve. He turns and gives his teammates a toothy grin.

"Game's called, guys," he says matter-of-factly. "On accounta the fuckin' dog. Come on—less go swimmin'."

Mavis, watching, presses Jacqui's hand in her own.

"Come on now, Mavis," says Grammock. "Listen up. The preacher, he heads for the winder, but the farmer's in there afore he can git it open. The farmer—listen up now, Jacqui, you're gonna like this—the farmer, he flops down on the bed an' says, 'Maw, stop lollygaggin' around that winder an' git your pud over here.'

"Well, the preacher, he don't know whether to shit or go blind. He kinda slinks over to the bed and giggles in a high-pitched voice, playin' for time, and then all of a sudden he feels somethin' strange in the middle of his wad a clothes. It's a bowl a cornmeal mush—the farmer's most favorite meal—that the farmer's wife'd covered with a towel an' left on the table an' that'd got all bunched up with his clothes when he picked 'em up. Well, we already seen he's a quick 'un, this here preacher, an' he tosses his clothes aside an' scoops out a

106

big pile a mush with that towel, rollin' it all up into a big ball. He sidles onto the bed and stuffs that there wad between his legs, an' in no time a-tall the farmer's on top a him whisperin' sweet nothin's in his ear an' rammin' his tallywhacker into that towelful a mush. He's workin' so hard on it that he tears a hole in the towel. That don't faze him none, though. He's so liquored up he thinks he done hit pay dirt. But that there mush, the way it sloshes around in that towel, well, it jist don't got what you might call real *substance* to it, an' that farmer bangs away on into the night—one hour, two hours, three hours, on an' on, while that skinny preacher is a-moanin' underneath the load, a-wigglin' his skinny ass around to save his life.

"Well, finally, the farmer, he jist give out an' rolls offa the preacher, kinda mutterin' to hisself, an' he falls asleep. The preacher slips outta the bed, a-countin' his blessin's. He picks up his clothes an' tippy-toes into the kitchen, headin' for the door. But the farmer's wife is layin' for him with a fire poker. Ya' see, when she got back from the outhouse, she didn't take too kindly to what she heard a-goin' on in her nuptial bower. She winds up an' gives that preacher a whack on his tool that sends him screamin' out the door, his clothes flyin' ever' which a-way, an' he tears off acrost the field with his ass a-gleamin' in the moonlight. Folks say he ain't been seen nor heard in them parts ever since.

"Well, the next mornin' the farmer stumbles outta bed with a moan, his head a-fillin' the room an' a ache in his crotch runnin' up his belly an' down his legs, so he's feelin' purty bad all over. He drags his overhalls on an' kinda slumps into the kitchen, where his wife is firin' up the stove an' wonderin' what he's gonna say 'bout last night. *She* ain't gonna say nothin' if'n *he* don't, that's for sure. The farmer sets down at the table, a-throbbin' all over, an' jist stares at the table kinda blank for a while, tryin' to figger what's ailin' him so bad.

"'Maw,' he says—it's funny how he always calls his wife

'Maw,' like maybe he's fond a reminiscin' 'bout good times in the sack with his real mama—'Maw,' he says—"

"*Stop!*" shrieks Mavis, pressing her hands against her ears. Grammock looks at her, perplexed. Jacqui takes advantage of the interruption and jumps up from the table without a word. She hurries into the house after Eddie. Edith sits very still and blinks nervously. Ellie has managed to tune out much of the tale, for the sake of the twins, so that they won't be marked.

"Hang in there," says Grammock. "The punch line's comin' right up."

Mavis looks at him and hisses, "This is the most disgusting thing I've ever heard."

"Purty good, ain't it?"

She jerks to her feet. "You're an ignorant slob." She glares at him a moment and turns away, calling loudly and desperately for Narvel.

Grammock sits with the pained, uncertain look of a man who has just swallowed his chaw. Ellie suddenly stands up from the table and hurries over to the climber, where Tina has become entangled and is in need of help. This leaves Grammock with Edith.

"*But the punch line,*" he yells to the air. He scowls after Mavis, then turns to Edith. "Ya' ever see such a bitch?" he says to her.

She throws him a quick, tight smile before turning away. Grammock glowers at her profile and looks back to the house.

On the porch, Mavis remonstrates with Narvel, jabbing her finger repeatedly at Grammock, then sweeping her hand over the entire back yard. Eddie strides out the back door in his swimming suit with Jacqui right behind him. She reaches out and touches his arm, gently, but he yanks it away and hurries on across the yard to the pool. Mavis turns to her, talks to her briefly, gives her a hug, and steps to the door. Narvel looks somewhat longingly toward Eddie, or perhaps toward the pool, since he too is in his swimming suit, but Mavis grabs his forearm and pulls him into the house with her. Jacqui follows them inside. Before the door closes, Frank and E.T.A. come out with towels draped around their necks, and they head for the pool.

Bubba, a non-swimmer terrified of death by drowning, stands at the hors-d'oeuvres table, popping peppery radishes into his mouth, one after another. A thought strikes him. He turns and looks at the Great Dane, which seems to be looking back at him. Then he stuffs a huge handful of radishes into his pocket, takes three more from the plate, and begins to juggle them.

Grammock finally abandons Edith at the table without formally taking his leave and ambles over to Apples and the dental assistant, who again lie fused in their lawn chair and are chatting with Ellie and Tina. Grammock makes a bit of small talk, his eyes running up and down and around the dental assistant's compact body, until his envy of Apples is so great that he wants to heave the lawn chair over and steal the woman and take her home with him. Seeing that he will never get their full attention, he looks around desperately for someone else to cheer him up. He spies Scrappy, still dressed in his street clothes, sitting alone on the porch steps.

When he is gone, the dental assistant says to Apples, with an air of authority, "Wow. He's a real tooth-grinder."

Bubba, still juggling so as not to arouse suspicion, works his way slowly over toward the fence.

"Whatcha up to, Scrapola?"

Scrappy, his head cocked back and his eyes half-closed, looks up at Grammock. The bright sun behind his head darkens Grammock's face demonically. Scrappy fully opens his eyes and sits up a bit. He cannot tell Grammock the complete truth—that he is afraid to put on a swimming suit in front of these women, ashamed to show them his body, scarred and burned with the record of his childhood—so he says, "Jist soakin' up a little sun, I guess, Skip."

"Mind if I set a spell?"

"No, Skip. I don't mind."

Grammock sits on the second step from the top, leans his elbows back against the porch, and lets his legs sprawl down the steps. His hands inch forward and go to work on his belly, circling in nervous agitation over the white T-shirt stretched tightly over its expanse. He chuckles hollowly.

"Them gals didn't seem too taken with my story 'bout the skinny preacher. You know, the one where—"

"Yeah, I know it, Skip."

Grammock sighs. "That wife a Narvel's is a bitch on wheels, ain't she?"

"I don't know her too good."

"She looked like she'd a liketa take my head off." He spits. "No wonder Narvel don't never talk. She's broke him of it. Jesus H. I'd hate to come home to that every night."

"You never got married, didja, Skip?"

Grammock looks at him sharply a moment, his hands freezing atop his belly. Then he relaxes and falls into his rhythm again. "Nah. I got enough family right here in this back yard. I done my share a livin' too, Scrappy. Don't you never think different. I plowed a twitchet or two in my time."

Scrappy winces. His eyes drift over to Ellie—gentle, good Ellie—and he thinks, whatever sex and marriage and love are supposed to be about, Buford and Ellie surely come closer to it than Grammock ever did, or ever could.

"Ya' tongue-tied, Scrappy?"

"Sorry, Skip. Jist thinkin'." He clears his throat. "Ya' know, we got people from all over the U.S.A. in this here back yard. Them ladies ain't used to stories like me an' you was brung up on. But that's okay, seems to me. It takes all kinds."

"I expect so, Scrappy. Hell, you're right. You 'n' me *are*

different from the rest a them. Jist a coupla peckerwood boys. Lookit this here picnic. Lookit the shit they cooked up for us. Christ, if I don't puke my guts up into the swimmin' pool before the day's over, I'm gonna be real surprised. Now, you take them Fourth a *July* picnics back home, an' the cookin' we enjoyed there. You know what I'm talkin' about?"

Scrappy grins, warming to Grammock's enthusiasm. "I sure do. My grandma told me all about 'em."

"An' the gals comin' from miles around. That was livin' the way livin' was meant to be. I always done my best sparkin' at them picnics. How 'bout you, Scrappy? You ain't exactly my idea of a ladies' man, but you musta done some tail-chasin' in your day."

"I dunno, Skip. I never got outta the house much."

"We got roots, Scrappy, you 'n' me. You take Narvel there. Raised up in California like that, where you got a mixed litter of people from all over hell an' creation, it's no wonder he got all fucked up 'n' went 'n' married a bitch like that Mavis bitch. You 'n' me, we got our heads screwed on right, all on accounta our deep roots. I thank Jesus H. Christ ever' day a my life for that. Was you brung up religious, Scrappy?"

"Oh, sort of. My grandma believed in lotsa stuff."

"E.T.A. was tellin' me the other day that she was a real Ozark granny woman. That musta been somethin'."

"Yeah. That was in her younger days, though, before she took me in. E.T.A. told you 'bout her?"

"That's another fine old custom. Them granny women knew more about ketchin' babies than many a college-educated doctor today, I'll bet." He pauses and sucks his teeth appreciatively.

"I don't know, Skip," Scrappy says tentatively. "There was a lotta superstition in them days too."

"What's wrong with that?"

"I dunno, exactly. Seems to me—"

111

"Like puttin' a ax under the bed to cut the labor pains. That's real colorful, an' there jist might be somethin' to it."

"Yeah, maybe. But some a the things that Gram' told me about sounded downright dangerous."

"Like what?"

"Like, well, she told me she useta make tea outta chicken droppin's for the babies, to quiet 'em down."

"Naw," Grammock says skeptically.

"Yeah, an' she'd also put cow dung on their raw little belly buttons to stop the bleedin'. Geez, that's colorful, all right, but—"

"Naw, Scrappy. She musta been pullin' your leg."

"Honest, Skip. She done it, an' lots a others done it too."

"Naw. She was jist outta her mind." He gives Scrappy a knowing grin. "E.T.A., he told me all about her."

Scrappy gives him a sharp glance. "He did?"

"Sure. Don't act so surprised. There ain't no privacy on a ballclub, Scrappy. You oughta know that. He told me all about her. Like about her hair. That innerested me a lot. It was real long, wasn't it? Clear down to her waist?"

"Yeah," Scrappy says dully, his gaze seeking out E.T.A. on the pool deck and resting on him.

"An' she made you brush it ever' night?"

"Yeah."

"An' come mornin', she'd wake you up by swingin' it back an' forth in your face, like cobwebs?" He chuckles. "I can jist pitcher you swattin' at it in your sleep, dreamin' up a storm."

Scrappy is silent.

"An' when you went an' got yourself in trouble, like you're always doin' with me, she'd pluck one a them long strands out an' make you eat it? Am I right? That's what E.T.A. told me. That innerested me a lot, Scrappy. Ya' see, my mama had long hair like that too. She always said the Bible taught us a woman's hair is her glory. That's a beautiful thought now, ain't it? Yessiree." He pauses meditatively. "I don't recall her ever servin' any of it up for supper, though." He smiles and gazes up toward the sun in contentment. His hands continue to circle his belly, more slowly and peacefully than when he first sat down.

Bubba stops his wandering-juggler stroll about ten feet from the fence. He locates the dog's precise position, turns his back to the fence, and continues to juggle. He suddenly catches all three radishes, gives a furtive glance around the yard to make sure he is not being observed, and then pivots and wings a radish at the dog. It finds a hole in the cyclone fence and strikes the animal on the thigh. The dog gives a yelp and leaps to his feet, growling and searching the air around him for the enemy. His sudden motion catches the attention of a few in Eddie's yard, but by then Bubba has pulled a new radish out of his pocket and is juggling again.

Jacqui suddenly appears on the porch in a minuscule silver-colored bikini. She walks gingerly down the steps between Grammock and Scrappy, giving off a rich perfume scent. Their eyes dance all over her as she eases across the lawn to the swimming pool, Grammock feeling aroused to violence of some kind, Scrappy feeling a sad, lonely longing. Grammock sees Bubba bobble and drop his radishes. He laughs and says, "Lookit that Bubba itchin' to get aholt a some a that."

When Jacqui reaches the pool, she calls out something cheerful to the men splashing around with Frank's sons and E.T.A.'s son, but Eddie's loud voice fills the air with inarticulate cries that drive her away. She runs across the lawn in tears, her arms crossed over her breasts and clutching at her shoulders. Ellie, holding Tina's hand, hurries after her. Grammock inhales deeply after Jacqui passes up the steps again, but Ellie is right behind her, and all he can smell is the complex bouquet of Play-Doh, milk-breath, and urine that Tina carries with her.

The ancient caterer begins bringing hot dishes out from the kitchen to the buffet table, their earthy, vital aromas mingling in Grammock's nostrils with the smell of Tina. Grammock wants to trip the old woman and send her tumbling down the stairs.

"Jesus H., Scrappy," he mutters. "Okra in a Hog's Head, Okra Surprise, Okra Funcakes." Another yelp pierces the air. "What the hell's buggin' that dog, anyway?"

Buford looms on the porch, his beefy torso above his swimming suit dazzlingly white and homely.

"You gonna swim, Bufe?"

"Yeah, Scrappy. I had a real nice nap upstairs. I'm feeling pretty peppy now. I think maybe I've got this thing licked."

"That's great, Bufe."

Grammock says, "It'll be good to have ya' back, son," and mentally revises his starting line-up for tomorrow's game.

Buford strides vigorously across the lawn, raising his towel above his head and pulling on it with hands held wide apart, stretching the muscles in his arms and shoulders.

Jacqui hurries down the steps again, this time covered with a sheer bathrobe, and she runs to the pool.

"Uh-oh," says Grammock. "Fireworks time again. Listen up, Scrappy."

Eddie's shouts can be heard again, but Jacqui doesn't back down. Eddie pulls himself out of the pool and hurries across the lawn. He bounds up the stairs, his jaw set with determination. Jacqui is right behind him, looking helplessly bewildered. Grammock listens for sounds of violence from inside, and, disappointed, watches E.T.A. and Frank climb out of the pool, dry off, and work their way to the buffet table, where, after a moment, Edith, Apples, and the dental assistant join them.

Bubba, his ammunition spent, turns around and faces the fence. Several radishes lie on the gravel around the dog, a few in the yard beyond him, and some in Eddie's yard—those that struck the fence and bounced back. He creeps over to these and begins to collect them. A low growl rises in the dog's throat, then, as their eyes lock, in Bubba's. Bubba takes another step forward and chances to look down the length of the fence and beyond, down the driveway separating Eddie's house from his neighbor's—the dog owner's house, he suddenly realizes—and he sees a police car parked at the neighbor's curb. His eyes bug out. He throws the handful of radishes to the ground and sprints to the gate at the rear of the yard.

Ellie is suddenly at the back door, calling for help. "Buford! Scrappy! E.T.A.! Come here! Quick!"

But Jacqui is right behind her, again in tears. "They took him away. There was a struggle. Oh God . . ." Ellie seizes hold of her and presses Jacqui's head against her shoulder.

"What the hell?" bellows Grammock.

The players rush to the porch and surround Ellie and Jacqui, exploding with questions. What happened? What did Eddie do? Where is he?

"The police came to the door," says Ellie as she helps Jacqui back into the kitchen. "Because of the dog. The owner saw Eddie trying to hit him with the bat and called the police. Then, I don't know, he must have lost his temper. Come on, Jacqui." She gets her away from the others and finally settles her into bed upstairs with Tina. Jacqui says she wants a Valium pill, and as Ellie is bringing it to her from the bathroom, the idea of medication makes her realize with panic that a full ten minutes have passed without her thinking once about Buford. She summons Edith to stay with Jacqui and hurries out of the bedroom and down the stairs, past a frantic Grammock swearing into the telephone, and then through the kitchen, where Eddie's teammates sit morosely while the ancient caterer resolutely packs the untouched main courses into containers to be put in the refrigerator. As she hurries

115

across the lawn, Ellie spies the Great Dane watching her, and her hands fly protectively to her abdomen.

In the pool, while E.T.A.'s boy clings nervously to the edge, Frank's sons splash and paddle their air mattresses around Buford's, on which he lies on his back, fast asleep. They have used his belly to stack face masks and snorkels on. Then they used his massive whiteness in a game of "Thar she blows," feigning thrusts into his sides with make-believe harpoons. Now he is a human torpedo, which they propel back and forth across the pool with huge noises of destruction.

Bubba is three blocks away by now. He has stopped to buy an ice-cream cone, which he plans to be eating when, having circled around, he walks up the street in front of Eddie's house to his car. No one will suspect him of anything if he is eating an ice-cream cone.

○ ○ ○

"E.T.A., I didn't wake ya', did I?"

"No, Skip," he says into the phone. "What's the situation?"

After a brief flurry of obscenity, Grammock says, "I finally got him outta there. Judge let him go without no bail."

"What's the charge?"

"Assault. They're sayin' he went an' slugged a policewoman. Crazy goddamned nigger."

"A woman?"

"You heard right."

After a moment of silence, E.T.A. says, "Can he play?"

"Yeah. No sweat, far as that goes. An' he ain't gonna come into trial for two more months at least. Then I'm jist gonna hafta see what comes down the pike. But even if I end up tradin' him to Sing Sing, I'll have this season under my belt. It'll be history—somethin' no one can ever take away from me."

"How is he?"

"Fucked up, as usual. I got him home to his old lady. I don't know what's happenin' there now an' I don't care. But I think bein' arrested kinda took the tuck outta him. What I'm callin' about, E.T.A., is somethin' else. I'm callin' about you."

"Me?"

"We're gonna need a leader now."

"You've *got* one, Skip."

"Yeah, but he's a loco nigger. I mean we need a new one."

"I thought . . . well, I always saw myself as the leader anyway, Skip. But if you wish to formalize it in some way—"

"Jesus, E.T.A.," he says angrily. "Whatever give ya' the idea *you* was the leader? Everybody an' his uncle knows it's been Eddie all along. Hell, what kinda leader you gonna be if you're so outta touch? I'm beginnin' to think I called the wrong guy. Maybe Frank, or Jaime—"

"No, no," E.T.A. says quickly. "I won't quibble over this point, Skip. Whatever you say. I'll be happy to assume a more important role. Are you planning to make some sort of announcement to the guys about it? Perhaps I could help you with the wording."

"Yeah," Grammock says sarcastically. "I'm gonna see if the King an' Queen a England can be on hand too. Jesus, E.T.A., smarten up, will ya'? Do I have to spell it out? You become a leader by *bein'* a leader. All's ya' gotta do is be more active. You know—take charge, like Eddie always done. But don't for Christ's sake act like ya' *know* you're the leader."

"I understand perfectly, Skip."

"An' work on your goddamn vocabulary."

"Right, Skip."

"Ease up on it a little. Shorten your sentences."

"Gotcha."

"Don't go on and on. Be subtle."

"Mmm."

"Swear."

"Fuckin'-A."

"Another thing. I want ya' to talk to Eddie. Git to know him. Find out what the hell's eatin' him. We got a certain magic on this club, an', the way I see it, he's got more to do with it than anybody else. I want that man happy. If that woman a his is what's ailin' him, tell him to dump her. If it's somethin' else, find out what it is an' cure him of it. Ya' understand? If he beats this rap, I want him back for next year, an' not jist as a player, neither. I mean as a leader. Ya' understand? Your job is to work yourself right out of a job as team leader, okay?"

E.T.A. swallows hard. "The team comes first, Skip. Whatever you say."

Within seconds of Grammock's call, E.T.A.'s phone rings again.

"Hello?"

"E.T.A. Hey, man, how ya' doin'?"

E.T.A. tenses. "Hi, Eddie."

"E.T.A., ya' ever been in jail?"

"No, Eddie, I haven't."

"I don't recommend it." He gives a brief, empty laugh. "It don' make ya' feel too tall."

"I'm sorry about what happened, Eddie."

"*You're* sorry. Man, I don' know what got into me, between the dog an' . . . that other shit. I guess you all didn' have too good a time, huh?"

"Don't worry about it, Eddie. These days none of us *ever* has a good time."

Eddie laughs loudly. "Man, you so cool an' even-tempered. You the Ice Man, all right. I *know* I called the right guy. Listen, I got a favor to ask."

"Anything, Eddie. Anything."

"I'd 'preciate it if there wasn't no talk about this. I don'

118

feel too good 'bout what I done today, an' I'd like to jis' forgit it. Besides, I been talkin' to my lawyer, an' he say I'd be smart to not talk to nobody about it at all. Could you kinda let the guys know the subject is, ya' know, off limits?"

"Sure, Eddie. I understand."

"You know how I like to needle the guys, an' this is a golden opportunity for 'em all to git back at me. Hell, if it'd happen' to someone else, I *know* I couldn't lay off it. But I don' think I could take it, even in fun, ya' know?"

"Yes. I hear you, Eddie."

"I'm workin' on this shit. Believe me, I'm workin' on it. I jis' don' under*stan*' it, thas all. But I'm tryin'. I already been on the phone to Buford tonight. I'm gon' call his doctor tomorrow an' see if I can git some a them pick-me-up pills. But I need some peace too. I don' want no distractions. I don' want the guys ridin' me. So, listen, I'm gon' make a point a comin' in a li'l bit late tomorrow. That'll give you a chance to talk to 'em. Okay?"

"Sure, Eddie. But . . . listen, if you ever *do* want to talk about it, or about anything, well, you know where my locker is, so to speak."

"Hey, I jis' might take you up on that. I'll catch you later, E.T.A."

"Goodbye, Eddie."

As E.T.A. hangs up the phone, his thoughts drift back to the run-down play in May and his bitter argument about it with Eddie in the shower. How wonderfully leader-like of him, he thinks, to be willing now to overlook the way Eddie shamed him and essentially ruined his season with that play and that argument. What a majestic gesture he is making toward Eddie now. What a prince he is.

○ ○ ○

Grammock scowls down the length of the dugout. There's no denying it: his bench isn't worth a fart in a tornado, and this is exactly when it shows. Buford's left-field replacement is good with the glove but can't hit a lick, and he's due up now, with the bases loaded, one out, and a tie score in the bottom of the tenth. Grammock has called the incompetent back into the dugout. He wants another hitter, but he can't stand to look at his bench, they stink so much. He can see one after another of them doing something useless: striking out, popping up, or hitting into a double play. Certainly not getting a base on balls—no, they're too eager for that, the goddamn brats. And God forbid they should lay a decent bunt down and score Bubba from third. No, that's not important to them. Nobody ever got any snatch after a game from a fan of the bunt. They like to muscle up and try to knock the stuffing out of the ball, the short-sighted bastards. Someone like Buford, though—if he told him to turn around backwards in the batter's box and hang his ass over the plate, he'd do it. He's that kind of boy, always laboring for him, and with love. But Buford is still beany, what with his mono and his goddamn wife about to calve. His timing's still off, and he's not supposed to run at all. Hell, any sort of grounder would be a sure D.P. But oh how he would like to send his boy Buford up there. That'd scare 'em.

A smile appears on his face. He thinks of Buford's soft streak, his surprising ability to be gentle. He sees a perfect bunt rolling along, scoring Bubba, winning the game. Buford can deliver. He looks down the dugout. "Jesus H.," he mutters, for Buford is sound asleep at the far end, his head leaning against the wall and his mouth wide open. He looks completely torpid, as if he has just put down three whole chickens served up at Denny's.

"You got a hitter, or what?" the ump yells into the dugout.

"*Ellenbogen,*" shouts Grammock. Buford wakes up gazing into center field and begins to smack his lips like Gabby Hayes. He thinks he has awakened naturally, so he continues

120

to stare at mere vacancy while the entire team in the dugout looks at him. *"Buford!"* shouts Grammock. Buford turns, sees his teammates' eyes on him, realizes something is going on without knowing what, feels with certainty that this will always be the case, and vows to have himself institutionalized as soon as the game is over. He rises and works his way toward Grammock, hoping he is doing the right thing. As he moves, he half-listens for a roar of laughter from the stands at the grotesqueness of his behavior. But he makes it to Grammock without this happening.

Grammock puts an arm around him. "You can bunt pretty good, ain't that right, Buford?"

Buford thinks that "bunt" might have some new meaning that he hasn't picked up yet, but he responds as if Grammock is using the word in its older sense, just in case.

"Yes, sir," he says, but his throat, as thick with sleep as his mind is, gives the words a pale, voiceless quality. He clears it and speaks more loudly. "Yes, sir."

"Shhh," says Grammock. "Jesus, they'll hear you all over the ballpark. I want you to bunt."

"Yes, sir."

"Don't show it too soon."

"Yes, sir."

"You've got to let 'em think you're gonna swing away."

"Yes, sir."

"An' don't run. Don't even try for first. Let 'em throw you out, or even tag you. I don't wanna see your spleen busted all over the base line."

"Yes, sir."

"Now don't fuck up, Buford. You're a good boy, I love you like a son. But don't fuck up."

"Yes, sir." He takes his bat from the rack and steps out of the dugout toward home plate.

"Git in the on-deck circle an' take some swings!" Grammock yells. "Jesus . . ."

Buford suddenly realizes that as he walks he is holding the bat out in front of him, level with the ground, his right hand cradling its meat end: the bunting grip. Grammock's words light up the stadium for him and he recognizes the pattern. He looks at the men on base—Bubba at third, Jaime at second, Eddie at first—he looks at the scoreboard and sees he has slept through five innings, and he feels his brain growing with new understanding. How awful it must be to be insane, he thinks. How thankful he is that he is not.

Confident now, he strides boldly to the on-deck circle, where he grabs three bats. He begins to warm up, slowly at first, gradually accelerating until he is a blur of rotary flamboyance. By the time he is in the batter's box, the third baseman is poised on the backs of his heels like a man with ten bee stings on the bottoms of his ten toes.

His bunt is deadly. When the ball begins its slow roll down the line, the third baseman might as well be in Crimea for all the chance he has to make the play at the plate. The pitcher tries a desperate scooping of the ball home in one swift motion with his glove, but the ball stays in his glove too long and rises almost straight up. While the catcher gazes up longingly at it, Bubba scampers for home and knocks him unconscious with a slide that, were the ball involved in some way, could be called constructively play-busting.

Buford watches it unfold with paternal pride from a position eight feet down the first-base line, where he has paused in his slow progress to first. His teammates are suddenly upon him, clapping him on the back and slapping his hands.

Grammock watches and grins with pleasure. They are in first place by seven games now. *Seven*. And forty-nine games to go. And *seven* times *seven* is forty-nine, which is exactly *seven* years less than his age, and . . .

He decides it is time he told Buford of the phone call that came in just before the game started: Ellie is in labor and has gone to the hospital. The crowd of players sweeps Buford past

Grammock down the runway, and he follows after. By the time he gets to the locker room, he sees that he won't have to tell him after all. Buford is hanging up the phone. His face white as milk, he announces to his teammates loudly that (a) Ellie's water has broken, (b) her cervix is three centimeters dilated, and (c) she is presently being coached by a very able nurse but would very much like him to be there. Grammock hurries to him and signals to E.T.A., who is standing nearby.

"Help me git this boy into a cab, E.T.A. An' I'm goin' with him. The shape he's in, he's liable to fall asleep an' end up in a whorehouse."

The cab ride is a verbal stew of unintelligible post-game analysis by the cabbie and profane hand-wringing over the upcoming series with the Mets by Grammock. With Grammock's help, Buford makes it to the hospital information desk. Then Grammock hustles him into an elevator and pushes the button for him. But at the last instant he jumps out of the elevator and shouts back to Buford, "Hang in there, son."

When the doors open, Buford steps into the hall and is dazzled by the color-coding on the walls. He has no idea which color to follow and chooses to stand erect, just outside the elevator, waiting for something to happen. A nurse addresses him by his first name and leads him down the hall. Buford, forgetting that he is loved locally, figures Ellie has circulated a picture of him among the staff, just in case he turned up in the hall.

When he comes into the labor room, Ellie is in the middle of a contraction. The nurse with her watches a machine that shows the hills and valleys of her pain. In a reversal of what is supposed to happen, Buford responds to the sound of Ellie's deep breathing with automatic encouragement. The nurse steps aside and lets him take over. Ellie focuses on his wedding ring to take her mind off the pain. His job—a feeble contribution, he says to himself—is to hold it steady for her.

After the contraction Ellie sighs and squeezes his hand.

She looks awful—like Narvel after catching a July double-header in St. Louis. She tells him she will be able to push soon, and she seems to look forward to it. Then another contraction comes. She congratulates him on the game, and another one comes. Then another. He whispers encouragement, thinking that it must be horrible for her, knowing it will get worse before it is over. But a doctor swoops in, appears incredibly delighted to make Buford's acquaintance, examines Ellie, and gives her a shot that makes her face look more like the one Buford knows.

The nurse is back, then she is gone, then she is back again, telling Ellie to push. Ellie grabs her thighs and does it. This goes on for an hour. Her pain seems to have lessened, and Buford allows himself to relax. Shortly thereafter, it is all he can do to keep himself from asking her to scoot over so he can nap on the labor bed beside her. The doctor is back. He examines her and says, "Let's do it."

"Here?" says Buford, wondering where they will put all the babies when they come out.

The doctor laughs and disappears. The nurse pulls up the side of Ellie's bed and begins to wheel her out. She directs Buford to the doctors' locker room, where he finds a green smock and green paper shoes to put on. When he returns to the hall, there is no sign of Ellie or the nurse. He freezes and stands in place. Someone in a surgical mask beckons him from beside a huge sink. It turns out to be the doctor, who tells Buford he looks worn out. Buford tells him of his mono-nucleosis and asks if it is possible he could give it to his newborn children. The doctor says he doubts it very much. Should he wear a mask? It's not necessary, says the doctor. But he wants to wear one, he says, just to be on the safe side. So the doctor gives him one.

The delivery room is filled with so many people that Buford looks around for other expectant mothers besides

Ellie. Incredibly, she is the only patient. Buford feels a burst of gratitude for the attention.

The first baby, a girl, comes out in total silence. Buford is sure there is something wrong. But there is nothing wrong, the doctor says. Some babies just come out quietly. Buford watches her airborne progress to a brightly lighted tray, where two young men begin swabbing her down. Between babies, the doctor asks Buford what he knows about discount flights to Mexico City. Buford has little to say on the subject. He is busy rooting for a boy to come out, wondering what is keeping him. Finally, another girl is born—a screamer. Buford looks at her as the doctor wrestles with the umbilical cord. For a moment, he is misled by a labial swelling and protrusion into thinking the doctor must have made a mistake. Surely that's a boy. He steps forward and looks more closely. No. The doctor was right. Two girls.

Now that it is over, Ellie sighs a sigh that to Buford's ears condemns him for not participating more. He stands beside her mutely and wonders if she will reject him now. He becomes aware of his fear and begins to hate himself for it, when he suddenly feels Ellie tugging at him. She wants to kiss him, and she does, through his mask.

In the recovery area, Ellie shakes for an hour while Buford watches. Then they are upstairs in her room. She is eating, a pediatrician is machine-gunning her with instructions, and Buford is falling asleep in the other bed. As he drops off, he wonders if maybe girls are good things to have, and if having two at once is better than having a silly old single one.

A faint light is streaming through the windows when he awakens. All is still. Ellie is asleep, her back to him. He slips out of his bed and pads in his dirty baseball socks around her bed to look at her. Her eyes pop open as he bends down to

125

her and she whispers, "My baby," reaching out to him and then wincing with pain.

"You okay?"

"I had a rough night, Buford. These stitches. And this tube."

"And I slept through it all," he says bitterly.

"You're a sick man, Buford," she says. "Until you're over this mono, I don't expect too much from you. I've got three babies to take care of, the way I see it."

He softly touches her arm where it lies on the pillow beside her hair, which is tangled from a long day of sweat. She moves her arm and he fears he has touched her too hard, that she hurts even there, but then he sees that she only wants to take his hand. As he reaches out and moves a strand of hair to the side of her forehead, their eyes meet and lock for a moment.

The door crashes open, and a nurse shouts, *"Brehfas'*—an' I ain't talkin' 'bout *yours*. I'm talkin' 'bout dese here double whammies. Girl, you got de notion you gon' have 'em in yo' room, you got to *deal* wid it."

Buford watches in mild terror, shaken by the violence of her entrance, as she wheels in two glass cages full of blankets. He squints at them. An ominous bit of flesh shows in each.

"We'll need some formula too," Ellie says, slowly sitting up in bed. "My husband will take one of them." Buford searches frantically for his surgical mask and finds it tucked in the elastic waistband of his pants. He quickly puts it on and stands erect, ready for orders. The nurse says that everything they will need is on top of the dresser. Before she leaves, she says the Swede will be in soon.

"The Swede," thinks Buford, imagining some agent of torture employed by the hospital. But before his fear can grow, a gray-haired woman enters the room, smiles at Buford, and begins to talk in a quiet lilt with Ellie. Buford stands in place, not wanting to bother anybody. From the glass cages, silence. He wonders why they don't just let them sleep if they want to. Then he is startled by a blasting cry from one of them. He looks to the Swede for help, but she is still with Ellie. He hesitates, then walks over to the cage. He stares. It is impossible for him to pick her up.

"We'll start you with this one," the Swede says, for she is suddenly there, handing Buford a bottle and scooping the baby out of the cage. Buford sits down on the edge of the bed and moves his arms around a bit, warming up. It is hot in the room and he begins to perspire. The nurse slips his daughter into his arm—Marie or Sally, he doesn't know which—and helps him guide the nipple into her mouth. The child sucks, coughs, spits, rolls her eyes, and falls asleep. Or perhaps she has dropped dead. The nurse, busy with Ellie and the other baby, has utterly abandoned him. Buford touches his daughter's lips with the nipple and she takes a few more sucks and turns away to sleep again. The sweat drips off his forehead into her blanket. A drop lands on her cheek and he wipes it away with a huge thumb. He wonders what to do next and impulsively begins to rock his arm slowly back and forth, back and forth.

In a sudden flood tide of boiling warmth, with sweat and tears pouring down his face, he chokes, then bellows to the wall, "Oh Lord, I love these children. Oh Lord, I do."

And he does.

6

It has been asked if a team can be a contender without the big stick, or with a weak bullpen, or with rookies at the corners. A related question that has not been asked is if it is possible for a team to be a contender with two of its three outfielders on Elavil.

"You poppin' pills, Buford?" asks Grammock as he stalks through the clubhouse and sees Buford and Eddie comparing labels. "Ya' finally found somethin' that's gonna wake ya' up?"

"They ain't uppers, Skip," says Eddie. "The doctor says—"

"You got a prescription for this?" Grammock asks, ignoring Eddie as he grabs Buford's bottle and squints at it.

"Sure do, Skip," Buford says with animation.

"E.T.A., what do you know about this?"

"Nothing, Skip. I—"

"It's your job to know about stuff." He turns back to

Buford. "Do these pills interfere with your fielding, throwing, running, hitting for average, or hitting with power?"

"No, Skip," says Buford. "No problem there. They just give you a wee touch of constipation," he adds, pinching a thumb and forefinger together like a merry chef.

"Yeah," says Eddie. "The doc says—"

"Constipation?" Grammock says suspiciously. "That slow you down any, Buford?"

"No, sir."

"Then I don't give a shit what it is," he says, handing the bottle back to him. "I got enough problems with this team without worryin' 'bout you guyses' bowel situation. I got a losin' streak of four games doggin' my heels, the longest of the goddamn season. I got a front office always talkin' trade, trade, trade, when I love all of you boys and wouldn't part with none of ya', not countin' my bench, which stinks so bad I can still smell 'em on my clothes when I take them off at night. I got a horny pitcher that you'd think he was gittin' laid in the tooth dentist's chair for all the clubhouse meetings he's missed. I got Chicago starin' at me, which we ain't beat the bums but twice all season. So, Buford, as long as what you're puttin' in your mouth ain't illegal, I got nothin' to say to ya'. Jist all of ya' for the sake of Jesus H. Christ gimme a break an' jump out on top tonight instead a raisin' wind on my stomach by mopin' around for half the game an' then playin' catch-up ball." He storms on through the locker room to his office and slams the door.

Eddie breaks the silence left behind by Grammock with a long, low chuckle. "That man's somethin' else, ain't he?"

"Hey, Eddie," says Buford. "Let's see your imitation of him. You haven't done it all season."

"Nah," Eddie drawls uncertainly.

"Come on, Eddie," says Scrappy, trying to pick him up. "Us new guys—me 'n' Frank—we ain't seen it yet."

Eddie gives a self-conscious grin. "Ya' know, I do kinda miss doin' it. I wonder why I . . . Hell, I'll give it a try. I'll give it mah bes' shot." He stands very still for a moment, thinking. Then he tries to puff out his bare stomach above his warm-up shorts, but his body is too taut for this to have much effect. He slowly walks over to where Narvel sits and places a fatherly hand on his shoulder. When he speaks again, his voice is high and gravelly.

"Narvel, I know the fans been startin' to git on ya' lately. I know they been callin' ya' ugly names an' all. I know that that one guy shouldn't a hadn't a oughta brung a crossbow into the box seats, but, listen up, Narvel, I don' wanna upset our rhythm none. Ya' think ya' can go another coupla innings with that there arrow in your butt? We got a good thang goin' here, a real magic, an' I don' wanna mess it up, ya' understan'? Can you be a good boy fo' me an' show me what you're made of an' hang in there another coupla innings, huh?"

He suddenly steps back from a diffidently smiling Narvel and adds another physical touch. One hand rubs his stomach steadily while the other flies back and forth from his lip, where he moistens a fingertip, to his right nipple, which he stimulates—not strictly part of the Grammock repertoire, but it seems right. "We gon' change some signals now, mah boys—an' I hope you niggahs on the club don' git all uppity 'bout me callin' you 'boys.' I sure don' mean no *of*fense by it. Ah sure don' mean you jis' a buncha jungle-bunny spade spooks that had oughta should go 'roun' all the time bein' humble an' thankful 'cuz ya' ain't been strung up from the stadium rafters by now. Naw, Ah sure don' mean that a-*tall*. Now, we's gotta change some a our signals, 'cuz the opposition ain't as ignorant as Scrappy here, so listen up, Frank, if'n ya' can stop your jabberin' a minute, for the sake a Jesus H.I.J.K.L.M.N.O.P. Christ. Now, the indicator—that means the next signal is valid, okay? Scrapheap, 'valid' is a big word that means ya' gotta do what it says, okay? The indicator useta be skin on skin, like mah finger touchin' mah nose. Thas too simple. From now on, skin on skin don' mean nothin'. What counts is skin on *fo*'skin, like this." In a flash, he pulls the front of his shorts and jockstrap down and gently taps his foreskin before quickly snapping them back up to his waist and resuming his belly and lip-to-nipple rhythm. "Ya' gotta be lookin' for it, 'cuz it's gon' happen real quick—I show too much a my tallywhacker an' them young twitchets in the stands is gon' be slobberin' an' maulin' me. Now, if'n I hafta give a lotta indicators, I jis' might git a boner inside a mah pants, which is always kinda awkward. If'n that happens, the indicator switches to . . . ah . . ." He breaks into laughter. "Hey, Bufe," he says in his normal voice. "What's it switch to? I done forgot the routine."

Buford, laughing, says, "I don't know, Eddie. That's okay. You'd better stop anyway, or *I'm* gonna have twins."

E.T.A. watches, slightly amused, but mainly distressed by Eddie's domination. It was his impression that Eddie was going to ease back and let him take over. At the same time, though, he grudgingly admires the way Eddie handles the guys. Yes, he thinks—good-natured abuse is definitely part of the team leader's arsenal. He sits quietly, his nose twitching under his glasses, as he waits for his chance to take over.

Scrappy's smile slowly dies. He has enjoyed Eddie's performance, but he is troubled. He watches Eddie sit down on a stool, flushed and laughing, and then he can see Eddie's face fall as he lapses into introspection. He knows Eddie is thinking what he is thinking, maybe what all of them are thinking: that this is the old Eddie they just saw, the Eddie that is no more. He feels as if, leafing through a scrapbook, he has suddenly come upon a snapshot of a dead man.

As the players settle down and begin suiting up for the game, Scrappy speaks up with unaccustomed frankness. He asks Eddie how he thinks he can ever truly know himself if he relies on drugs. "'Know thyself,' that's what Abe Lincoln always said," he informs Eddie. "He knew hisself, you can bet, and was a purty happy man too."

Eddie shrugs. "An' you know *yo*'se'f?" he asks with a playful smile.

"I'm workin' on it," Scrappy says matter-of-factly. "I'm learnin' some things. It takes time."

"*Ha!*" E.T.A. shouts, leaping to his feet. "But how *much* time?"

Scrappy's eyes dart nervously from Eddie to E.T.A. "A year, maybe. Maybe longer."

"Seem like a lotta talkin', Scrappy," Eddie says in a gentle way.

"My guy says I got a lotta issues to work through," says Scrappy.

"*Issues?*" E.T.A. says in a high-pitched voice. "Issues of what—the *Sporting News?* What kind of word is that for *you* to be using?"

Scrappy's face collapses and he begins to whine his arguments out, speaking with a tentativeness bordering on total capitulation. He says that his guy says drugs just cover up the sickness. Eddie says he personally feels that if depression is bad only because of the symptoms, and if drugs take away the symptoms—as his doctor says they do, in most cases—then it's a harmless disease. It's as harmless, suggests Eddie, as being allergic to moon dust: it makes no difference if you never go there.

"*Yeah*," E.T.A. snarls vehemently, drawing several frowns.

Frank, who has been oiling his glove, throws his red, square face into the debate. "Lay off, E.T.A. Scrappy's right. He's just got the wrong kind of therapy. What is your guy—an analyst?"

"I dunno," says Scrappy.

"You lie down?"

"Nope. Sit right up."

"How often do you go?"

Scrappy shrugs. "Our schedule makes it kinda unregular. Maybe once a week, average."

Frank purses his lips. "Maybe he's not, then."

"But he wants me to come a lot more when the season's over."

"Ah. Does he ever talk about the here-and-now?"

Scrappy looks deeply uncertain.

"You know—about what's going on in your life today," Frank explains.

"Sometimes. But he seems more innerested in, I dunno, my life before kinnygarden, I guess."

"Yeah," Frank says knowingly. "You got the wrong persuasion, Scrappy. You should get into cognitive therapy."

"And just what might *that* be?" snaps E.T.A., thinking what a good target Frank would be for him.

"It's clean and simple," says Frank, warming to the subject. "People get depressed because they constantly have bad thoughts about themselves. Cognitive therapy helps the patient see that these thoughts are distortions of reality. Like if Jaime here thought he was a for-shit ballplayer, if I was his therapist I'd remind him of some of the great catches he's made this year and of his record for doubles last year. Stuff like that."

Jaime smiles, dimly sensing good vibrations.

"Thas got a nice ring to it, Frank," says Eddie.

"But does it *work?*" asks E.T.A., his eyebrows dancing demonically. He looks right at Frank, into the soul of his depression.

"Well, it's *working*," says Frank.

E.T.A. snorts. "And what if the bad thoughts are true? Like Jaime's home-run total is way down this year, and he lost us a game last week on a shamefully incompetent throw. What's your therapist going to say when it looks like his patient's truly a loser?"

Jaime stops smiling.

Frank is not prepared for this objection. "Maybe he kind of puts things in perspective," he says uncertainly, gesturing broadly with his hands—hands that he proudly remembers have been called "soft" for the way they absorb ground balls.

E.T.A. snorts again and looks at his teammates for supporting snorts, but they are silent. Frank sits quietly, searching frantically for another good thought to think about himself.

"Yeah," Eddie says thoughtfully. "I kinda wonder 'bout all this talkin' stuff too. Seem to me we got to find us all a sure way of gittin' over this shit so we can be whole again, you know what I mean? An' so we can play complete ball. You take me, now. How can a po' niggah like me keep his mind in the game when he's so fucked up he beats up on a dumb-ass dog, gits his ass throwed in jail fo' all the worl' to read about, an' has all sorts a other shit comin' down? Thas what this sickness done fo' me. You guys know it, an' I know it. An' how in hell can I deal with it without some kinda help? Me an' Bufe got us a doc that says pills can do it, an' I believe him."

"Are they working for you, Eddie?" Buford asks.

"I jis' started on 'em, Bufe. I expect 'em to. I'm real hopeful."

E.T.A. glowers at Eddie. He finds it criminally unfair that Eddie has brought up this subject after asking him not to. He feels scooped.

"My guy says a *lot* of good stuff," Scrappy blurts out, fearing he has let his guy down by defending him so poorly.

"My guy didn't say diddly-shit," Narvel says bitterly. "What's *your* guy say?"

Scrappy starts to speak, but he draws a blank. He can't separate his therapist's words from his own. "We jis' mainly talk a lot about like how I was brung up an' all."

"I'm not sure how much stock I put in all this childhood stuff," says Buford.

E.T.A.'s hand darts to his glasses to adjust them—a purely rhetorical move. "Would you care to elaborate, Buford?" He says this as if Buford's claim has deeply offended him. It hasn't. In fact, he was about to make it himself. But he wants to take him on.

"Huh? No, E.T.A. Not me. It was just a thought."

"And not much of one, Buford," says E.T.A., unbothered by the fact that his abuse thus far has been thoroughly ill-natured. "I am prepared to say that I, for one, believe strongly in parental responsibility."

Eddie shakes his head. "Thas jis' the easy way out, E.T.A. Thas jis' shiftin' the blame. Thas chickenshit stuff, seems to me. I got no bitch against my folks. They did a good job a raisin' me, under the circumstances, which was that they couldn't hardly stand the sight a one another. They never let that git to me none, though. I had to listen to 'em fightin' every fuckin' night, but they never took it out on me none. You gotta respec' that."

"But look at your marital problems now," says E.T.A.

"What's it to *you*?" Eddie says, rather sharply. Then he looks away, down to the floor, suddenly frightened by the direction of their talk. But he trusts E.T.A. to steer it away from this course.

"You can't all of a sudden withdraw from the discussion like that and pretend I'm being too personal," E.T.A. says in a snide, sing-songy fashion. "You can't do that, Eddie, especially after getting so . . . so *confessional*. My point is that even as you disclaim the molding influence of childhood, you have described a pattern that you yourself are repeating at this moment in your life."

"Shit, E.T.A.," Eddie drawls, trying to find a smile. "Gimme a break."

E.T.A. snorts. "That's not much of a rejoinder, Eddie. Haven't I spoken with deadly accuracy about your marriage?"

"Come on, E.T.A.," says Eddie with a mixture of embarrassment and fear.

"If you're not comfortable speaking directly to my point, that's fine with me, Eddie," E.T.A. says with a veneer of equability. "That's just fine and dandy." He turns to Buford. "You're another example, Buford. Here you have had the audacity to question the importance of childhood, when you've been boring us all season with your anxiety over your twins. Now, wouldn't you say it's reasonable to assume that your own parents' bungling is the root of your exaggerated fears?"

Buford gulps and runs a paw through his blond hair. "I don't rightly know, E.T.A. I always thought they gave it their best shot, but I could be wrong."

"You're damned right you're wrong," he says. He turns his attention to the entire group. "Let me expand a bit, if I may. Let me share with you the history of my thought on the subject of clinical depression." He senses no objection. In fact, he feels that they have all been waiting for just this moment. "For much of the season now, I have been grappling with the issue of my intellectual competence. This must come as a surprise to many of you, but you also should remember— and, indeed, your recent experience qualifies you better than others to understand—that, if I might follow up and improve on what Frank has tried but failed to say, for a depressive what counts is not objective reality but his misperception of it."

Bubba farts.

E.T.A., momentarily discomposed, glances at his cruelly expressionless face before continuing. "Lately, my thinking has focused on the key role played by aggressiveness in life both on and off the field. Success demands an aggressive posture, by which I mean not a predilection for random destruction"—his lingering look at Bubba is, he hopes, devastating—"but a recognition of one's right to compete actively in the arena of life and to claim one's winnings without apology."

Bubba farts again. Eddie and Buford laugh.

Jaw set, E.T.A. continues. "I am particularly interested in the mutually destructive interaction of aggression and success. Apples is a good example. In his last outing—"

"I don't like the idea of talking about Apples behind his back," Frank interjects.

"And I know why you don't, Frank," E.T.A. says. "You fear the very same thing yourself—not without reason, I might add."

Frank withdraws into himself in silent, ardent resentment.

"Not much gets by me," E.T.A. says, allowing a self-adoring little chuckle to escape his lips. "Really, Frank, sometimes you're as transparent as a jellyfish. Let me hurry to move on to someone more interesting. It is obvious that Apples is most in danger of losing his stuff in the late innings, when he has a lead and victory is within his grasp. Does he grow tired? I think not. No, for it is the threat of being successful that undermines him. But this means he is caught in a perilous dilemma, *as we all are*. Losing isn't a solution. Losing will only raise havoc with our already fragile self-esteem. But if we continue to win, oh beware ye the psychic perils of success. And if we win the big one? Disaster. For a baseball team sickened by success, winning the World Series is definitely contraindicated."

Bubba farts again. This time, Frank joins Eddie and Buford in laughing.

"Bubba, I'm going to have to address you. If with that noise you mean to imply that my speech is somewhat flatulent, then the onus is on you to elaborate." E.T.A. is beginning to look a little strange. His words are coming out calmly, but his face is reddening while his neck tightens rhythmically. "I might add, Bubba, that, in your own way, you are demonstrating another element fundamental to depression: *anger*." He bites the word out so viciously—his voice having suddenly caught up with his body—that it is totally unintelligible. So he says it again, this time with a halting, dying fall to it that enrages him. "Anger. All of us are angry, but anger, being a form of aggression, makes us un-*com*fortable and we turn it *in*ward against our*selves*." He has hit a strange rhythm, speaking with an accentual violence that is foreign to him but that sweeps him along of its own power. "You ap*pear* to be an exception, Bubba, because your anger is vented daily on everybody you come into *con*tact with, but that just shows you are crazier than the *rest* of us and have a *sur*plus of anger even after you have turned it *in*ward. *I* am growing angry too. You can *see* it. I can *see* that you can see it, and that makes me even *an*grier. To think that an animal like *you* can do this to someone like *me*."

And again! His teammates are amazed at the abundance and timeliness of his eruptions, not to mention their forensic effectiveness, and several of them laugh and talk about it.

E.T.A. runs off the rails. Moving with the monstrous frenzy of a man to whom anger has been a stranger for far too long, he grabs a bat from his locker and raises it high over his head with both hands, bringing it down like a battle-ax, meaning to split Bubba's skull. Bubba's eyes bug out. He darts aside and raises his hands in a panic of self-defense, and the blow catches him along the length of his upper left arm. He sprawls to the floor screaming in pain as E.T.A. is subdued by his teammates.

"*I'll kill him*," shrieks E.T.A. "*I'll kill him. I'll kill him if you let me go. Don't let me go. I'll kill him.*"

Bubba howls, moans, and whimpers as he is lifted to his feet. Grammock is suddenly upon them, shouting them all down, demanding to know what has happened. Secretly, though, he is delighted with the violence. His boys needed a shaking up like this. And, he notes with pleasure, it looks like E.T.A. is finally taking charge. Grammock bellows obscurely for a while, creating a calming confusion, and then he hustles Bubba into the trainer's room.

E.T.A. twists free of the men still holding him and spins away down the aisle in the opposite direction, kicking stools all the way, sending a Mexican utility infielder who has been cutting his toenails at the far end of the room scrambling for cover. The men see E.T.A. turn the corner and they listen, gauging his movements from the noise. There goes the large candy barrel by the door, they think, and . . . yes, that would be the stretcher that hangs in the runway, and . . . what's *that?* Oh—the clatter of bats being heaved out of the dugout by the handful, a sight that must surely be a surprise to the groundskeepers preparing the field. Then they hear nothing, for the sound of a bat being repeatedly smashed against second base is not audible in the clubhouse.

"Who rattled *his* cage?" says Frank.

"Someone oughta go after him," says Scrappy, sitting glued to his stool. No one moves.

"Whew," says Buford. "I've never seen him like that."

"He'll git over it," says Eddie. "I know. I can relate to it. Shit, lately I'm always burnin'."

"But why?" asks Scrappy. "What are you mad at, Eddie?" Then he quickly raises a hand, palm outward. "No. Never mind. I shouldn't ask. Forgit it, Eddie."

"You can ask, man," Eddie says softly and simply.

"Well, I jist been worryin' if you was mad at *us*. Are you?"

"No," says Narvel, answering for Eddie and looking at him. "Not us."

"The queen of bitches," Eddie says, nodding slowly. "How 'bout you, Narv'? You mad?"

"Sure," Narvel says with a shrug. "But I don't know why, exactly."

Eddie looks to Buford. "Bufe? You ever mad?"

Buford's big face goes blank under his blond hair, which is matted from nervous sweat. He has been thinking about parental responsibility ever since E.T.A. uttered the words. What does it mean? What does he know about raising kids? He wants to abdicate. Let Ellie raise 'em, he thinks. He's on the road a lot anyway. If he meddles with them only now and again, they'll just get confused. Hands off—that's the best policy. In the off-season, he can play winter ball in the Dominican.

"I'm not mad, Eddie," he finally says. "I've got no problem with anger."

"Scrappy?" says Eddie, turning to him.

Scrappy looks at his teammates. Should he tell them the full, grim story of his life? His sense of team spirit makes him want to. But he gets all that he needs from his guy, who once spoke scornfully about group therapy. He can see why, when he thinks about E.T.A. Open up his heart to a guy like that? No thanks. It is clear to him that they cannot possibly help one another.

"I pay for treatment, Eddie. And I don't chew my cabbage twice."

Eddie shrugs. "Have it your way."

"I'm mad at just about everyone I can think of from my childhood," says Frank, though nobody asked. "I was an Army kid, and we moved around a lot, so I was switching schools all the time. As soon as I made friends, I moved away and had to start all over. And it seemed like I'd never studied what the other kids had, so I was always behind. Couldn't draw or sing, either. The teachers always found me handy as a negative example. They must have figured, 'What the hell, he's just passing through,' and they would talk about me all the time in front of the other kids." He pauses, then says with a dreamy smile, "I hate a whole shitload of people."

Eddie surveys his teammates. "So some of us is mad and some of us ain't."

"We'll check with Bubba later," says Narvel with a small chuckle, "but I think I know what he's going to say."

"You combersá me nada."

They wince with pain. Then they force themselves to look at Jaime.

"You combersá me nada nada."

"Say *what?*" says Eddie.

"Esaqui no ta gustámi."

"Get one of his countrymen over here to translate," suggests Narvel.

"Me no surdu. Me no muda."

"But he don't got none," says Eddie.

"Me no gagu. Scuchámi."

"I mean another Spanish dude," says Narvel. "That's close, at least."

They call on the utility infielder at the far end of the room—an undepressed, altogether uninteresting man. He exchanges several sentences in Spanish with Jaime, interrupting him frequently. Jaime speaks with animation, apparently ranging far and wide before settling on one long sentence, which he says over and over. The infielder flinches and frowns, then shrugs before turning to the others to give a translation: "A burro is not a beautiful animal, but neither is it an ugly one."

"Great," mutters Eddie.

"Yeah," says Narvel. "That helps a lot. Let's just forget him and keep talking."

"That's *it*," says Frank. "He's saying we don't talk to him. 'We converse with him nothing nothing.' I had some Spanish at one of my schools once."

"He wants us to *talk* to him?" Narvel asks with disbelief.

"It ain't no *point* in it," complains Eddie.

"I don't know," says Frank. "Jaime's not such a bad guy."

"Sure," says Eddie. "He jis' *might* be the mos' wonderful person in the worl'. But how the fuck we gonna know that?"

"It's hopeless," says Narvel. "Let's forget him."

And they do. They form a tighter circle and continue to talk, developing their thoughts. Grammock steps out of the trainer's room, planning to tell them Bubba has the biggest bruise in history but otherwise appears to be okay. He's eager to joke with them, get them loose again after the fight, maybe get going on Scrappy.

But the words don't come out when he sees them all hunched together. He listens. What are they talking about? He hears the word "depression" and thinks, Hell, that's okay. They're talking about Eddie's private depression in the turf out in center field. That's good. They got their minds on the game. But now they're talking about other things—feelings, and all sorts of crap. He squints at them, his belly starting to churn at the way they're all bent over and muttering. Jesus H., he thinks. They're as freaky as a bunch of goddamned Christian athletes in Bible study.

Something's gone wrong with his boys.

○ ○ ○

Chicago. They have squeaked a victory out of the first game but have lost the second in miserable fashion. The rubber game of the series is an hour away. The time is right for it.

"I dunno, I ain't much for speech-makin', but I was sittin' in my office last night thinkin' that the somethin' that's ailin' my boys is maybe somethin' the ol' skipper can try an' set right with a coupla well-chose words. I don't know rightly where to begin, so lemme jist jump right in an' start off by sayin' somethin' about bad breaks. We've had our share lately, sure, but lemme tell ya' somethin'. Good breaks come to good teams an' bad ones to bad teams, don't ask me why.

You play smart, an' the cards'll start comin' your way. Ya' make your own breaks is what I'm sayin'.

"Okay. That's point number one. Point number two is ya' gotta think you're hot shit. Deep down, ya' gotta think ya' got somethin' comin' to ya' because you're such hot shit. Point number three has to do with bein' cool. Now, I been in this game a long time, an' I know bein' cool is a awful important part of it. If you're cool an' ya' know you're hot shit enough so's to deserve to win, then when you *do* win you can more or less take it in stride, on accounta you're both hot an' cool, ya' know what I mean? But there's such a thing as overdoin' the coolness, of bein' *too* blah-zay. Somethin' about this team: you guys act the same, win or lose. When you're back in the clubhouse, if I didn't know you'd won, there's no way I could know from watchin' ya'. Sometimes it's okay to celebrate, is what I'm sayin'. Sometimes it's okay to be *glad* you're such hot shit.

"Next point: you guys are *thinkin'* too much. I can feel it in my bones. Sure, ya' gotta think about where you're gonna be goin' with the ball when you're in the field, an' when ya' stand in at the plate, ya' gotta be thinkin' about what that pitcher's gonna bring to ya', but you guys seem to be off on the wrong track somehow. I look in your faces an' it's like lookin' at the moon. There's a lotta spare time in this game, let's face it. Time for thinkin'. So you gotta watch out, is what I'm sayin'.

"Now, the next an' I guess last thing I got to say is pretty personal. I ain't ashamed to say it, though. I ain't ashamed a-tall. Here it is, now, so listen up. I love you boys. Maybe I love ya' too much. Sometimes when I git riled up, maybe ya' think I don't love ya'. Maybe I say things I shouldn't oughta an' it upsets ya'. Well, I'm human too. I make mistakes—all managers make mistakes. But I hope that *most* of the time I'm lovin' ya', an' showin' it. You're good boys, all of you. But my oh my, how you do fuck up sometimes, so I can't help but blow off a little steam an' smoke. Way I see it, so long as ya' know ya' got my love, it's okay for me to git on you a bit. Now, I don't wanna single no one out, but like when you, E.T.A., dumb up an' make two mental errors in one game, I swear I'm tempted to think you're so ignorant you couldn't lead a little baby's tugboat across the kitchen floor. I dunno, now I think about it, sometimes you guys make me so mad I'd like to come out an' jist kick every one of your butts all over the infield. I'm thinkin' a you, Scrappy, though I don't wanna pick on nobody. I'm thinkin' how you somehow can't never git our signals straight, an' I swear, some days I wanna slap you around until ya' wake up to how worthless you are.

"Now, I know I ain't perfect—hell, they don't make 'em that way no more—an' maybe some a you guys don't like my way a doin' things. Apples, I know you're a religious man, your father bein' a flaky California preacher an' all, an' maybe you don't like my occasional takin' a the Lord's name in vain. Well, you gotta take the good with the bad, way I see it. Here's a for-instance: I'm willin' to overlook Frank not knowin' when to shuddup, which in my humble opinion is about a hour before he ever gits started. I'm willin' to overlook Narvel's lousy father in San Diego bellowin' at me from the stands like I'm a goddamn Little League coach. I'm willin' to overlook the fact that, for all your thinkin', you boys can't seem to keep your mind in the game—sure, Buford, you've brought a couple little buggers into this stinkin' life, an' when their caterwaulin' at home throws you outta bed after a tough loss, you're naturally gonna wanna blow your brains out, but you gotta try 'n' keep your mind in the game too. And sure, Eddie, maybe you got problems with the law an' your neighbors an' your temper an' with the little woman at home, but I also happen to think she's a helluva good-lookin' gal, an' I know I ain't alone in thinkin' that way—right, Bubba?

"Well, hell, I dunno—I can't say I ever give a pep talk before, but I guess I'm a-givin' one now. I been real careful not to forgit nobody that's worth rememberin', so all's I can say now is git out there an' whup their butts or I'll whup yours an' enjoy doin' it too."

○ ○ ○

On the day of Grammock's pep talk and their subsequent 16–0 loss to the Cubs, they head out for the Coast, where they rebound and take three from the Padres, two of three from the Dodgers, and two from the Giants. The biggest contributors are Bubba, who pretends that every pitched ball is E.T.A.'s head; Frank, who since the clubhouse discussion has been encouraged by the fact that he has come very close to discovering one more good thought about himself; and Buford, whose mononucleosis and depression seem to have disappeared simultaneously, as if the one absorbed the other. After their first win against the Dodgers, he cheered the Los Angeles sewer system no end by flushing his remaining tablets of Elavil down the toilet.

On the eve of their last game on the road—after a painfully frustrating loss to the Giants, in which Frank committed two errors, one a game-losing mishandling of a bunt—Apples and E.T.A. step out for a few drinks. Apples spends the time dreaming about his dental assistant and relishing his absence of discomfort with the obviously homosexual clientele in the obviously homosexual bar, recommended to him as a joke by a bullpen asshole, while E.T.A. bends Apples' ear with a tedious lecture on team leadership, desperately hoping for and utterly failing to get acknowledgment from the inattentive Apples that he, E.T.A., is now the undisputed team leader.

When they return to the hotel, they see Bubba leaning against a pillar and nod to him. He nods back and, when they are past him, silently mouths obscenities at E.T.A.'s head. Just beyond him is an open elevator, and they speed up to catch it. It is packed full of people, mainly nurses attending a convention, and after causing a bit of shuffling, they find room for themselves just inside the doors.

As the elevator begins to rise, Apples takes up the conversation where they left off. "Why did Frank's old man move around so much?" he asks, speaking in a loud voice to display his masculinity to the nurses, who arouse him to a point of extreme agitation.

"Army orders, I guess," says E.T.A., whose frustration with Apples' inattention at the bar now inspires him to roast Frank. "Maybe because of his father's personality too. You know—like father, like son. Maybe his superiors couldn't stand having him around."

The elevator proceeds slowly, stopping at each floor, often without any shifting of its population. They look at the panel displaying the floor numbers and see that it is completely alight.

"Bubba?" Apples speculates.

"Yeah," says E.T.A. "It's one of his favorite tricks. What a child he is."

The nurses see it now too and moan to one another good-naturedly. Apples looks to each side of him and favors them with a toothy grin.

"I wonder if they called Frank's father 'Suitcase' too," E.T.A. says.

"Not in the Army," says Apples. "Maybe 'Knapsack.' Or 'Duffelbag.'" E.T.A. chuckles. Apples feels really good. He feels important discussing something he knows the nurses don't understand, especially because he made E.T.A. chuckle in front of all of them. "To give him his due," he continues, "he seems a little less gabby lately."

"Nah," says E.T.A. "Besides, even when he's not jabbering, it feels like he is. You look at his face and your ears start ringing, even when he's not talking."

Apples chuckles. Softly. He wants the nurses to know his joke was funnier than E.T.A.'s

The elevator bumps upward, and the nurses disembark in a jovial mass on the eighth floor. To let them pass, E.T.A. scoots aside, squeezing into the front corner facing the display panel, where he is blinded by the lights of Bubba's anarchism. Apples, however, remains standing in the very center of the front of the elevator, so that the nurses must pass on each side of him. Many of them brush against him on their way out. He runs the tip of his tongue across the smooth surface of his new incisors while his cheeks redden with mounting lust.

"Where's he from anyway?" asks E.T.A.

Apples eases back into reality. "Everywhere, I guess." His speech is more subdued now, for only a few people remain in the elevator behind them.

"I mean where was he born? He must consider some-place home."

"Nah," says Apples. "Just the hotel lobby."

"Yeah," says E.T.A. "Hoping for someone to sit down beside him. Fat chance."

Behind Apples and E.T.A., pressed against the rear wall, stands Frank, red-faced and breathless. This is *it*, he thinks. There can be no sugarcoating of it. This is what he figured went on all along, without ever being sure. The purity of the slander gives him surprising pleasure. He wants them to continue, to get really mean about him.

On the fourteenth floor, Apples and E.T.A. step out, and, after a calculated pause, so does Frank, jostling the two remaining passengers in a way that he is sure will have them talking about him after the doors close behind him. Padding softly on the rug, he hurriedly follows his teammates and slows to their pace when he is a few steps behind them. But they are talking about something else now. The nurses in the elevator. Then someone in the San Francisco line-up. Then the question of why Narvel always insists on sitting by the door in taxicabs. Then the nurses again. Frank is disappointed. But even so, he rejoices in those words in the elevator. They were almost perfect. If the conversation had gone on a little longer, if it had not suffered a change of scene, if they had ridden on for ten more floors, he is sure their words would have exactly matched his worst thoughts.

E.T.A. fishes his key out of his pocket and turns to the door of his room. He catches sight of Frank and feels a small surge of panic. Frank slows and nods to him once, saying nothing. Apples looks back to say good night to E.T.A. and sees Frank.

"Hi, ya', Frank," he says innocently, stepping back to the two of them. "Your room on this floor too?"

"No."

"What're you doing here? Just kind of roaming around? Looking for some conversation?"

"I was in the elevator," Frank says coolly.

"Yeah?" says Apples. It hasn't sunk in. He is too fogged up with his nurses.

"With us?" E.T.A. asks, recalling the words, wondering if he can explain them away, finally concluding it is hopeless.

"That's right."

Apples finally gets it. "Geez, Frank. Uh . . ."

"I heard everything you said." Frank states it as a bald fact. He will let them give it meaning.

"Man," moans Apples. "Oh, man." The color is gone from his face. He wants to hug Frank, clutch his curly hair in his fists, smother his square face with kisses.

E.T.A. is suddenly resentful of Frank for putting them in this plight. Frank is a jerk, he thinks. The sooner he knows it, the better.

"So what do you want us to say, Frank?" he asks.

Frank's face narrows and collapses into a mournful oval

shape. "*That's* your attitude?" he whines. "That's all you've got to say to me?"

"No!" Apples blurts out, stepping toward him. "Frank, we were awful. I don't know what I was thinking. I don't believe any of that."

"Then why did you say it? And why did you let E.T.A. say it?"

"I don't *know*. Geez, I could kill myself. Frank, listen, you've got a lot going for you. Really."

E.T.A. is repulsed. "Come on, Frank. Give us a break."

Frank looks at him without expression.

"It's late," says E.T.A. "We can talk about it tomorrow."

"Thanks a lot, E.T.A.," Frank says peevishly. "You really care a lot, don't you?"

"Okay okay okay. Tell me what you want me to say and I'll say it and that'll be the end of it."

"Thanks a lot. Thanks a whole hell of a lot, E.T.A."

Apples says, "Listen, Frank—"

"Well, it's true, isn't it?" says E.T.A., getting hot. "Come on, Frank. Go ahead and deny it. What did we say that was false?"

"Geez, E.T.A.," says Apples.

"Don't you care about me, E.T.A.?" Frank's lips barely move to let the words by.

"Oh, Frank," E.T.A. groans loudly. "Frank, Frank, Frank. Do I ever seek you out for a chat? When I'm down and I'm looking for a sympathetic ear, do I ever say to myself, 'Hey, how about ole Frank? He'll give a listen'? Hell no, I don't. The day you start showing some interest in other people's words, I'll change my view of you. But I'm not going to do it just because you heard me talking about you. No way." He looks at Frank steadily for a moment. Then he unlocks his door and goes into his room. As he closes the door behind him, he feels a surge of pure exhilaration.

Outside in the hall, Apples is wiping his palms on his pants. "Listen, Frank. Listen, now. I love you. I really do."

"Nice try, Apples," Frank says with profound dignity. He turns away and walks slowly down the hall, leaving Apples standing there in utter despair, his hands working spastically in the air as he searches for words.

○ ○ ○

Eddie takes the sinking line drive on a dead run, just inches above the wet turf, and then pulls up into a slow, casual trot before flipping the ball to the second-base ump, who examines it as if searching for blackheads to pinch. Eddie trots on in, feeling good, looking forward to his first at-bat of the double-header, hoping that Bubba or Jaime or both can get on base before him. Things are going well. The newspapers have finally run out of things to say about his arrest and probably won't bring it up again until he comes to trial—November, at the earliest. The hometown fans have been good to him about it, and the opposition's fans don't bother him too much with their shouts of "Hey, Eddie, wanna buy a puppy?" and "Hey, Eddie, got to see 'The Man' about a dog?" And although the bitch is still a bitch, his medication seems to be kicking in, and she may look better under its influence. And, further down on the list, if they win both games tonight and Atlanta beats Los Angeles on the Coast, they will clinch the division title.

Initially, he is not surprised to see Tina in the dugout. There is no sense of incongruity at all. She is often pleasantly underfoot. But when he recognizes her familiar dance of discomfort and speeds up to get into the dugout to ask her if she needs to go potty, he realizes he has never taken her potty in the locker room before because she has never been here before—moreover, she is not supposed to be here now. At this moment, she should be with the bitch, who planned to do some of her perpetual shopping during the first game and then, after dumping Tina with a sitter, stroll into the stands to make a rare appearance at the second game, her plans implying—as do, he thinks, all of her words and deeds—boredom with the game and presumptuous certainty that he will be playing it forever.

Tina squirms next to the bat rack, tightly holding the hand of a stadium guard and yet standing a little apart from him. The guard is pointing to Eddie, her daddy, and her eyes search among the bewildering array of uniformed players tumbling into the dugout emitting spit. She finally sees her father. She has been holding it all in, and now she cuts loose, filling the dugout with a wail that sends Grammock's buttocks creeping up his back.

Eddie hurries to her and bends at the knees to be near her. "What is it, babe? What you doin' here?"

She presses her lips together and hugs him tightly around the neck.

"A cop brought her to the gate, Eddie," says the guard. "He said she was wanderin' around Saks by herself. Said a saleslady recognized her as your girl because she'd seen her in there before, with your wife. I don't know no more. They found a cop and brung her to the stadium. I don't know no more."

Eddie thanks the guard. Then he sits down with Tina on the bench. Her tearful story makes little sense to him, and he is still trying to sort it out when Bubba flies out and he must go on deck. He explains to her that he has to leave her for a second, but promises her that she will be able to see him the whole time. She sniffs.

Buford scoots over to her and tries to cheer her up, telling her about his twin girls. In Buford's opinion, Eddie's treatment of Tina in her crisis has been adequate but short of perfect. He feels that under the same circumstances with one of his daughters he would be handling it much more sympathetically, though if pressed he would not be able to give specifics.

Scrappy, who has also been watching attentively from farther down the bench, sees it differently. "Ya' know, Apples," he says, "when I first seen Tina here, I thought Eddie was gonna blow up."

"Yeah?"

"I thought he was gonna spank her—you know, for bein' somewhere she hadn't oughta been."

"Nah, Scrappy. He really loves that girl."

"I never seen anything like it. Never in all my borned days. I useta sometimes wonder 'bout Eddie, on accounta the way he needles me an' all. But this—man, don't it jist warm your heart up? Don't it?"

"It sure does, Scrappy."

"So *that's* what love is. I always kinda wondered."

On deck, Eddie makes silly faces to Tina, who sits dwarfed beside Buford, his large hands sweeping the air as he goes on and on about his girls. Grammock, leaning against the water cooler, looks at Eddie mugging and moans while a taste of Maalox burps up to the back of his mouth. After Jaime singles smartly to left field, Eddie bounces into a double play. Tina claps as Eddie returns to the dugout to check on her.

"She can't stay in here, Eddie," Grammock snaps at him. "You know the rules."

Eddie looks at Grammock a moment, then bends down to Tina. "Daddy's gon' put you in a big chair jis' inside this open door, babe. You still gon' be able to see me. Okay?" He reaches for his glove and asks the trainer to scoot Grammock's runway stool closer to the dugout door—the stool Grammock sits on out of sight of the umps when he has been ejected and wants to continue to direct the club. Eddie throws Tina a kiss and runs out onto the field.

Grammock watches Tina's progress to his stool in resentful silence. No one else ever sits on that stool. It's *his* stool, and Eddie never even asked for his permission. What's she doing here in the first place? What's he running here—a goddamn orphanage? Reasoning like a petticoat-phobic sea captain, he has already put both games of the double-header into the lost column and calculated that it will take another week at least to clinch the division title, which will mean painstaking shuffling of his starters, no chance to rest any of his regulars, and many more innings of gut-wrenching ball. He glares into the runway door at Tina, who has located a candy bar and looks up from it, timidly meeting his gaze. What a big wet load of snot under her nose, he thinks. He orders the trainer to go wipe it off.

Between pitches, Buford looks from deep left field into the dugout, trying to see the dark little girl in the runway behind Grammock. He waves now and then, hoping she can see him even though he can't see her.

In center field, Eddie is talking to his wife, calling her every name he has saved for their very last fight. He is kicking her butt all over Saks, knocking her into smiling mannequins, pitching her head-over-heels into the Clinique counter. It's *his* turn now. She's had her turn at hurting him, meeting his honesty with her fake sympathy, cuddling into him when he has told her of his pain, offering him her worthless, skinny body when he wanted so much more. But it will be *his* turn now. Just what the fuck does she call herself doing, losing her like that? Her own child. Her *only* child—it's not as if she's got a decent-sized family to worry about. She's seen to that, cutting off her tubes and having herself froze up inside. But it's *his* turn now. She's going to try to talk about *us,* but he'll say it *ain't* no us 'cuz that's all *use*ta be. Then she won't say a word, or if she does, it'll be her last.

Nothing comes his way. A strikeout and two ground-outs. He trots back in, carrying the huge crisis of his crumbling marriage back into the dugout.

Buford stands in the batter's box, whiffs, and returns

eagerly to the dugout. He tosses his batting helmet into the rack and hurries over to Tina. Eddie and Grammock are arguing farther down the dugout—Buford hears Grammock say "got to look like you have an *idea* out there"—and Scrappy is lurking ineffectually near Tina, as if he wants to relate to her but doesn't know how. Buford does. He just had a brainstorm so profound that he forgot about the opposing pitcher's deceptive change-up and found himself falling down in the box from his huge swing at mere air before the ball arrived at the plate. "Nice anticipation," the catcher jeered, making the ump chuckle. Buford didn't care. He was already on his way to Tina, his daughter three years from now.

"Listen, Tina," he whispers hotly. "Watch out for those four big men dressed in black out there. Especially the one with the mask. He wears that because he has to hide his face, which has no eyes at all—just skin there, you know? And he's mean and crazy. Swings his arms and screams now and then for no reason at all. And look at him now, taking those balls away from our little bat boy. He ate our last one. Just chewed him right up and spit out his ears. We've put you back here in the doorway so he can't get to you. If he saw you, I don't know what he would do to you. I just don't know." He puts a dreadful look on his massive face, which is inches from Tina's.

Scrappy, seeing a small puddle seeping through Tina's tights onto Grammock's stool, says, "I think maybe ya' might be scarin' her a little there, Bufe."

"Nah," Buford bellows confidently, but Tina fills the stadium with six sudden shrieks. Eddie runs to her while Buford backs away, lamely protesting that Eddie told him she likes scary stories, and that Ellie says imagination is important to youngsters. He didn't mean any harm. Honest, he didn't. Grammock yells at Buford to sit down and shut up, then clears his end of the dugout when he explodes into a squeaking, fat tornado of fury.

Jaime, seated nearby, has calmly been studying the situation, trying to learn from it, striving to lift himself out of his eternal cloud of unknowing. He has seen the little one. She looks much like Eddie's woman—the masha masha bunita lady who eats little and would not work well in the hot aloe field. He has seen Eddie standing out on the funny grass and watched him beat his fists against his legs like un homber loco and sway with dolor like the twisted divi-divi tree. He has seen boss man Skeep Gruñón kicking water engine in unhappiness. He has seen grandi grandi blancu mericanu combersá with the little one, trying to make his words fly with butter wings, but it was no good. Jaime knows one must be careful, because por ehempel small kittens can sneeze. Masha tristu for the little one so wet in the nanishi, for he knows it is easy to find a stick to beat a dog with. Masha tristu for all forgotten little ones.

Thinking and remembering, he watches E.T.A. single and Frank ground into a double play. He knows a lot, this Jaime Jan Orguyo van der Pijpers—not about the world, but about forgotten little ones.

The next four innings are painful to everybody but Tina, who has gradually come to enjoy the stimulating spectacle. Her daddy is there a lot, touching her and making her feel happy, and the man with the orange pants is very nice about keeping her face dry with his hankie, and she also likes the funny-looking little man who plays with the mud stuck in his shoes, because when the orange-pants man is busy squeezing some other man's arm, the mud man gives her his shirtsleeve to wipe her nose on, and he smiles a lot and wipes his own nose on it too, and it's fun taking turns like that, sharing. She's not too sure about the man who keeps his coffee cup on his tummy. He kept giving her a Mr. Yuk face at first, but he doesn't anymore, so maybe he won't yell at her the way he yelled at her daddy, but she's still not sure. Some of the white people are afraid of the tummy man—she can tell. Maybe he is their daddy—a mean daddy, like some of her friends have.

She is most afraid of the man who reminds her of milk, the one who told her about the bad man with the mask. But the milk man is leaving her alone, and so is the masked man with skin for eyes, so maybe she will be okay until her momma comes for her.

"An interesting pattern," Frank says to nobody, hoping someone will ask him to elaborate. He has resolved not to force his opinions on people. The elevator incident and E.T.A.'s amazing refusal to back down have had an effect. But it is hard for him to change. No one responds to his trial balloon, so he adds, "The double plays."

Silence.

"We've grounded into six consecutive double plays," he says.

"Who gives a fuck?" snaps Grammock from his end of the dugout twenty feet away.

Frank is quiet for a full minute. Bubba grounds out and Jaime walks to the plate.

"The record for most double plays in a game is seven," Frank says more softly.

"Who gives a flying fuck?" snaps Grammock.

Frank hesitates, then whispers, "One more and we'll tie it. Two more and we'll break it."

"You whammying sonofabitch!" Grammock screams, jumping to his feet and putting a foot on the first step of the dugout, refusing to dignify Frank by looking at him when he speaks to him.

"I thought maybe talking about the pattern would bring an end to the pattern," Frank protests mildly.

"You thought, you thought," Grammock says to the field. "You don't think when you talk, Frank. Everyone knows that. Your goddamn tongue wags at both ends."

Jaime singles. When the brief applause in the dugout dies down, Frank says, "All I can say is my understanding of a

156

whammy is when talk about a pattern changes a pattern, and if we want *this* pattern to change—"

"You're thinkin' of a negative whammy on a positive pattern," shouts Grammock, his tone pedantically sing-songy with much learning. "How can you not know about the positive whammy on a negative pattern? You've stuck us in the pattern, Frank. Down fucking 4–0 and you've fucking guaranteed us more of the same."

"That's an interesting concept," Frank says as they watch Eddie bounce into a 1–6–3 D.P.

Grammock flops back onto the bench in defeated misery, his fingertips slipping beneath the elastic of his pants, seeking comfort in the tangles of his pubic hair.

In the top of the eighth, after two opposing batters reach base with nobody out, Scrappy takes five-and-a-half seconds from the crack of the bat to retire the side all by himself. The batter lines what promises to be a sure single up the middle, but Scrappy is miraculously there to take it on the fly. His body is parallel to the ground, yet somehow he manages to land on his feet, run across second base—killing the lead runner with the air of a very busy junior executive still with much to do—and dash after the other runner, who is doing cartwheels in the slippery base path as he tries to reverse direction and scramble back to first. Scrappy reaches him before he makes much progress, diving to tag him for the third out. He bounces to his feet with a broad grin.

"Why'n't ya' tag me while you're at it?" the first-base ump says to Scrappy in good-natured admiration.

So quickly have they moved from a no-out jam to the bottom of the inning that the rest of the team takes an extra moment to begin to come off the field, each man counting to three over and over, just to be sure.

"An unassisted triple play," shouts Apples in the dugout

amid the flurry of handshaking and backslapping. "Nice work, Scrappy. You don't see those very often."

"Before today, five in the American League, three in the National," Frank says crisply, instantly spoiling the moment for everyone. He sees what he has done, and his face reddens with shame.

After they have settled down on the bench, Apples says to a still-beaming Scrappy, "That was pretty smart of you to chase him down instead of throwing to E.T.A. That made it your solo all the way."

"I wasn't really thinkin' a that," says Scrappy.

"You weren't?"

"Naw. I never throw to nobody 'less I have to. The safest play is to run after the guy an' tag him if ya' can. I ain't no genius, but I know that much."

Apples says, "Well, whether you planned it or not, you're in the record book now, kid."

Scrappy grins at Apples. Then he perks up even more as he sees Grammock approaching—to say something nice to him about the play, he figures. But Grammock stops when he gets to Buford and puts his arm around his shoulders and tells him something about where to play a certain hitter. Scrappy waits, forever hopeful, but Grammock just spits, turns around, and goes back to his end of the dugout.

While the opposing pitcher warms up, the thought occurs to many of them that Scrappy's defensive triple play might end their own string of offensive double plays. Of course, this does not quite follow as the night the day, but they're convinced, or at least hopeful—provided Frank doesn't kill the possibility by talking about it. Buford steps into the batter's box, and every time Frank shifts his feet or leans forward as if threatening to speak, cough-barrages and chatter fill the air. But Buford, still in a funk from his inept venture into the field of children's literature, strikes out for the third time that day.

"That boy's gonna lose my love," bellows Grammock. They all hear it, but for Scrappy, who can also hear Eddie chatting with Tina in the runway, it has special meaning.

They're all nervous now. The lead-off man is out once again. If E.T.A. singles, as he has done twice already, they know he is doomed to erasure in a subsequent double play. Frank can hardly hear himself think for all the noise the guys are making around him, and he is due to bat next, so he rises from the bench. His teammates in their panic think he must be bent on walking down the dugout to share the forbidden thought with Grammock. Bubba sticks a foot out and trips Frank, bringing him crashing to the wooden floor of the dugout amid much apparent solicitousness. While Frank struggles to his feet, E.T.A. doubles up the right-center-field alley. The team goes crazy with cheers, and Tina, sensing something good has happened, silently pours forth a fresh load of mucus in celebration.

"Whaddya know?" says Frank as he hurries out to the plate.

After a conference on the mound, Frank, a .297760041 hitter, is given an intentional base on balls so that the pitcher can work to Scrappy. This is yet another resounding statement about his worthlessness, Scrappy thinks bitterly, and his anger triples the strength in his swing at the first pitch. As the ball clears the fence just inside the left-field foul pole, he glances back with hatred at Grammock, who is standing and clapping without emotion. It is only Scrappy's second home run of the year, but he runs the bases with the slow, cocky trot of a power hitter like Eddie or Buford. In the dugout, he ignores Grammock's outstretched hand and rushes to embrace his teammates.

Narvel walks, a pinch hitter singles, advancing Narvel to second, Bubba drives Narvel in with a single, and Jaime's smooth double puts them ahead by two.

"Ain't it easy, though!" shouts Scrappy. "Ain't it!"

After Eddie grounds out and Buford whiffs for the third out, one of their relief pitchers—an undepressed, altogether uninteresting man—shuts the opposing side down in order, bringing it to an end.

As they pour off the field into the runway, Grammock pauses at Tina's stool. "You can move around now, honey," he says, patting her hair, amazed at the way his hand bounces back off it. "You're a good-luck bird, you sweet little thing."

Scrappy hears this and scoffs right at him as he brushes by.

Not much happens in the second game. Tina naps (and wets) on Grammock's office couch while her daddy wears the collar again. "Pick me up, guys," he says after every one of his at-bats. "I been havin' troubles, but I'm beginnin' to see straight now. Pick me up." He finally asks Grammock to take him out in the seventh. In the top of the eighth, when Eddie is told his wife is on the phone, calling in tears from a police station, asking if he has seen any sign of Tina, he laughs and yells down the runway, "Tell her to go fuck herse'f. Ain't no one else who want to—'ceptin' Bubba, an' he's out in the field."

Jaime goes four-for-four. Scrappy goes two-for-three. They help them win it, 5–3.

While they shower and dress, they listen to the Braves-Dodgers game over the clubhouse speakers. Then they stick around, quietly joking with one another as they await the outcome. They moan when the Dodgers come back to tie the score at four-all in the bottom of the ninth, sending the game into extra innings. It drags into the tenth, the eleventh, the twelfth. A few of the guys head home. Then a few more. When the last of them leaves, the game is in the fifteenth inning. Then, as they drive home, each player alone in the dark listens on his car radio to the delightful sounds of Atlanta scoring three runs in the sixteenth and of Los Angeles going down in order.

"Howcome you honkin', Daddy? Howcome you honkin'?"

"Because yo' daddy is a winnah, babe. Thas why."

"Thas good, Daddy."

7

"Where is he?" one of the sportswriters asks. "If he calls a press conference, he should be here on time, damn it. Who do these guys think they are, anyway?"

"I can't imagine he's got much to say," says another. "Crummiest copy in the National League. I'd sooner sit through one of Grammock's raunchy stories than listen to him."

"You know why he called it?"

"No idea. I don't know what makes these guys tick. Buncha prima donnas. Arnie, you got any dope on this?"

"No, Bob," says another, taking a pipe from his mouth. "Maybe he's unhappy. Maybe he's going back to wherever the hell he came from. I just wish the sonofabitch'd—" He stops speaking and prepares a smile as the door from the locker room opens.

Jaime walks in without looking at any of them, striding with an easy, confident grace. He walks to the front of the room, turns, and faces the crowd of reporters and photographers. He studies them for a moment, then speaks.

"Me Jaime Jan Orguyo van der Pijpers."

The writers wait, pens poised.

"Me Jaime," he says. "Jaime. Jaime."

A few of them exchange frowning glances.

"Jaime," he says. "You say."

They shift their feet, hungry for a story, eager for it to begin.

"Jaime," he says again. "You say."

"We say *what?*" one of them calls out belligerently.

"Jaime," he says. "You say."

"All right. I mean, what the hell, huh? *Jaime.* Okay?"

Jaime nods. "Sí. *Jaime.* No Jamey. No Jamey."

"What is this, Jamey?" one of them asks. "Something about your name? You changing your name?"

"No Jamey. *Jaime.*"

"I think it's about how to say his stupid name," the one with the pipe says. "You're getting it wrong, Fred. It's *Jaime,* you know? Like H-I-M-E-Y. Not Jamey."

"Jaime sí," says Jaime. "Jamey no." He lifts his chin, exposing his long, dark neck, and he runs the tip of his finger up and down its length as he produces a sustained H-like sound from deep within it.

A photographer impulsively gives it a try. "Jaime," he says, lingering tenderly on the rasping initial consonant.

"Sí sí sí," says Jaime.

Several others try it. One mutters, "Sounds like a hawking-and-spitting competition."

"Sí," Jaime says to the group, cutting them off with a conductor's wave of his forefinger. "Eesa goo." He pulls the shirt of his uniform over his head, exposing the rippling muscles of his upper arms, of which he is particularly proud.

"What now?" mutters a reporter.

Jaime shakes the shirt out, then turns it around to show

163

them the back of it. Above his number is his name: in small letters, VAN DER, and, below this, in larger letters, PIJPERS.

"Van der Pijpers," says Jaime. "No Pijpers. *Van der* Pijpers."

"I guess he wants us to write 'van der Pijpers' from now on," says one of them.

"Looks like a new shirt," says another.

"Hey," calls a third. "Look at the scorecard for today's game. It's there too. Not just 'Pijpers,' but 'van der Pijpers.'"

Jaime spies the raised scorecard and beams radiantly. "Sí." He puts his shirt back on, tucking it in very carefully. He reaches out both hands before him and clasps them together in a gesture of profound gratitude and goodwill. "Dankee," he says.

"Whoa," one man cries out. "That's *it?*"

"Dankee," says Jaime. He walks to the door.

"Hold it, Jamey," another shouts. "You've got to give us more than this. What's it all mean? Are other changes in the offing too? Your fielding position, for example? Your place in the line-up? Can you give us a run-down on that?"

Jaime pauses at the door, confused. "Me Jaime," he says.

"Sure, Jamey, but can you give us a little background on this? Someone on the club suggest it? You getting along with everyone? Any dissension? Speak freely, now."

"Me beeg league."

"Did Grammock order you to do this? Is he cracking down on you? Do you have any beef about the way Grammock is handling you?"

"Me beeg show."

"Jamey, did this come down from the high and mighty front office? Feel free to unload on them."

Jaime slowly spreads his long arms out, palms up, and delivers his final statement with all his heart. "Me masha goo." He turns away and he is gone.

After a moment of stunned silence, one of the writers

calls out melodramatically, "Where's a phone? Quick! Stop the presses!"

They all laugh at this and fall into carefree, easy abuse of Jaime.

○ ○ ○

"Like what he says about fishin'. You ever fish?"

"I have, in the past."

"Well, Grammock says he likes it 'cuz it's nice an' peaceful. My way of thinkin' is . . . an' you don't fish no more?"

"No."

"Well, I useta fish too. Right in Licking Creek—the one Gram' was so het up about starin' at from her grave so's she could live forever. I know what fishin' is, an' when I hear Grammock talkin' about it, I always end up lookin' at it from the fish's point a view. Jist think about it. You're lazyin' along in the cool, clear water, enjoyin' life, an' then you're snappin' at that flashin' thing, jist because you're ignorant—or maybe you're kinda slowly driftin' up to snake a fly that you're lucky happened along—an' all of a sudden ya' got a hunk a iron in your cheek an' you're bein' drug all over hell an' creation. Then your head's bein' slammed against a rock an' your eyes bug out like a coupla marbles. Then you're tossed in a bag with grass in it, like that's your grave or somethin', an' every now an' then ya' got this Grammock peerin' in, checkin' on ya' to see if you're movin' at all, an' if you are, it's *whack* against the rock again. Now, that ain't my idea of peaceful.

"I dunno. I can't stop thinkin' about that man. I'm watchin' him all the time, hopin' he'll be friendly someday, lookin' for him to say somethin' nice, somethin' other 'n 'Scrapheap' or 'Scabs' or 'Scumbag.' Like when I pulled off that triple play. He didn't say diddly-shit all through the rest of the game, an' nothin' through the next one neither. So later, when we was in the locker room, I asked him what he

165

thought of it. I jist *had* to. I couldn't take it no more. Know what he said? Said I was lucky to be in the right place at the right time. That is exactly what he said. Big deal, he was sayin'. It's like he wanted to take it away from me, an' that don't seem fair.

"Or like when the guys in the other dugout git to ridin' me, callin' me 'rat face,' or talkin' 'bout my chin, which they do 'cuz it don't really amount to shucks, ya' know? Ya' see it? It ain't much."

"Mm-hmm."

"So the guys'll yell, tryin' to razz me when I'm up there takin' my cuts, sayin', 'Hey, you with the chin,' or 'Hey, Four-Oh'—that's my number, forty—'Hey, Four-Oh, what happened to the bottom of your face? Too much chin music?' Now, the way I see it, they can ride me if they want to—hell, that's part of the game—but Grammock shouldn't oughta *laugh* when they do. Jesus, you'd think he was on the enemy team. Sometimes he sounds jist like Gram' the way he cackles, only his voice is higher."

"Higher than your grandmother's?"

"Yeah. He's a real pussy. Him an' Gram'—what a pair. That's somethin' new I been thinkin' about—them bein' a pair. I first thought about it at Eddie's barbecue party, an' then later, durin' that game when Eddie's little girl was in the dugout, that's when it come home to me, real clear an' simple. Another thing too—I come to realize I ain't free an' clear a them superstitions neither, not a-tall. Hell, you're raised on a steady diet a that shit, you don't shake it off jist like that. Like when Gram' died—when I got back home for the funeral, I made a point a findin' out the exact moment she died, an' I figgered out exactly what I was doin' at the time, which was fieldin' ground balls on diamond number two in Sarasota, an' it's been botherin' me all season that my ears didn't ring when she died. They're supposed to do that, ya' know, when someone close to ya' dies. Now, I been askin' myself, lately at

166

least, if I was free a this shit, why exactly would that a been buggin' me all season, ya' know?

"I guess I hate his guts, when I think of it. But what can I do? Jist a .200 hitter an' sinkin' all the time. The day I don't git to the ball the way I should'll be my last, you can bet. He's jist waitin' for it to happen too." He sighs. "It's more 'n that, though—I mean more than me bein' afraid he's gonna bench me. I want him to *like* me, even now after I seen through him. Ain't that somethin'? Me worryin' 'bout bein' liked by a shit like that? See? It's me 'n' Gram' all over again."

"Mm-hmm."

"If only I could hit the damn ball a little better. Maybe then he'd like me."

"You talk as though you're a poor hitter."

"Because I *am*. Bubba, Jaime, Eddie, E.T.A.—they're all hittin' over a hunderd points better 'n me."

"But you hit a home run last week."

"Big deal. Two in the whole season."

"But didn't it save the game? Didn't everybody rally behind you?"

"Oh, yeah. It really picked 'em up. Narv', he give me the nicest hug at the plate, an' when I come into the dugout, you'd a thought . . . I dunno . . ."

"Yes?"

"I was gonna say you'd a thought the guys all loved me."

"Maybe they do."

"Don't be an asshole."

"I'm not being an asshole."

"You find somebody who loves me an' I'll believe it. Nobody loves me."

"Says who?"

"Says Gram'. Every goddamned day of my life." His voice catches. "What's that box a Kleenex doin' here?"

"It's for summer colds."

167

"Yeah, well, I'm catchin' one." He yanks a tissue out of the box.

"Scrappy, Gram' was a very sick lady who is dead."

"Yeah? She's fuckin' got a long reach, though." He sniffs, winces, blows his nose. "She ruined my life, didn't she? I'm a goner, ain't I?"

"I don't think you're a goner."

"I'm fightin' a fuckin' ghost. Jesus, back in April I was dumb enough to think I was all fucked up in my mind because she'd jist died an' I was gonna miss her. The fact a the matter is she ain't dead enough, not by a long shot."

"What about Miss Eula, Scrappy?"

"What about her?"

"Don't you think *she* loved you?"

"Nah. She jist felt sorry for me."

"Maybe she did. But she could have loved you too. She spent a lot of time with you, and, from what you say, she seemed to enjoy it."

"Nah."

"She didn't enjoy it?"

"I don't know if she did or not. All's I know is she didn't love me."

"How can you be so sure?"

"Because I'm *me*—Scrappy. The worthless piece a scrap. The chinless muggins."

"That's Gram'-talk, Scrappy."

Scrappy laughs bitterly. "That's the only way I know how to talk. See what I mean when I say I'm a goner? She's got them bony hands reachin' out right now, right into this office a yours. She's dead an' she *ain't* dead. What do I gotta do—kill her all over again?"

O O O

"E.T.A., how's it goin'?"

E.T.A. doesn't look at Eddie, but continues to watch the

Atlanta pitcher take his warm-up throws. "Not bad," he says guardedly.

"E.T.A., who'd ya' mos' like to face in the playoffs?"

He shrugs. "I don't really care."

Eddie watches the catcher fire the ball back to the pitcher. "Listen, E.T.A. Ya' ain't been your ol' se'f lately." He laughs softly to himself. "A course, none of us have, but I mean you seem kinda withdrawn from the guys lately. Anything you wanna talk about?"

"I've been fine, Eddie," E.T.A. says coolly.

"I been thinkin' 'bout what happened in the clubhouse a while back. I don' mean I been *dwellin'* on it or nothin', an' I'm sure the other guys ain't been neither, in case you been wonderin'."

"I haven't given it a moment's thought."

"What I want ya' to know is, it ain't important. Ain't nobody gon' hol' that against you for long. Hell, look at me— beatin' on a damn dog an' . . . that other shit. But the guys are willin' to forgit stuff like that. They don' be walkin' 'roun' thinkin', 'Uh-oh, here come that loony again. Got to keep mah distance.' Hell, you goin' after Bubba ain't no worse 'n what I tried to do to that fuckin' dog. Matter of fact, they pretty much alike, ain't they? It's almos' like you been takin' lessons from me."

E.T.A. is silent. He watches Bubba stretch in the on-deck circle. Finally, he shifts on the bench a bit and says, "How about you, Eddie? Any progress?"

"I'm doin' okay, man. I'm holdin' mah own."

"How about your trial?"

Eddie laughs. "I got me a lawyer, he's the magician a *stall*. Time it come to trial, hell, I mon' be in the Hall of Fame."

E.T.A. nods. "You're going to plead not guilty?"

"Yeah. I done that already."

"What's your defense?"

"I can't really talk 'bout it, E.T.A."

"Why not?"

Eddie sighs. "'Cuz my lawyer, he say . . . Aw, hell, E.T.A. Ain't no use lyin' to you. 'Cuz I *done* it, thas why."

"You did?"

"Yeah. When that bitch in uniform come to the door to ask about the fuckin' dog, somethin' jis' popped inside a me. I didn't know what I was doin'."

"So you hit her?"

"Yeah. Once. Slapped her." He laughs self-consciously. "Big man, huh?"

"So what's your defense—insanity?"

Eddie laughs, but a glance at E.T.A. tells him he wasn't joking. "I don' know, man. My lawyer, he say it's an advantage if I say I was actin' under the influence a some kinda 'motional disturbance, or some shit like that, but, *man*, I don' want that shit all over the newspapers. My lawyer, he say we can go with another plan too. I can plain an' simple say I didn't do it."

"But the policewoman *knows* you did it. And wasn't there another cop there?"

"Nah. The other one was in my stupid-ass neighbor's house."

"Anyone else see you do it?"

"Jis' the bitch—I mean *my* bitch, Jacqui—an' my lawyer say she don' got to testify."

"So it's your word against the policewoman's."

"Thas right. *Shit*, E.T.A., I know it's dishonest, but I 'uz all fucked up. An' my lawyer, he say it's the smart an' legal thing to do. I don' *need* this shit right now."

"I don't see why a judge would take your word over that of a police officer."

"Well, you got a point there, but I got a li'l somethin' goin' fo' me. My lawyer say this policewoman got a lousy reputation. It's been a lotta complaints 'bout her harassin' people an' generally fuckin' up. Only problem is I ain't exactly

170

gon' he'p her rep none by testifyin' that she made it all up, so I ain't too proud a the whole idea, if ya' know what I mean. To be honest, I jis' don' know what the fuck I'm gonna do. I got these two ideas poundin' on me from different sides—do I say I'm crazy or do I say *she* crazy—an' it feel like some heavy-weight slugguh been workin' on me fo' ten rounds."

"How does Jacqui feel about all of this?"

"We don' talk about it. We don' talk 'bout *nothin'*. Thas another thing I been seein' my lawyer about."

"You're finally going to cut the knot?"

"You got it."

"What about Tina?"

"Man, you got all the right questions, don't ya'? I'm lookin' into that. She the mos' important thing in the world to me."

"Is she really?"

"Shit yes, man. What the fuck kinda question is that?"

"Well, even assuming for the moment that she is, I seriously doubt that you can get custody."

Eddie rises to his feet. "Hey, E.T.A., next time ya' see I need cheerin' up, why'n't ya' take a hike out in the middle a the ocean somewhere? *You* sure ain't the one I need to talk to."

○ ○ ○

After having clinched the division title nearly three weeks before the end of the regular season, they lose every single remaining game, coming within four games of tying the major-league record for most consecutive games lost, as Frank almost points out a dozen times, fighting his nature and finally defeating it, ultimately sharing the statistic with his reflection in the mirror when he shaves. Grammock cannot believe they have won it. He is convinced more than ever that he is a born bad-luck bird. As he watches the performance of his boys

171

plummet, he counts the regular-season games remaining over and over, forever fearful that some unsuspected quirk of mathematics will rob him of it in the end.

Eddie blames himself for their losing streak, loudly and frequently. His batting average slips twenty points in the last two weeks. The guys try to keep his spirits up. They tell him every player has brief slumps. This is his first, so it is especially frightening to him, they say. He should be happy that it came when it did, at the end of the season. They remind him of all that he has done for the team all year.

When they're not trying to pick Eddie up, they talk about the losing streak in an effort to understand it. They conclude that now that they have won the division title, they are free to show their true colors and become what they really think they are—losers—at no real cost to their self-esteem. Just to prove that they are in full control of their destiny and can still win when they want to, they go all out in the last game of the regular season. When they lose that one too—an error-riddled, 12–1 laugher—they begin to wonder about themselves more deeply.

Not E.T.A., though. Like an overstaffed think tank funded by a computer's error, he has generated yet another new idea. He believes that second place is the best place in life to be. It carries honor without the awful burden of excessive excellence. In his view, first place in the Western Division is still not really first place, and they can cope with that. But to be first in the National League would be to tempt fate, and he figures that his mentally pedestrian teammates must unconsciously know what he in his brilliance is able to take a step further to full articulation—namely, that being number two is the only healthy destiny for them. His interpretation of their losing streak at the end is that they have all been practicing to lose the National League playoffs. But he keeps this view to himself. Since the clubhouse incident, he has made a temporary tactical retreat in his campaign to prove he is the

172

true team leader. Also, he finds all of his teammates beneath contempt.

In addition to his abiding penchant for silly theorizing, E.T.A. has a new problem. Having gotten in touch with his anger (at Bubba's expense), and having fondled and caressed it (at Frank's expense, in the hall of their San Francisco hotel), he now finds himself entirely *stuck* to it, as if to some huge, ugly piece of bug-spotted flypaper. In the last weeks of the season, he spends lots of time barking contradictions back at smarmy political thinkers on television, throwing his head back in braying laughter at his own wit. His timid wife and withdrawn young son tiptoe around the house, scurrying out of a room as soon as he enters it, taking refuge in each other's arms and exchanging desperately hopeful whispers that they are sure it is a phase that will soon pass. In the clubhouse, he says little. Now and then, though, he will spout a false baseball record he has made up just for the sheer aggressive fun of it, just to watch Frank chomping down on his tongue. On the field, he is like a spring-loaded giant toy that flips and jerks unpredictably. He argues with umps for the first time in his career, backing them up with his spitting sallies. When he bumps one and gets run out of a game, he finds he likes the feel of it and gets ejected from the next game as well. And from the next. He has found his rhythm. Grammock stops going out to take E.T.A.'s side in the disputes, because he can never figure out what they are about. Neither can the umps, and E.T.A., hitherto renowned for his quiet dignity, has them talking to each other after the games, reviewing the rules, making sure they in fact understand baseball as well as they thought they did.

The hometown fans in their ignorance appreciate the new E.T.A. for his spirited devotion to the game. Simultaneously, and to the surprise of everyone but the object of their scorn, the fans turn against Narvel. Yes, Narvel. What a strange thing for them to do. Can't they handle the success of

173

their team? Must they now turn against a part of this extension of themselves? Certainly Narvel's snake-bit squirminess behind the plate has something to do with it. But judging from their comments, his bitter boredom with the game, now obvious to all of the fans, has even more to do with it. They utter clichés at one another, talking about his salary, the thousands of young kids behind him who would be proud to be a big leaguer, and what a shame that the game isn't what it used to be. Even as they complain about his bored attitude, they bore one another with their words, which makes them even angrier.

In a curious way, one boo at Narvel begets another. A fan hears a boo, spots the target, looks at Narvel with newly critical eyes, sees a little something there he doesn't like, and joins the bloodthirsty throng. This is hardly fair. That fan would probably get some boos too—say, from his father evaluating him as a son, or from his son evaluating him as a father—if he were given the same unsympathetic scrutiny that he gives Narvel. All of mankind deserves a boo, in fact. The boos multiply in another way too. When they rain down on Narvel, he seems so oblivious to them that the fans go crazy in their raging impotence, demanding some sign of repentance from him.

How does Narvel take it? He responds in his typically pale, potato-faced way. That is, he fails to find it new or interesting. Life has always been this way, he thinks.

The hostility toward Narvel mounts in the first of the best-of-five playoff games against Montreal, the winner in the Eastern Division. They play at home, with Apples on the mound. Narvel is booed for the way he puts on his shin guards, for the way he walks onto the field, and for the way he swallows his saliva. In the game itself, he gives them endless material—a passed ball, a wild throw into center on an attempted steal, and catcher's interference with the bases loaded in the seventh, which scores a run and ties the game at

3–3. It is almost as if he is looking for ways to get the fans on his back.

In the eighth, leading off, he drives them into a frenzy. He takes a called third strike, and when the Montreal catcher drops the ball on the ground a little to one side, rather than sprint to first as he should, especially in such an important game, Narvel moves in a slow, shuffling trot down the first-base line and, worse still, removes his batting helmet as he shuffles along and sets it atop the narrow end of his bat. Being a catcher, Narvel is conscious of having to don and doff his equipment in a hurry, so when he strikes out, he *always* takes his batting helmet off right away, setting it atop the knob end of the bat before handing it as a sort of package to the bat boy. But he does it too soon after this at-bat, before the out has officially been made. The image of him shuffling down the line and carrying his equipment that way, the helmet twirling atop the bat like the head of some skinny wooden sidekick of his, is too fatalistic even for his few remaining supporters in the stands, among whom can be found his parents, who have flown out from San Diego for the playoffs and now join the crowd in denouncing their son. As Narvel is easily thrown out at first and veers off the line into the dugout, he hears his father's jeers among the others and feels right at home.

But Jaime picks him up. Jaime has been a one-man team lately, hitting over .500 during the losing streak, quietly going about his business with a new sense of who he is, doing things at the plate that would have ended the streak if only the rest of the team had been able to contribute. In this game, he has driven in two of their three runs, and with the score still tied in the ninth, he wins it for them with a home-run blast as ear-shattering as his consonants. It is such a clean and certain blow that it seems to say, "¡Ándele! Not to worry, boss man Skeep Gruñón. Eesa goo baw cub, ¿no?" Narvel is the first to greet him at the plate with an embrace, but many of the fans don't like the moves he puts on Jaime, finding even his skills as a hugger lacking.

After the victory, alone at home talking loudly to himself in his den while his wife and son cower in their beds, E.T.A. decides that it will be all right for them to win the League pennant, provided they go on to lose the World Series and can view themselves as second in the major leagues. He is so taken with this idea that he decides to go on the offensive again and calls up several of his teammates to enlighten them, getting them out of their beds and swearing at them when they fail to be sufficiently appreciative.

The second playoff game is a rather nasty affair. It is endlessly scoreless—scoreless in a tense way. There are, on the one hand, pleasantly scoreless games, where good pitching combines with good fielding, where few batters reach base (ideally, none until the middle innings), and where the game seems to progress in a natural, classic fashion. But when, as in this game, runners are stranded by both sides in nearly every inning, everyone on the field and in the stands grows edgy with a bitter sense of bungled investments.

The team's mood sours more with each new inning. When, in the second, Frank is knocked down by a high, inside fast ball, the game is still too young for them to protest. Besides, who cares about Frank? Likewise when a pitched ball almost kills Bubba in the third. But when Buford is brushed back in the fourth, the dugout slowly begins to gush bile. The Montreal pitcher is a plump creature with a sad dough-face, and they go to work on him. In keeping with tradition, Eddie leads the verbal charge, but his many preoccupations have dulled his needling. He has obviously lost the knack. As if sensing this himself, in the next inning Eddie silently yields to his distinguished colleague E.T.A., who sprawls forward on the steps of the dugout like a bespectacled predatory insect and goes to work.

"Hey, Porky," he yells at the pitcher. "Hey you, side-meat. Hey, wart hog. Whaddya call that—your squeal ball?"

Bubba singles.

"Hey, Angus," yells E.T.A. "Hey, bull-brains. Hey, you grain-fed mother of kine. What's that soft stuff you're throwing there—cow pies?"

Jaime singles to left. Bubba advances to second.

"Hey, Leviathan. Hey, manatee. Hey, you hippopotamic sea cucumber. We're gonna light our lamps with your sperm."

Eddie pops up to the shortstop. One out. E.T.A. crouches in the on-deck circle.

"Hey, Dinosaur National Monument. Hey, you Mesozoic creampuff. Hey, you megatherian dumpling. I'm the Ice Man, and the Ice Age is comin'."

Buford walks, loading the bases.

E.T.A. digs into the batter's box, one ear cocked toward the dugout as the pitcher goes into the stretch. E.T.A. is surprised that his teammates have not taken up the chatter where he left off. He is even more surprised to see the pitch flying toward his head, and he throws his legs out from under him and drops to the ground, just barely escaping with his face. "It's all part of the game," he says to himself as he rises and dusts himself off. "I can dish it out and I can take it." On the next pitch, he sprawls on his fanny again, regretting it even as he descends, sensing it was a curve, not a fast ball.

"*Steeee*," wails the ump, with a tiny "rike" tagging along like an afterthought.

E.T.A. steps out of the box and dusts himself off again, regrouping. "Bases loaded," he thinks. "Got to get those men in. Got to back up my words with *action*. Got to hang tough."

He jumps back from the third pitch, which is two feet outside. The pitcher grins as he takes the throw from the catcher. "Why is he grinning?" wonders E.T.A. as he looks for the ball coming out of his hand.

"*Steeee*," he hears again from ground level, then "rike." That one wasn't even a curve, he thinks with shame. A fast ball right down the middle. Again he rises and dusts himself off. All aquake with unresolve, he stands in on jelly legs, a little whining moan of terror escaping his lips, and he puts the bat out in front of the next pitch from a powerless, backward-teetering position. The ball dribbles back to the pitcher, who throws home for the force out and whose laughter E.T.A. hears as the throw from the catcher to first beats him by five steps, retiring the side.

"Hey, Four-Eyes," yells the pitcher, who is not an original thinker. E.T.A. looks up from first and sees the pitcher wagging a schoolmistressy "that'll teach you" finger at him. E.T.A. feels the top of his head blast off and begins to charge across the infield. But Scrappy has seen it coming and inserts himself between the pitcher and E.T.A., embracing his teammate and walking him away back to first base.

The home crowd cheers E.T.A.'s gutsiness. Narvel looks up at them in disgust as he walks to his position behind the plate. He thinks, "Yeah, way to go, E.T.A. Way to ground into an inning-ending D.P. with the bases loaded."

In the sixth, after they retire the side in order for the first time all day, Frank goes up to bat. There is scattered chatter in the dugout, but no real good abuse of the pitcher. No one wants to compete with E.T.A., who they feel has redefined bench-jockeying in such bold new terms that, Frank-like, he has taken all the fun out of it. As for E.T.A., he sulks in silence, loathing them for not following his lead, loathing himself for being craven, loathing them *and* himself for being depressed.

Frank flies out, Scrappy walks, Narvel hits into a double play, and the boos rain down on him.

"You had your chance, boy," his father bellows to him

from his seat twelve rows behind the dugout, "and you blew it." Narvel glances at him as he returns to the dugout for his tools of ignorance. *You ought to know, Pop,* he thinks.

In the seventh, each side strands two men on base without scoring any. In the eighth, they each strand three. Still no score. To Apples, resting in the dugout and alternately contemplating the game and his dental assistant, the action on the field is like an orgasm taking twenty-three years to happen.

In the top of the ninth, Montreal has what in any other game would be called a scoring opportunity. With one out, a man singles and then steals second, just beating a perfect throw coming in at his shoetops from Narvel (*Boo!*), and then advances to third on a ground ball to Bubba. Montreal's rookie catcher comes to the plate with two outs.

E.T.A. studies him from first base. The freckle-faced young man seems nervous. He seems weak. Apathetic. Doubtful of himself. Stooped shoulders. Winding sheet for a face. Furtive looks to the side. Heavy sighs. What a pathetic patsy the kid is, E.T.A. thinks. A cruel leer disfigures his face and he goes to work.

"Hey, you with the slump in your mind."

The batter takes a called strike on the outside corner.

"Hey, you, snap out of it. Stop staring off into space."

The batter takes a called strike on the inside corner.

"Hey, Slumpy. Hey, Slumpy-slump-slump. No more bad thoughts about yourself—starting right after you fail in this at-bat." E.T.A. follows this with a braying cackle.

The batter swings tentatively at a high pitch outside the strike zone, missing it by a foot.

"Clear the field," E.T.A. says to himself, as he trots into the dugout. "I can annihilate 'em all by myself."

Jaime triples to lead off the bottom of the ninth. The fans go wild. Surely the team can get a man home from third with no outs. Surely this awful ordeal is about to come to an end.

Eddie, hitless so far in the playoffs, goes up to bat. He fouls off the first pitch. The second pitch is outside and in the dirt, and the rookie Montreal catcher does a nice job of blocking it, preventing Jaime from scoring—for the moment, saving the game. E.T.A., smitten with an idea, sprawls on the dugout steps and stares at the catcher, committed to whammying him with the sheer force of his thought. And, indeed, it is almost as if the youngster behind the plate cannot handle the success of the way he overmastered that bad pitch, because he allows the next one—a slightly high-and-away fast ball—to glance off his mitt. Jaime dashes for home as the ball rolls toward the backstop. The catcher charges after the ball, lunges for it in a panic, crashes into the backstop, and collapses in a heap.

The team rushes out to pound Jaime on the back after he crosses the plate. A passed ball is a rotten way to win a game, but he *did* hit the triple that set it up, and they want a hero.

E.T.A. is not with them. He remains in the dugout and watches the Montreal trainer rush to the aid of the catcher, who lies on his side, one leg rigidly curled up to his chest as if frozen there, the other scraping aimlessly in the dust. E.T.A. continues to watch, without expression, as his teammates pour into the dugout and down the runway, exuberant in celebration. A stretcher is brought out from the Montreal dugout, but the catcher finally manages to stand up with the aid of two teammates.

Narvel is back in the dugout, concerned about the rookie. He knows about the punishment a catcher has to take. He watches him walk slowly off the field. "He okay?" he says to E.T.A.

E.T.A. says nothing.

"Hey, E.T.A. What do you think? He looks okay, don't you think?"

A ghost with E.T.A.'s face turns toward him. "I did that," he gasps. "I did that with my *mind*."

180

Narvel frowns deeply and watches E.T.A. walk in a daze down the runway toward the locker room.

○ ○ ○

E.T.A.'s daze, which consists of one part sympathy for the freckle-faced catcher and ninety-nine parts megalomania, persists as they board the plane for the flight to Montreal for the third and potentially last game of the playoffs. He takes a window seat and gazes dully out at the airport lights. Eddie takes the aisle seat in the same row and studies him across the empty seat between them.

"E.T.A.," he finally says as the plane taxis out to the runway. "You was right."

E.T.A. turns and looks at him.

"About custody. About mah Tina. I been talkin' to my lawyer all week. Man, I don' know what I'm gon' do."

"You've got a choice, Eddie. You can go on living with someone you don't love for the sake of someone you *do* love, or you can free your life of someone you don't love at the expense of someone you *do* love."

Eddie nods. "Thas about it."

"You could get visitation rights, of course, but I imagine that can be pretty frustrating."

"Thas what I imagine too, E.T.A. Shit, I tried everything. My lawyer, he ask me how can I show the judge that the bitch ain't fit to keep mah Tina, an' all I can think of is she's a bitch, ya' know? He say that won' hol' up in court. I say she always be dumpin' Tina at the daycare center. He say ever'body be doin' that. Yeah, I say, but jis' so they can go *shoppin'?* He don' know 'bout that, he say, but it still don' mean nothin'. I say how 'bout her losin' Tina at Saks like she done. That sound like neglect, don' it? That sound like a momma puttin' the ig on her own chile, her own li'l girl. He

181

say, nah, folks be pullin' that shit all the time. He ask me do she beat up on Tina. I say, fuck no, man, I wouldn' 'low that. He ask do I think if I wasn' aroun' would she beat up on her, an' I gotta say, no, I don' suppose so, an' he say I ain't got shit. I begun to see I'm up against a system, E.T.A. I'm up against a whole way a thinkin'. Mommas rule the world, thas what it's all about. They can git away with all kindsa shit an' society say, thas okay—she the momma. You take them mommas that go shoppin' fo' they groceries an' be puttin' they babies on the roof a they car when they loadin' the bags in, an' then they git to thinkin' 'bout somethin' else, like the lates' fashion in nylons, or fuckin' *per*fume, or some other dumb shit, an' they forgit what they doin' an' drives off with that baby still flappin' aroun' on de roof—*shit*, man, they gon' be voted fuckin' mothuh-of-the-year. Thas what I'm up against."

"It does look pretty hopeless for you, Eddie. Besides, there's the whole issue of your being on the road so much. What would you do with Tina then?"

"Yeah, my lawyer, he was real quick to point that out too. I tole him I'd take her with me. He say that kinda shit went out with vaudeville. I say I can quit playin' ball. He say I ain't got no college. He ask what am I gon' show the judge fo' income. I say what's the bitch gon' show. He say not a fuckin' thing. She don' got to. She keep the baby, I work my butt off payin' chile support. Thas the way the world turn. He say he can git me a divorce all right, 'cuz ever'body an' they mommas be gittin' divorces, but I'm livin' in a crazy man's dream if I think I can take mah li'l girl with me. Thas what he say."

"You hate women, don't you, Eddie?"

"*What?*"

"Don't fight me, man. I'm trying to help. I think you hate women. All women, not just Jacqui. Look at that police-woman you roughed up. You think you would have done that to a man?"

"You tell me, E.T.A. You got all the answers. You the smart-ass on this team."

"Tell me about your past, Eddie. I get the impression that you had a father who perpetually ridiculed his wife, which no doubt affected your view of women, and you had a mother who did the same to your father, with whom you identified, bringing him down all the time and bringing you down with him. I see a childhood of perpetual symbolic castration. Tell me about it, Eddie."

"Shit, man . . ."

"Come on, Eddie. Talk to me."

○ ○ ○

Some of the club's fans follow the team north, but most stay home, so when Narvel pops out in his first two at-bats, he must do so without the support to which he is accustomed. His parents have returned to San Diego to await the outcome of the games in Montreal. His father, by way of encouragement, told Narvel he expected the series to go all the way to the last game, and even though his son was willing to foot the bill, he refused to spend that kind of time in a country that couldn't even decide what language they want to speak. Narvel's mother, vaguely fearful that once out of the country she could never get back in, was relieved to hurry back to the banality of their sunny retirement home.

An odd thing happens in the sixth inning. When Narvel bats with the club down, 4–2, and swings and misses under a letter-high fast ball, falling down with the force of his swing, he hears, *"Way to take a cut, bay-bee!"* from someone high in the stands behind him, and he smiles, figuring it is a sarcastic Montreal supporter poking a little fun at him. But when he takes a called second strike and hears, after the cheers, *"Way to wait for your pitch, bay-bee!"* he begins to wonder. He wonders even more when he watches two pitches just miss the outside corner and is praised from the same quarter for the way he looks them over, bay-bee. Then he lines out hard to the pitcher, a shot that is caught while he is still in the batter's box, and as he walks toward the dugout and the Montreal fans' cheers fade, he listens.

"Way to get good wood on it, bay-bee!"

It is a high, penetrating voice, with vowels so pure they sound almost foreign. Narvel looks up and by the end of the sentence locates the speaker high behind home plate: a rotund black man wearing a bright yellow beret, a black turtleneck shirt, and some sort of necklace made out of bones. The man meets Narvel's gaze with a big grin, then shakes a fist in passionate encouragement.

"Ya' got a friend up there, Narv'," Scrappy says to him in the dugout.

"You heard him too?" asks Narvel, sitting down beside him and buckling his shin guards. "Geez, what do you make of it?"

"Ya' got a friend. That's all."

"Yeah?" says Grammock. "Well, ya' better start hittin' the ball someplace useful or ya' won't have *me* for a friend."

"What the hell, Skip?" Narvel asks, his thin voice showing the injury he feels. "I've been playing steady ball all season."

"Yeah?" says Grammock. "What about today? And two days ago. And—"

"Lay off him," Scrappy says coolly. And Grammock, bewildered by this unprecedented challenge, scowls and watches the rest of the inning in silence.

In the ninth, with the club still down by two and Scrappy on first with nobody out, Narvel walks to the plate. Scrappy shouts encouragement, but he is soon outdone by the mystery fan.

Narvel fouls the first pitch weakly into the stands down the right-field line.

"Way to get a piece of it, bay-bee!"

He offers at the next pitch. Indeed, he does everything involved in swinging short of actually swinging—leaning in, stepping forward, bringing his bat back a bit before beginning the swing, only to stop it at the last instant in a way that leaves him tottering on his toes. He looks like an indecisive house-wife fretting over a cantaloupe purchase and finally deciding against it. He looks silly.

"Way to look 'em over, bay-bee!"

He fouls the next pitch down hard, right on his instep. He hobbles around, dragging his bat with him, working off the pain before he finally steps back into the box. As a rhyth-mic clapping starts up—the Montreal crowd wants the strike-out—Narvel figures his friend cannot possibly say anything good about the foul ball, but before the clapping builds, he hears from him:

"Way to shake it off, bay-bee!"

He fouls another pitch to the backstop.

"Way to hang in there, bay-bee!"

He fouls a bouncer down the third-base line.

"Way to hang tough, bay-bee!"

He guesses curve, guesses wrongly, and takes a called third strike. The cheers for the out are loud and long, so he must walk slowly back to the dugout to give his friend a chance. As he reaches the top step, he hesitates, and, while Grammock tries to pierce him with a glare, he hears the voice for the last time.

"Way to be, bay-bee!"

"Way to be?" he thinks as he hands his bat and helmet to the bat boy. "Way to *be?*"

A beefy, undepressed pinch hitter singles to right, and Scrappy goes to third. Grammock replaces the beefy pinch

185

hitter with a lean, high-on-life pinch runner. Bubba walks. The bases are loaded, but they are still down by two. After a new pitcher is brought in, Jaime drives a shot to the wall down the third-base line. Scrappy and the pinch runner score easily, tying the game. Bubba, his body churning like a demon's, runs through the third-base coach's stop signal and crashes into the catcher—yes, the same unhappy goat of the previous game—who has the ball, but not for long. It squirts away in the collision, and Bubba, sprawled on his chest behind home, gropes back for the plate and finds it with his fingertips, scoring the go-ahead run. By the time the pitcher retrieves the ball, Jaime is at third, pounding his chest with pride.

The dugout goes wild with celebration. If they can keep the lead, they will be in the World Series. They send Eddie to the plate with passionate encouragement to do more damage. He strikes out. But Buford hits a home run into the left-field stands, putting them up by three.

It looks bad for the Montreal club, especially the catcher. After E.T.A. pops up to end the top of the inning, Montreal comes to bat and goes down in order. Owing to the luck of the line-up, the catcher, to his credit, does not figure in the final three outs.

The guys celebrate raucously in the clubhouse, spraying champagne on one another and on the camera crews and sportswriters crowding around them, pausing at moments to wonder who they are now and what they may yet become, then celebrating some more.

"We don't deserve it, bums that we are," Apples shouts at the top of his lungs as he grabs two bottles of champagne, "but I'll sure take it."

"I'm gonna be in the World Series," Scrappy shouts to Buford. "Worthless ol' rookie me is gonna be in the World Series."

"Gee," Buford says softly. "Me too."

Scrappy grabs an open bottle of champagne sitting on Narvel's stool. "Is this your'n?" he asks him.

Narvel, strangely elated by much more than their victory, laughs and says, "No. It's champagne." Scrappy frowns, then gets the joke and laughs, feeling like a genius.

"*Offrez-vous une autre!*" Apples says to Eddie, quoting a beer ad on the Montreal scoreboard that E.T.A. once translated for them. Eddie looks up from his locker and sees Apples holding an opened champagne bottle out to him. He smiles weakly, shakes his head, and begins to undress. Apples, undaunted, moves on to Jaime and says it again— "*Offrez-vous une autre!*"—confusing the hell out of him.

Grammock grins as he passes through the clubhouse and pats his boys on their fannies. He turns off his grin when he gets to Scrappy and Narvel, and turns it back on again when he approaches Buford, his very best boy. He notices with disappointment that slumping Eddie is already in the shower, all by himself, or he would make a point of ignoring him too.

8

They have three days of freedom before the World Series opens at home.

Bubba roams the streets, dodging phantoms. He pushes buttons on the traffic-light posts at corners with no intention of crossing, just to stop the traffic. To hapless souls asking him for the time or for directions, he willfully gives false information. He waits at bus stops and simply stares up in silence when the driver wheels over and opens the door for him. These are the games of his childhood. This is his way of taking action.

Frank talks to the walls. No one, not even his sons, has called to congratulate him on his team's winning the National League pennant. This is fair, he thinks, considering what a bore he is. But he will change. He talks to the walls so that when he goes outside for walks he can be ostentatiously silent. His neighbors, however, continue to avoid him. His walls crack and peel.

Jaime thinks about the last game with Montreal. He remembers the ball girl who pranced by the dugout in her short-shorts in the third inning. He remembers watching her and becoming aware of ancient stirrings deep within. He remembers how he chased a foul that dropped into the stands and then, as he turned to go back to his position, contrived to bump her gently. He fell down with her, atop her in fact, but he managed to cushion her tumble to the ground with his hands cupping her buttocks. He remembers this play well. He goes to his closet for his very best flowered shirt. It is time for him to visit his marshas.

Narvel writes a letter to his parents. He tells them to stay in San Diego during the Series. He will not give them any of his tickets to the games. He doesn't want them in the stands. He doesn't want to see them for some time. He doesn't want his mother's silliness confusing him. He doesn't want his court jester of a father fouling his air with his stupid pipe—and it really is a stupid pipe, Pop, he writes, with that idiotic perforated tin cap that clips over the bowl, as if you want people to see you as a fun-loving Bavarian, Pop, when you know damn well you're a bumbling arsonist who destroys other people's lives with your dumbly dropped sparks of stupidity, right, Pop? He addresses and seals the envelope, calculates the number of days before the Series will begin, wonders what the postage for a special-delivery letter is, and tears the letter up with a shiver of fear.

E.T.A. broods in his den, surrounded by his books, none of which he has had the concentration to read for six months, while his wife and son wonderingly whisper to each other about his strange new silence. He thinks about the team's crisis of leadership, and, with bitterness, of Grammock's demeaning view of his reign as a mere interregnum. In a Platonic heaven of self-absorption, his mind broods in contemplation of itself.

Apples works out with the dental assistant. During the day, while she is at work, he alternately reviews the Yankee hitters he will be facing in the first game and gazes out her apartment window to the street below, shooting beaver from seventeen stories up. He sighs, bemoaning his twenty-three years of sexual idleness. He pities the women he sees below on the street for never having had him. He thinks of his elevator-full of nurses, all agiggle, all goosing him and groping at him as they ride with him up to his hotel room.

Buford bungles a diapering, is gently chided by Ellie, and storms out of the house in sweat and tears. Ellie fetches a neighbor to watch the twins and drives in the pouring rain through their suburban neighborhood in search of him. She finds him jogging up a steep hill and pulls alongside him. As they move slowly up the hill—she driving, he plodding—she shouts her encouragement to him, confesses to numerous diapering bungles of her own, and renews her vows of love for him as a husband and father to their children. He jogs, and through the sweat and tears and rain matting his blond hair he bellows to her about his dread of the future, when the twins are no longer babies, when they will need a better man than he is to guide them. She tells him the very same thing that Eddie had the wisdom to tell him long ago—that he will know what to do when the time comes; that he is doing fine now; that he will always know what they need today, if not tomorrow; that thinking about tomorrow has never been a talent of his. This time, coming from Ellie, backed up by evidence he cannot deny, the words take.

Eddie takes Tina to the zoo and has a god-awful time. She drops her ice-cream cone on the pavement, she whines, she wets her pants. They miss the chimp show and the lion-feeding. She demands that her father tell the uniformed engineer that she wants to drive the zoo train, and, when Eddie gently explains it cannot be, she denounces him for a boody-butt. These things happen, he says to himself. Nobody is to blame. When he gets home, he studies his notes of his conversations with his lawyer. They make his brain reel. He paws through his fan mail, most of which is supportive or downright adoring. He ignores this bunch in favor of another much smaller bunch.

And, finally, Scrappy, who works with earth. He quietly catches an afternoon flight to Little Rock, where he rents a big black Lincoln Continental. He drives north, through Grammock country, across the Missouri state line, and then he angles east, traversing the Ozarks, arriving along with the full moon at the playground of his childhood. The highway takes him by the old place—a gray, three-story house of horrors, empty and rotting. He slows the car and pulls to the side of the road. Beyond the split-rail fence choking with bittersweet vine, he sees the barren yard and the moonlight reflecting back at him off the filthy windows. He imagines the cracked flowered-linoleum floors inside. The calendar and the picture of Jesus. The weird ornaments—wasps' nests, hair balls, and hazel-stick crosses on every wall.

He pulls his car back onto the highway and drives on down the hill into the town, across the bridge, and up the next ridge, climbing, climbing, finally wheeling the car into the rear lot of the county maintenance garage. He easily jimmies open a window and climbs in, finding the keys on the nail where they have been hanging for the past eight years. Nothing changes here, he thinks. If Gram' were still alive, she would still be taking in little neighborhood babies and pinching them and loving them up. He pushes the button to raise the garage door, climbs aboard the bulldozer, starts it up, and waits a few minutes while it warms up.

A butterfly in the house, Scrappy! They's a-gonna be a weddin'!

He wheels the bulldozer out of the garage, taking the gravel road down to Bud Hotchkiss's driveway, which he follows a short distance before angling off to circle around the lower edge of the farm, well out of sight of the farmhouse. At the edge of the field, he crashes through a barbed-wire fence and skirts the edge of the Dunlap property, chugging slowly and quietly in the moonlight.

A centipede, Scrappy! Shet your mouth tight! Don't let 'im count your teeth or you'll die sure!

He knocks through a rock wall and aims for and finally finds the dirt road leading to Licking Creek and then paralleling it upstream. He squints into the darkness ahead, climbing with the creek. When he reaches the cemetery gate, he cuts the motor and stands up on his machine, surveying the land. He looks up the steep hill. In the moonlight, the tombstones—some black, some white—jut up irregularly, pointing in all directions. They remind him of her teeth when they were still good.

He starts the motor and, remaining at the same elevation, wheels the bulldozer exactly halfway around the hill, away from the water. Then he angles down and easily finds the long chute on the other side—empty now, for the water is low—which he follows, letting his machine push aside stray boulders and logs, all the way to the point where it meets the creek coming in from the east. He climbs down and studies the job before him. Perhaps he should have cleared the chute more thoroughly as he followed it, he thinks. Then he decides it is all right that he didn't. The water will do that. He will let the water work for him. His job is elsewhere, just over the little tapering spur before him, where the water flows.

He goes to work, driving the bulldozer up the side of the spur and lowering the blade when he reaches the other side. He begins to move the mountain. He sends earth, rocks, and debris cascading down the hill into the water, alarming the night creatures of the woods and sending them scampering for safety.

You don't know what death is, Scrappy! I do! I do! Promise me! Promise me!

He works, gutting the side of the hill, plugging the creek, redoubling his efforts when a persistent trickle tries to cut around the mass he heaps up. Finally, below him, the water lies in still puddles. Behind him, on the other side of the spur, he knows the creek is dancing down its new home. He continues to work, building a ten-year wall, a twenty-year wall, a hundred-year wall.

When he is finished, he eases the bulldozer down onto the drying gravel and chugs down the former creek bed. He cuts the motor when he is due south of the cemetery and walks up the hill, through the gate, all the way to her grave. He looks at it a moment, then sits down on the grass a little distance away from it, leaning back on one elbow. Below, the moonlight glistens on the remaining puddles of the savaged creek. All around him, silence reigns, save for the chirp of a cricket, the call of a screech owl—harmless sounds of wholly natural, physical creatures struggling to survive.

As he rises to his feet, he spies some wild chamomile growing on her grave. He plucks these from the earth and walks over the top of the mountain to the north-facing slope. He takes the flowers halfway down the hill to another grave. Farther below, the water dances.

"These are for you, Miss Eula. They say it's bad luck to take flowers from a grave, but that don't worry me none. I don't believe in bad luck no more."

○ ○ ○

Game One. The box score shows that Apples pitched a shutout and that Scrappy drove in three of their four runs. The box score does not show that as Scrappy clattered into the dugout after the final out of the game, he greeted Grammock by yelling into his face, "You're gonna die before me, you potbellied sonofabitch, an' you better watch yourself, 'cuz I'm Scrappy, an' that means I'm a fighter. I can move the *earth*."

○ ○ ○

Game Two. The box score shows that they lost the game, 2–1, and that Narvel made the last out with two runners on base.

The box score does not indicate how much Narvel was booed by the home crowd—perhaps their last chance at him this season, because the team will play the next three games in New York. The box score does not show who attended the game—two of Jaime's marshas, for example, to whom he had given free tickets. It does not show that he spotted them in the second inning as he came off the field, and that they waved and blew him kisses. It also fails to show that in the course of the rest of the game, his erection pushed restlessly against the inside of his brand-new cup jock, groaning and stretching like Alice outgrowing her house in Wonderland.

○ ○ ○

Game Three. The box score shows that they won this one in New York on Buford's twelfth-inning grand slam. It does not show that afterward, when they took the field in the bottom of the inning, Frank whispered into his glove that Buford had hit the thirteenth grand slam in World Series history and the very first grand slam in extra innings in a World Series game. It does not show what Buford was thinking during the game. It does not show that he was filled to bursting with pride in himself as a father, joyfully dwelling on the memory of his being up to his wrists in a diapering the night before (for Ellie, wanting to be at Buford's side for every Series game, has traveled to New York with their daughters). The box score is an inflexible, shabbily incomplete record, and it does not show that the scent really stays with you, and that when Buford gunned down the potential winning run in the eleventh, the ball he threw on the fly to Narvel had a measurable trace on it.

○ ○ ○

Game Four. The box score shows that Apples didn't get past the first inning, giving New York a lead that they kept for the rest of the game. The box score doesn't show that Apples spent the night before the game thrashing around with a compact little physical therapist attending a convention in his hotel. It does not show the massive burden of guilt and sorrow he carried out to the mound with him. The box score shows that Eddie got his first hit of the Series. It does not show that it was a measly, ignominious, checked-swing single down the opposite-field line, nor does it show that the night after the game he went directly into the hotel bar with the intention of drinking himself into weeping oblivion.

○ ○ ○

The bartender, a barrel-chested, friendly-faced man, tries to pick him up. First, he chases a couple of heckling Yankee fans away from the bar into a corner booth, telling them to leave Eddie alone or he will throw them out. Then he chats with Eddie about post-season slumps.

"Hell's bells, Eddie. Don't you worry about going one-for-sixteen. I've seen many a Series in this town, and I've seen many a star player struggle through the first three or four games and then just come to life for the rest of the games. You can still be the one to win it for your guys. I've seen it happen that way many times."

"What the hell you tryin' to cheer me up fo'? You a Yankee fan, ain't ya'?"

"Sure am."

"Well?"

"Oh, hell's bells. I hate to see a good ballplayer get down on himself. I want the Yanks to win, sure, but not at anyone's expense."

Eddie looks at him across his bourbon. "Say, thas mighty white of ya'."

The bartender laughs uncertainly. "I don't know how to take that, Eddie."

"Take it good, man. Thas how I meant it."

195

The bartender looks over Eddie's shoulder. "Here comes one of your colleagues."

Eddie swivels on his stool, a bit unsteadily, and sees him. "Hey, E.T.A. Got any battin' tips for me?"

"Hi, Eddie."

"Sit down, E.T.A. Have you a papaya juice or somethin'." He looks to the bartender. "E.T.A., he don' indulge."

"Just a Tab, please," E.T.A. says to the bartender.

"E.T.A., what am I doin' wrong? Been four weeks now, an' every time I stan' in there, it feel like my uniform's on backwards."

"I know. You're struggling, Eddie."

"I can't kill nothin' an' won't nothin' die."

E.T.A. looks off into the distance abstractedly. Then his eyes fall back on Eddie. "It's just finally caught up with you, Eddie. That's my theory."

"What's caught up wit' me?"

"The whole thing. We've all been holding it off—you know, *functioning*—but it's finally overpowered you. The same thing could happen to any of us tomorrow."

"Yeah? When's it gon' be *my* turn again? I mean, when am I gon' overpower *it*?"

E.T.A. shrugs and reaches for his Tab. "Who knows?"

"Yeah," Eddie says thoughtfully. "Who knows?" He sighs. "I think I got to talk to someone, E.T.A."

"I'm here, Eddie. I'm right here."

"Yeah, I know, an' you done hipped me to a lotta stuff. But I mean I got to talk to a doctor a some kind. Like Scrappy been doin'."

E.T.A. emits a little snort. "I wouldn't take my lead from Scrappy, if I were you. He can hardly tie his shoes."

"Nah, E.T.A. He's got his smarts, in his own way. An' I think he been on the right track all along. These pills—I can't really say they doin' a whole lot for me."

"That's something I'm not qualified to comment on."

"I know. But I been thinkin'. Even if this medicine is

rewirin' mah brain, I still don' know shit 'bout why I turned out like this in the firs' place."

"You want knowledge."

"Yeah. Right on. Thas what I want."

E.T.A. nods deeply. Then he goes to work. "You know, love is a pretty mysterious thing, Eddie."

"Love?"

"Yes. There's a lot of talk about it all the time. Buford loves Ellie. Apples loves his new girlfriend. You love Tina. Grammock loves his team."

"Yeah?"

"Think about it. Does that jerk really love us?"

Eddie chuckles. "It don' seem too likely."

"But he's always saying he does."

"Yeah, he sure is."

"So you can't believe that someone loves someone else just because he says he does."

"Thas true."

"Grammock might even really *believe* he loves us, but we all know it's a fraud. So people can even fool *themselves* about who they love."

Eddie looks at him.

"Take you and Tina."

"Jis' wait a minute, now."

"Eddie, do you want to talk straight or not?"

"Yeah, but—"

"Do you remember what I said about you and women?"

Eddie sighs and runs a fingertip around the rim of his glass. "Ain't been able to think a nothin' else ever since. An' my fan mail been tendin' in that direction too."

"Do you have any reason to believe Tina would be an exception for you?"

"I sure as hell *do*. She's mah li'l girl."

"So what are you saying? Everybody loves their children? Narvel's father loves him? Scrappy's grandmother loved him?"

"*Man . . .*"

"I wouldn't be totally honest with you, Eddie, if I didn't think you could handle it. Take you and Jacqui, now. You don't love her, right?"

"Now you talkin' sense." He catches the bartender's eye and points to his empty glass.

"But you did once."

"Yeah. Leastways, I *thought* I did."

"Ha! See? It's hard to be sure, isn't it? If you did, what happened? Did she go and change on you?"

"Maybe. Maybe she did at that."

"Nah. People don't change, Eddie, not after about age two. You probably *never* loved her. You just managed to confuse yourself into thinking you did. I'll bet you were nervous about getting married. Am I right?"

"Yeah, but seem like probly everyone is."

"I don't mean the wedding *ceremony*, Eddie. Don't protect yourself by pretending to misunderstand me. I mean you were nervous about spending the rest of your life with her."

"Well, thas what *I* meant too. An' it don' seem unnatural to be a li'l worried 'bout that."

"Maybe it doesn't to you, but, to take myself as an example, I for one was absolutely certain about Edith. I knew what I wanted. And we have a good, solid relationship. My certainty was justified. Now, you—you were scared because deep down you didn't love her. That's why your marriage has been such a struggle for you all these years."

"You fulla shit, E.T.A., talkin' like this. If I don' love mah Tina, howcome it *feel* so much like I do?"

"There's a name for that. I forget what it is, but it has to do with being so afraid to face the truth that you end up exaggerating the opposite of what you really feel. And I'd say your love for Tina is definitely exaggerated. I've never heard anyone in my life go on and on about their kid like you. That's suspicious in itself. Me and my boy—well, I can take him or leave him, and if you talk to any other healthy parents, they'll say the same."

"Geez, E.T.A. Thas a hell of a pitcher you paintin'. Seem like a kinda ugly worl' you talkin' 'bout."

"Listen, Eddie. Don't you ever get mad at Tina?"

"Sure."

"Don't you ever want to flat out hit her?"

"I suppose so. But you know kids. They always be doin' one thing or 'nother, an'—"

"What do you do when you want to hit her?"

Eddie inhales deeply, then sighs with frustration. "I fight it. I go 'way an' be by myse'f. Or I try 'n' understan' her. Sometimes I try 'n' think how much I love her."

E.T.A. laughs aloud. "*Amazing!* Don't you see the pattern? You've repeated it perfectly, right here, right now. The hatred. The pumping up of false love to hide the hatred. It's as clear to me as that big, sad frown on your face."

The bartender, who has been drifting back and forth along the bar, always within earshot, steps in front of E.T.A. and points a finger into his face.

"You. You've had enough to drink."

"*What?*"

"This is a nice, peaceful place."

"*What?* What are you talking about?"

"Don't worry about the bill. I'll cover it. Now, do I have to help you out of here or can you go quietly?" He makes a move toward the end of the bar, as if he means to circle around it and come after him.

E.T.A. jumps to his feet and steps back. "I'll have your ass for this. I'll report you to the hotel manager."

"And I'll report you to *your* manager and tell him what you said about him. Now get out."

E.T.A. scurries to the door, his fists clenched in impotent fury.

Eddie watches impassively. The bartender reaches out

199

and touches his hand. "You too, Eddie. Go to bed. Big game tomorrow."

Eddie blinks and looks blankly at the man. He says, "Was he drunk?"

The bartender shrugs. "He's drunk with *some*thing."

Eddie rises slowly from his stool and turns to go.

"Good luck tomorrow, Eddie."

He turns back and gives him a long look. "Yeah. Yeah. Thanks, man."

○ ○ ○

The next morning—the morning of the fifth game—Grammock is thrown out of his hotel bed by the stereophonic wails of Buford's girls in the room next to his. He sits on the edge of his bed and lets loose a steady stream of curses, but his heart is not in it. He is really thinking about the New York line-up, about Apples' ghastly showing in yesterday's game—but because he pitched less than a full inning, maybe he will be ready to start in the sixth game?—about his stomach, and about breakfast. He thinks about Eddie's slump. He has decided Eddie is a bad-luck bird. He feels that he, more than anyone else, ought to know, because he is a bad-luck bird himself. But he knows how to fight it. He knows the signs.

Hunger competes with acid for control of his stomach. A fresh wail from next door gives acid the victory for the moment. Then all is silent. He listens. He hopes Buford has taken them into his bed and rolled over on them. He feels his beard and remembers he lost yesterday, but decides to put off shaving until after he eats some toast. He gets dressed.

Out in the hall, he throws a scowl at Buford's door as he passes it. Ahead of him down the hall, a door is yanked open and a gray head leans out and just as quickly disappears inside again. It gives Grammock a queasy feeling, as if the next thing he will see is a corpse being carried out of the room feet first.

200

But the head sticks out again and the man looks at Grammock. He finally recognizes him. It is Narvel's lousy father.

"I thought I heard a noise," he says when Grammock reaches him. He looks at Grammock with a weird smile.

"What?" says Grammock, looking with revulsion at the little old man's weak, soft lips.

"I thought I heard something. Someone fiddling with the door. You see anything, Mr. Grammock?"

"No." He starts to move on down the hall.

"You going down to breakfast?"

"Yep."

"Come on in here. We got Danish. Coffee. Juice. Coffee cake. You name it."

Grammock hesitates. He thinks of the coffee shop downstairs. Noise. Reporters. Frank. He thinks, "I didn't have breakfast with this man yesterday and I lost."

"The wife's dumb, but she's a great little cook."

Grammock shrugs. "Sure. Why not?" He steps inside.

Farther down the hall, Narvel emerges from the stairwell, alone. Mavis has not made the trip with him. She declined—as, indeed, he himself was tempted to do—when they learned his parents would be there. He tiptoes past the door of his parents' room and goes to Scrappy's room. Scrappy is tucking in his shirt as he answers Narvel's knock. They go downstairs for breakfast.

A few minutes later, E.T.A., refreshed from a good night's sleep, steps out of his room, walks to the elevator, and punches the button with crisp authority.

After breakfast, Narvel, Scrappy, and E.T.A., who joined the other two in the coffee shop, go to Eddie's room and knock on his door. Directly across the hall, Narvel's father throws his door open as if foiling a band of terrorists, and his face goes slack and foolish when he sees the trio. He invites them over for a snack just as Eddie opens his door.

"You too, tall man," Narvel's father calls out to Eddie. "We got plenty."

"We already ate, Pop," says Narvel.

"Have some dessert, then. Come on. It'll loosen you up."

"Give us a sec," Narvel says.

"Git back in here, Herb," Grammock's voice booms from inside the room. "I ain't done yet."

"Knock three times," Narvel's father says to them conspiratorially. "Two short and one long."

E.T.A. looks to Narvel with a question on his face as Narvel's father disappears back into his room.

"He's afraid of New York," Narvel explains, his face abject in apology.

"Hey, man," Eddie says to E.T.A. "About las' night—"

"Let's not talk about that, Eddie," E.T.A. says. "How are you feeling?"

"I jis' wannit to say—"

"Don't worry about it, Eddie," says E.T.A.

"You guys talking about me?" asks Frank, who is suddenly upon them.

E.T.A. gives him a great big smile. "Not this time, Frank."

"Listen," says Narvel, "my folks got some eats, and you don't have much time for breakfast, Eddie. It's horseshit company, but—"

"Lemme git my key," says Eddie.

A full minute passes. E.T.A., Narvel, Frank, and Scrappy wait in the hall. Finally, Scrappy knocks on the half-closed door, pushing it open all the way. Eddie is standing at the dresser mirror, looking into it and blinking rapidly.

"Eddie, you okay?" asks Scrappy as he steps toward him.

Eddie grabs his room key from the dresser in front of him and puts it in his pocket. When Eddie turns, Scrappy sees that his eyes are redder than they were when he opened the door.

"You wanna wait here a bit with me?" he asks. "You wanna talk, Eddie?"

Eddie shakes his head. "Ain't nothin' to say." He takes a deep breath and gestures to the door, indicating Scrappy should go ahead. The other three in the hall look closely at Eddie.

Narvel says, "Everything okay, Eddie?"

Eddie nods and takes another deep breath. "I was havin' some troubles. It's okay now. Less go eat."

E.T.A. pauses at the door across the hall, knuckles raised, wondering how to knock with two short knocks and one long one.

"Hey, Pop, it's us," yells Narvel, embarrassed by this nonsense.

Narvel's mother opens the door and smiles at them nervously. Behind her, they hear Narvel's father. "Ruth, I told you to let me—"

"Oh, it's just your poor son," she says. E.T.A. winces at the volume and pitch of her voice. She sounds like a megaphoned Betty Boop.

Narvel looks around the room as they enter. He sees vases and artificial flowers from their home in San Diego. Ill-composed snapshots from their mantel. A portable smoke alarm high up on one wall. A toaster oven they have brought with them. Failure has made them fearful of everything, he thinks, including travel. They take their shrinking world with them wherever they go.

"Sit down, boys," says Grammock, "an' don't interrupt. I'm almost done." He is sprawled on the far bed, his sport shirt unbuttoned and his undershirt rolled up to his breasts. A damp towel lies flat across his belly. He turns to Narvel's mother and father. "Well," he continues, "that there mush, the way it sloshes around in that towel, it jist don't got what you might call real *substance* to it, an' that farmer bangs away on into the night—one hour, two hours, three hours, on an' on, without no real usefulness to it, while that skinny

203

preacher is a-moanin' underneath the load, a-wigglin' his skinny ass around to save his life."

The ballplayers sigh and exchange weary glances. Narvel's eyes involuntarily begin to search the dresser top for loose change.

"Well, the farmer, he finally jist gives up and rolls offa the preacher, kinda mumblin' to hisself, an' he falls asleep. The preacher slips outta the bed, a-countin' his blessin's. He picks up his clothes offa the floor an' tippy-toes into the kitchen, headin' for the door. But the farmer's wife, she's layin' for him with a fire poker. Ya' see, when she got back from the outhouse, she didn't take too kindly to what she heard a-goin' on in her nuptial bower. She cranks up an' gives that preacher a whack on his jemson that sends him screamin' out the door, his clothes flyin' ever' which a-way, an' he tears off acrost the field with his ass a-shinin' in the moonlight. Folks say he ain't plowed a twitchet in them parts ever since.

"Well, the next mornin', the farmer stumbles outta bed with a moan, his head fillin' the room an' a ache in his crotch runnin' up his belly an' down his legs, so he's feelin' purty bad all over. He drags his overhalls on an' kinda stumbles into the kitchen, where his wife is firin' up the stove an' wonderin' what he's gonna say 'bout last night. *She* sure ain't gonna say nothin' if'n *he* don't. The farmer sets down at the table, a-throbbin' all over his body, an' jist stares at the table kinda blank for a spell, tryin' to figger what could be ailin' him so bad.

"'Maw,' he finally says, rubbin' his belly all confused-like, 'I reckon I'd kinda prefer havin' some sidemeat for supper tonight. Somehow that mush jist ain't satisfyin' enough.'"

Grammock's gut bounces under the white towel as laughter rises and rolls out of his mouth.

Narvel's father slaps his knees and laughs with piercing barks. "That's rich, Mr. Grammock. That's rich."

"I don't understand," says Narvel's mother. "What's a twitchet?"

Grammock and Narvel's father laugh some more. Narvel reddens and quickly begins serving his teammates packaged sweet rolls and instant coffee. While he is doing this, his father scurries into the bathroom, then out again. When Narvel looks over to Grammock, he sees, against the whiteness of the towel lying across his belly, a black revolver.

"A really nice piece," Grammock says as he fondles it.

Narvel closes his eyes tightly. "Pop," he moans.

"Don't 'Pop' me, boy. What do you know? Afraid of guns, afraid of everything." He turns to Grammock. "He's afraid to get in a goddamned elevator. What kind of boy did I raise, anyway?" He looks back at Narvel. "I got every right to carry this piece, coming to this snake pit."

"I don't know why you say that, Herb," his wife chirps.

"And there's a helluva lot else you don't know, Ruth," Narvel's father says as he reaches for his pipe and bangs it loudly into an ashtray.

"People have been very nice to us," she persists. "There was that lady in the elevator you told me about, the one who asked you if you were lonely last night, remember? I thought that was very sweet of her."

Grammock's frown gives way to a huge guffaw, and Narvel's mother smiles at him, evidently pleased that he shares her views. Narvel's father rolls his eyes to the ballplayers as if to say that if they have discovered that his son is dumb, they now know where the blame lies.

"You can't be too careful," Grammock says. He turns to Narvel. "Your dad an' me have been jawin' up a storm here. We share a lot of feelings. I like his thinkin'."

What thinking? Narvel wonders.

"Come on, boys," says Narvel's mother. "Dig into that food now."

Grammock sights the gun on Scrappy, grins, and sets it on the nightstand. Narvel's father, eager to repossess it, takes it and disappears into the bathroom. From the rattle in there, they all know he is cleverly hiding it in his shaving kit.

They eat. Six or seven topics are raised and discussed with complete failure. Scrappy observes Narvel's parents in action and wonders if Narvel might have been worse off than he was as a kid. E.T.A. watches Narvel's father and thinks, "A man can smoke a pipe and still be a chucklehead." Frank is aware of new advantages to his vow of silence. Narvel squirms agonizingly and decides to take a course in cardiopulmonary resuscitation, just so that if his father ever collapses at his feet, his inaction will be willful and not merely the result of ignorance.

"And what's *your* nickname?" Narvel's mother suddenly says to Eddie, her singling out of him and her excessive animation showing that she is uncomfortable with this big black man sitting on her bed as unequivocally as if she had pulled a Klansman's hood from her suitcase and wordlessly donned it.

"Ma'am?" says Eddie, who has said "ma'am" maybe once before in his life. He is searching for ways to be polite. He refuses to mock her, for Narvel's sake.

"I know you boys have nicknames. What's yours?"

He slowly sets his coffee cup down. "Sometimes E.T.A. here calls me 'Fast-Twitch,' but it never really took. Bubba don' got none neither." He looks at her and stops speaking, because he believes he has answered her question.

She frowns. "Which one of you is Bubba?" She looks at Scrappy. There is a pause as they all try to understand what is going on.

Eddie says, "Ma'am, didn't you mean us black players?"

"Eddie calls *me* 'Mr. Steady,'" E.T.A. says quickly. "Or 'Ice Man.'"

"Now we're rolling," Narvel's mother squeals.

"Scrappy's got a whole bunch of nicknames, don't you, Scrappy," Grammock says with a giggle, shifting on the bed and making it squeak.

"Last year they called me 'Two No-Trump,'" E.T.A. continues, over Grammock's squeaks and giggles. "That's because I was always wanting to get up a game of bridge."

206

"A pussy game," declares Grammock. "Hey, Scrappy, tell 'em yours. You got a whole junkyard of nicknames."

"Only to you," Scrappy says, calmly adding, "The guys know my name an' that's what they call me." He turns to Narvel's mother. "Jist plain ol' Scrappy, Mrs. Adams."

"Some name," mutters Grammock.

"This is fun!" exclaims Narvel's mother. "How about you?" she says to Frank, who reddens instantly.

"Frank don't got one neither," Scrappy says protectively.

"Hey, Herb," Grammock calls to Narvel's father as if struck with an unrelated thought. "When you take the team bus to the ballpark, jist leave your *suitcase* in the lobby with the ballplayers' suitcases. You'll see where they put theirs. Jist put your *suitcase* there with the others an' it'll git checked on the plane automatically. Your *suitcase* is what I'm talkin' about." He chuckles.

"That's real nice of you, Mr. Grammock," says Narvel's father.

Frank rises to his feet.

"Whoa, Frank," says Grammock. "You got plenty of time to pack, an' you oughta be purty good at it by now. An' there's somethin' I been meanin' to tell ya'. Ya' know what the record number of clubs is that any one guy has played for? Ya' know that?"

Frank stands in mute endurance.

"I can't recollect the number right off," Grammock continues, "but I got a bug up my ass about it the other day an' checked it out. I learned you're tied for it. There's a little bit a distinction in tyin' a record—like when we tied the D.P. record, with your help, remember?—but your real glory lays somewhere in the future, wouldn't ya' say?"

Frank whispers a "thank you" to Narvel's mother and silently leaves the room, closing the door soundlessly behind him.

"Hey," Eddie says to Grammock, who is one with the

bed as he and it quiver with his amusement. "Hey, Skip. What kinda brutal fuck done produced you anyway?"

"*Sir*," bellows Narvel's father to Eddie, "I demand that you apologize to my wife for your language."

"Your playin' days are over, Eddie," blusters Grammock. "I seen plenty a washed-up ballplayers, an' you're all washed up."

"That's bullshit," Scrappy snaps at Grammock.

Eddie looks dully at Grammock, his eyelids drooping heavily. He turns to Narvel's mother, who is smiling tightly. "Ah apologahze, Mrs. Narvel," he drawls.

"*Sir*, her name is Mrs. *Adams*."

Eddie rises from the bed. "Thanks fo' the eats, Narv'. See ya' on the bus. You too, Scrappy an' E.T.A." On his way out, he calls back over his shoulder, "Skip, yo' momma was a evil fuckuh, an' Ah apologahze again, Mrs. Narvel."

E.T.A. and Scrappy choke down whatever they find is still in their mouths and take their leave. Outside the room, they see Eddie carrying his bag and walking slowly down the hall toward the elevator. He turns and waves to let them know he is all right.

○ ○ ○

Game Five. Eddie rides the bench. They lose. They trail in the Series, three games to two.

On the flight home, Narvel's father makes a loud joke about a bomb and is whisked to the front of the plane by a plainclothes U.S. marshal riding in the seat directly in front of him. He is questioned, frisked, taken into the bathroom and subjected to a strip search, and then is returned to his seat with a reprimand that makes his ears burn on both sides of his indomitable foolish grin. Narvel slinks to the rear of the plane to get away from the taint of him. He plays cards with Scrappy.

Buford sits with Ellie and his girls. He helps a stewardess

put together two cardboard cradles, after first destroying one with his huge fists as he tried to punch it into shape, laughing at this minor incompetence, recognizing that it is trivial. When the twins awaken, he finds excuses for strutting up and down the aisle with one, then the other. He sees that Grammock is sitting alone and asks if he would like to hold one. Grammock declines.

Bubba sits next to an emergency exit over the wing and itches with the temptation to open it just to see what will happen—an impulse he successfully sublimates by taking a pillow with him into the bathroom and stuffing it down the toilet. Frank reads an article in the in-flight magazine on a French Trappist monastery. In the aisle across from him, Jaime jokes with a stewardess, or at least says things that make her lean down close to him and frown pleasantly. Eddie drinks. E.T.A. sits with him, an empty seat between them, watching him, planning to drive him home.

Apples sits alone, hating himself. When the plane lands, the dental assistant is there at the gate to meet him. When he hugs her, her body feels more familiar to him than his own. When he tells her of his infidelity and promises never to do it again, she cries and then is silent. As they walk down the concourse, he holds her tightly to him, tucking her head close to his ribs. She finally says she is not surprised. She understands that he needed to experiment. She gives him a glimpse of her own sexual history prior to meeting him—a history that makes him go weak in the knees until he finally begs her to stop. By the time they reach the baggage carousel, she has forgiven him.

As they all wait for their bags, it is obvious that Apples and the dental assistant are having a tender, private moment, and Apples' teammates respectfully keep their distance. Narvel's father, however, sits down directly in front of the two of them on the low railing of the carousel and tells them a little about himself and then asks Apples what went wrong with his pitching in the fourth game. Narvel watches. He sees the railing squirt his father's wallet out of his unbuttoned rear pants pocket. It plops onto the carousel and is partly obscured by a suitcase tumbling off the conveyor belt feeding into the carousel. The wallet goes round and round. Narvel watches, silently rooting. But Frank spots it, removes it from the carousel, opens it, and gives it to Narvel's father, who thanks Frank but eyes him suspiciously until he has his suitcase and he and Narvel's mother leave for their hotel.

○ ○ ○

At mid-morning of the next day—the off-day before the sixth game—E.T.A.'s phone rings.

"E.T.A. Hey, man. I'm all fucked up."

"Eddie." E.T.A. clutches the phone tightly. "What's the matter?"

"I'm in the hospital. All fucked up."

"What happened? What do you mean?"

"I busted my legs. Both of 'em."

"My God," E.T.A. says. "What happened? Where are you? Can I come see you?"

"After you brung me home, I went out for a stupid-ass drive. Run off the road. Fucked it all up."

"Geez, Eddie. Anybody else hurt?"

"Nah. Not even the team, seein' as Grammock wasn't gonna play me anyway."

"But he *was*."

"Huh?"

"He told me he was going to put you back in tomorrow. But that's not important. You—"

"You're right. It ain't, 'cuz I wouldn't a did shit anyway."

"I didn't mean that. I meant you shouldn't worry about tomorrow's game. The important thing is you're alive. You could have killed yourself."

"Tell the guys I'm sorry."

"Don't worry about that. What about next year, Eddie? Can you play next year?"

"I s'pose. I gotta go now, E.T.A. They comin' to stick my ass with a needle."

"Wait a minute. Where are you? I'll pick up some of the guys—"

"Whip up on 'em tomorrow, E.T.A. Pick me up, man."

"Wait!" says E.T.A. "Wait, Eddie!" But he is talking to a dial tone.

Eddie walks briskly from the phone booth back to his car. He slides in behind the wheel and looks at Tina, who sits on her knees beside him in the front seat, picking the caramel corn out of her Cracker Jack box, saving the peanuts for last. He watches her work intently, then leans over and kisses her on top of her head.

"You happy, babe?"

She nods without looking up.

"You got a toy in there?"

She reaches to the top of the dashboard and picks up a piece of cardboard still in its wrapper. "I'ma save it fo' Momma."

He watches her a moment longer, his eyelids drooping heavily. "This such a ugly worl', an' you such a good li'l girl. Thas why I wannit to be wit' you today. You such a good li'l girl." His eyes glaze over. He finally starts the car and pulls out of the rest area back onto the interstate, heading away from the city into the farmland.

○ ○ ○

On that same morning, at about the same time, Narvel sits in his parents' hotel room, just down the street from the stadium, trying to understand his mother while his father showers.

211

"It's just not fair," she says. "I believe it's important to be fair."

"They beat us soundly, Mom."

"But those Yankees didn't even take their bats at the end."

Narvel frowns. "What? Take their bats? Take them where?"

"They didn't go up and swing at the ball."

"How can you say that? They hit it all over the field. They hit the daylights out of it."

"I'm talking about the end of the game. It was their turn and they didn't even come out to take their bats."

Realization slowly dawns on him. He wonders why she even comes to the games. "They were the home team when we were in New York, Mom. The home team always bats in the bottom of each inning. When they are ahead in the last inning, they don't bat. There wouldn't be any point in it. They've already won."

"But *your* team batted," she says with a twinkle in her eye. She thinks she has caught him.

"But when we didn't score, the game was over."

"Everyone should have an equal chance."

"Chance? *Chance?*" He is almost screaming. "If we take the field in the bottom of the ninth, what chance do we have? There's no such thing as taking runs *away* from a team. Is that what you're thinking? Good God."

Naked and wet, Narvel's father dashes in a panic out of the bathroom to the phone. "Those goddamn nigger maids," he says, his teeth clenched.

"What is it, dear?"

"Those goddamn— hello? Give me the hotel detective, and I mean pronto . . . What? . . . What do you mean there is no such thing? Of course there is such a thing."

"What is it, dear?"

"Then get me the police . . . Ruth, what's our room number?"

"Five-oh-seven," says Narvel, slumping in his chair, bored by it all.

"Five-oh-seven," he barks into the phone. "And I mean pronto." He bangs the receiver down. "It just shows why you've got to stay on your toes. It shows it better than—"

"What is it, dear?"

"Some sonofabitch stole my gun, that's what it is, *dear*," he snarls at her. "It's gone."

"What?" says Narvel, sitting up.

"Are you sure?" says his mother.

"Ruth, you should have listened to me. I told you to bring extra bed linen. You just can't let them in your room like we've done. You can't let yourself be vulnerable like that."

○ ○ ○

Eddie pulls onto an exit ramp. At the top of the hill, he turns right, onto a small, two-lane highway. The road blurs before him as he begins to sob. Tina watches him, not at all surprised. She has grown used to it. She watches him and works on her peanuts.

"Jis' all fucked up," he cries out, over and over. "Jis' all fucked up."

"Daddy—"

He jerks his head and looks at her, his eyes wide. They narrow, then he says, "Babe, I change' my mind. This ain't safe. I want you in back. Git in yo' car seat."

"You said I could sit up here wit' you. You said—"

"Git in back."

"You said—"

"*Shut up an' git in back!*" he yells.

She begins to cry, bewildered by his screaming, angry at his broken promise. She struggles over the seat and climbs into her car seat, fastening the lap belt out of habit. She has spilled her peanuts in the process and she cries over this, but she is afraid to ask him if she can get out and pick them up.

Eddie slows the car as they approach a small town. He drives down the main street and spots a schoolyard filled with children playing during the noon recess. He pulls the car over and turns off the motor.

"You wanna play here a li'l while, babe? I'd like to watch you play a li'l while."

"You be wit' me, Daddy?"

"Yeah. I'll come an' watch. I be wit' you. Gimme a kiss now."

He helps her out of the car and they walk to the playground. Eddie sits on a bench at the edge of the grass while Tina tentatively works her way over to a tall wooden climber. She is the only child on the climber. Beyond her, far away on the other side of the field, the other children are playing a game that looks like baseball, only they use a big rubber ball, and they kick it.

Tina climbs to the very top and rests her chin on a wide wooden rail, watching the noisy game. She looks back to her daddy and sees that he is watching too, though he is leaning forward, not sitting back with his long arms across the back of the bench the way he usually likes to sit. She looks back to the game. She sees that the children are bigger than she is, and she is glad to be alone on the climber. She sees that only two of the children are black people, but one of the grown-ups, a lady, is black. She watches the lady help a boy who fell down and is crying. She takes him off the playground to a water faucet. His pants are torn. She sees the lady roll them up and splash water on his leg where his hurt is. It must be cold. The boy runs back to play some more. The lady wipes her hands on her skirt and looks across the field at Tina, high up on top of the climber. She probably can't believe Tina could be up so high. She looks at Tina for a long time, and then she starts walking over to her. Maybe she is going to tell her she didn't think such a little girl could ever climb so high. Maybe she is afraid she might fall and hurt herself. Don't worry, Tina will tell her. Her daddy is watching her. The lady comes near, and Tina turns around to point to her daddy on the bench, but she must be looking at the wrong bench because her daddy isn't there. But there are no other benches.

○ ○ ○

After talking with Eddie on the phone, E.T.A. wanders around his house. He dials Eddie's home number, but there is no answer. He calls Apples and tells him of Eddie's call. Then he calls Grammock, who spits and curses and condemns E.T.A. for not finding out which hospital Eddie is in. Grammock puts his flunky coaches on the job of making inquiries with the police and hospitals. They get back to him with their disappointing results in two hours: no trace of Eddie, no report of an accident involving him. Grammock threatens to fire all of them and calls the front office to have them put some of their flunkies on the job. When they get back to him in the middle of the afternoon with the same results, he calls E.T.A. to get his story again, but E.T.A.'s wife answers the phone and says he has gone out to pick up their son at school, so Grammock swears at her and dials Eddie's home number. Eddie's wife says she just got in and hasn't seen him since he went out with Tina after breakfast. Grammock eschews the stale custom of not saying anything to worry the spouse in such a situation and asks her pointblank if she knows anything about an accident. He tells her about Eddie's call to E.T.A., quickly and sloppily, for he is tired of telling this story to people over the phone, and when he sees that she is going to do nothing but scream *"My baby! My baby!"* he shouts a quick "Goodbye" into the receiver and hangs up, thinking, "Baby, my ass—that little snot-nose is three if she's a day." But then he remembers how Tina brought them luck in that double-header when she was in the dugout, and his heart softens. Not that he does anything about it, like calling Eddie's wife back to reassure her, but his heart does soften. He decides to take a nap.

After dinner, E.T.A. calls the front office and learns that Tina has been located. A schoolteacher in a small town eighty miles to the west found her playing alone in the playground. Tina claims her daddy left her there. The club has asked the police to look for Eddie, and the search is now going on. They have also notified the press of Eddie's disappearance. There is nothing more that can be done. E.T.A. asks them why Eddie would do such a thing, but of course they don't know. All they can do is hope he is found before tomorrow night's game.

E.T.A. calls some of the other guys, who in turn call the rest. That night they lie awake in their beds long after their wives and girlfriends and parents and children have fallen asleep, listening to distant thunder, wondering if it will rain, and wondering about Eddie.

The next morning, Grammock takes his phone off the hook and ignores his doorbell, dodging reporters, who have exhausted their material for off-the-field stories about the Series, have grown weary of reworking the same old subtly derisive stories about Jaime's name and Narvel's father, and want to know all about Eddie. Grammock spends the morning in his basement, listening to weather reports, cursing their vagueness, and cleaning his fishing equipment in anticipation of a consolatory ice-fishing trip in the off-season, because he can't trust his boys to win the next two and give him anything pleasant to contemplate in the long winter ahead.

After lunch, he drives through a misty rain to the ballpark.

9

"That about covers the hitters. Remember to watch your footing out there. And, outfielders, don't let that goddamn one-hopper skip by you. You're gonna have to adjust your approach a little. You're all big boys an' know how to do that, so I won't say nothin' more about it. Another thing: if there's a rain delay, I want you loose, but not too loose, understand? No TV. None of that goddamn heebie-jeebie music, neither. Cards is okay. Likewise okay is a little grab-ass in the clubhouse, only don't overdo it. And no thinkin'. I don't put no stock in thinkin'. Any questions?"

There are no questions.

"I know you're all wonderin' about Eddie, jist like I'm wonderin'. I'll let ya' know the minute I hear anything, I swear to God I will. I'm sure he's okay an' everything, an' I don't want none of you thinkin' otherwise, understand? Wherever he is, I know that Eddie would want us to go out an' give exactly a hunderd an' fourteen percent, so—"

"We don't know that," says Scrappy.

"—so jist go out there—"

"We don't know that a-tall," he says more loudly. Grammock turns to him. "I got no letter from Eddie sayin', 'Hey, Scrappy, I'm gonna be weird an' drive off with my kid an' dump her an' make myself scarce, but don't you give it no thought 'cuz I want you to give exactly a hunderd an' fourteen percent.' I got no letter like that. You got one, Skip?"

"What's your point, Scrappy?" Grammock says wearily.

"My point is it's bullshit to say stuff like what you was workin' up to say. I'm gonna play—hell, that's what we're all here for, what we was borned for—but don't give me no dedication crap."

"Right on," says Narvel, taking the steam out of Grammock's reply.

"As for you, Narvel," Grammock says, turning on him, "you keep your old man outta my sight. He's a bad-luck bird."

"I got no argument with that, Skip," Narvel says.

Grammock decides to end it there. He says, "Go get 'em" and turns and walks to his office. He hurries as he nears the door because his phone has begun to ring.

As they come out of the runway, Scrappy says, "Hey, Frank, wanna throw the old pill around?" Frank nods and they begin to throw easily in front of the dugout. Buford and Narvel take a few warm-up runs while the Zamboni machine circles in left field, sucking up water. In the bullpen, Apples brings his cheeks up to a reddish glow with his final warm-up throws. He puts his right arm into the right sleeve of his jacket and walks slowly to the dugout, meeting Buford and Narvel on their way back in, giving them a thumbs-up sign to let them know he has good stuff today.

The New York line-up is introduced and booed. Their own line-up is introduced and cheered, with the exception of Narvel. Grammock hasn't appeared in the dugout, and the umps and the New York manager wait impatiently at home plate for him to bring out the official line-up card. When he finally comes out of the runway, his face is a fish-belly white. He steps over to the water cooler in the dugout and leans against it out of habit. He hears the home-plate ump calling to him, blinks at him several times, drops his jaw, and hurries out to the plate. He gives the ump the card, stands silent and expressionless as the ump reviews the ground rules, fails to respond to a joke from the Yankee manager, and turns and walks back to the dugout when the meeting is over.

The ump studies the card Grammock has given him. He frowns. Is this some kind of joke? The public-address announcer calls out the names of the home-team players, bringing them trotting out of the dugout to their defensive positions. The ump hears a strange name called and sees a rookie running out to center field. What the hell is Grammock doing? He walks over to the dugout. Grammock stands by the water cooler, his hands under his shirt, stroking his belly aimlessly, while he gazes out to the playing field as if looking into an empty fish tank.

"Hey," the ump calls to him, "this line-up card you give me. What's the poop?"

Grammock's eyes dart nervously as he steps out of the dugout and takes the card. He sees nothing wrong with it. It is his regular line-up, the one with the boys he loves and has won with all year. But something must be wrong or the ump wouldn't be talking to him. He is helpless to figure it out.

"You got Eddie's name down here," says the ump. "You find him? If you did, what's that kid doin' out there?" He points to center field.

Grammock follows his eyes and sees a lean white youngster exchanging warm-up tosses with Buford. When he finally recognizes him and understands the mistake he has made, all he can do is gasp and shake his head quickly, then nod and point to the rookie in center.

"So you want *him* in the line-up, not Eddie, right?"

Grammock nods emphatically.

"Okay. Shake it off. Sit down. You look all tensed up. Relax. It's just a game." The ump returns to the plate. The announcer calls, *"Playeeee ballllll."* Grammock steps into the dugout and sits down very gently.

Apples does indeed have good stuff. Through five innings, he scatters three singles while his teammates score two runs, one on a combination of a teasing Bubba and a hard-hitting Jaime, who smacks doubles as if he finds something unpleasant or confusing about being at first base, the other on a lead-off round-tripper by Buford. In the sixth, the light mist returns and Apples struggles, finally giving up a run on a shot over the head of the rookie center fielder, who lost a step going back for it in Eddie's private dip in the field and watched the ball bounce off the wall before he recovered. Still up by one run, Apples just manages to retire the New York batters in order in the eighth before the rain begins to come down—in earnest, with a burst of pent-up power, as if nature, though desirous that the game be played to completion, like Narvel's mother is not exactly sure when it ends. The home-plate ump orders the ground crew to pull the tarp over the field, and the fans scurry for cover.

Grammock sits beside the water cooler, where he has sat, inactive, throughout the game. The players have interpreted his silence as some small part of a bizarre new design for inspiring them, and they have ignored it. But when they pour into the dugout, cursing the rain, Grammock suddenly comes to life.

"Nobody talks to nobody, got it?" he shouts down the length of the dugout. "You can talk to each other, but don't do no jawin' with nobody else. This storm's gonna pass, I can feel it, an' when it fairs up, I want your minds in the game."

They shrug and agree. There is no one for them to talk to anyway, apart from the cud-chewing deaf clubhouse man, who now stands at the door into the runway ready to hand them towels. Grammock brushes by him and beats all of them into the locker room. He hurries to the television set mounted high on one wall. It is on, but the sound is off. Someone is being interviewed by someone else. Grammock looks over his shoulder, sees that he is still alone and turns the sound up.

"—in a car in a dry-gulch well off the highway, about six or seven miles from—"

"*Jesus!*" he gasps, unplugging the television and carrying it under his arm to his office. The players come in and he shouts to them, "No TV. No radio. I want you in the game." He tosses the TV onto his couch and hurries to the exit leading to the interior of the stadium. The door is ajar. The clubhouse guard is talking with a mob on the other side of it. Grammock hurries forward, pulls the guard back in, and slams and locks the door.

"Skip, the reporters say—"

"I don't give a shit what they say. Your job is to keep this door closed and keep them out. An' keep your trap closed too."

"Yes, sir," he says.

Grammock eyes him coldly, assessing his loyalty, and finally turns away. As he heads toward his office, he sees Scrappy unbuttoning the shirt of his uniform. "You can take it off," Grammock yells to him, "but don't change it. I want you in the same uni when we git back out there." He slams his office door shut behind him.

Scrappy stares after him, open-mouthed.

"Isn't he something?" Apples says, laughing.

"Lives in a world a whammies," says Scrappy.

They settle down to the dull frustration of the rain delay. Scrappy hangs his shirt up to dry and gets up a poker game. E.T.A. strips to his shorts, takes out a book, and retires to the non-privacy of his locker. Apples and Narvel talk about the hitters.

"I'm gonna stretch out on the trainer's table," Apples says to Narvel when they are done. "Catch some winks."

Narvel nods to him and begins to walk around the clubhouse. He watches the card game a while, grows bored, walks by Buford's locker, congratulates him on his home run, finds that Buford has nothing to say other than "Thanks a whole heckuva lot, Narv'," and wanders down the runway to check on the rain. The dugout is empty, save for a few back-up players huddled near the bat rack. Narvel walks to the far end of the dugout and sits down. He watches the rain blowing back and forth in gusts, appearing to let up and then pouring down with renewed force, peppering the green tarp covering the infield. Some fans sail a few paper airplanes onto the field, the ones clearing the foul lines being cheered as if they were silent base hits in an unmanned game. A fan jumps out and does running belly flops on the tarp, sliding twenty or thirty feet each time before coming to a stop. It looks like fun. Two stadium guards chase him down and take him off the field.

Narvel looks out to center. Through the driving rain, he can almost see Eddie heading off a fly ball in deep right-center, then loping toward the dugout the way he does, his elbows cocked smartly and his wrists swinging high up on his body, deliberately slow after showing them how fast he can be: a man of many styles. He follows Eddie with his eyes all the way to the top step of the dugout, where Eddie's beauty melts into the ugly vision of his father standing before him.

"Hey, Narvel," he says, his slack mouth working foolishly under his wife's pink umbrella. "Lemme join you."

A stadium guard hustles over to get him back into the stands, but Narvel intercedes, saying that it is all right. The guard backs away, keeping an eye on them.

"Stay there, Pop," Narvel says. "You can't come down here. Grammock's rules." He wonders what his father wants to talk about.

"Your center fielder killed himself, Narvel." He nods furiously. "Honest."

Narvel thinks of the rookie who replaced Eddie and even looks out to center to see if he is there. Then he understands.

"Shot himself. They found him in his car out in the country somewhere. They just now said so on the radio." Narvel closes his eyes while his father goes on and on. "I've been keeping it from your mother. Didn't want to upset her. I mean, the guy was just in our hotel room, for God's sake. Something else, Narvel. They described the gun on the radio. It's *my* gun. It's just gotta be. Isn't that something?"

Narvel opens his eyes and stares at him.

"I got it all figured out. He was in the room when Mr. Grammock told me about putting our suitcases in the lobby with yours. The gun was in there, because you can't carry them with you on the plane—I've learned that—and I wasn't watching the suitcase in the lobby because there was a guy earning good money to do that. I figure Eddie must have told the guy watching them that he had to get something out of *his* suitcase, and then he took the gun out of *mine* and put it in *his*. He was a smart nigger."

"No, Pop." *You're the nigger*, he thinks.

"Huh? 'No'? What do you mean?"

"No." *Whatever "nigger" means to you, that's what you are.*

"What?"

You know what I wish, Pop? I wish it was Eddie here, alive, telling me you were dead. That's what I wish.

Narvel's father looks down at his son from under his pink umbrella. "What do you have to say, Narvel? Talk to me, boy."

Narvel stares at him. *I get more love from the guys I play ball with—hell, from a stranger in the stands way up in*

Montreal, a guy who loves me for who I am—than I ever got from you. He turns away and walks down the dugout.

"Narvel!" his father calls after him, taking a step into the dugout. The stadium guard begins to rush back to cut him off, and Narvel signals to him. The guard sidetracks to come close to Narvel, who points to his father at the far end of the dugout.

"That man has threatened my life," he says, very softly. "I want him arrested." He turns away and walks past the players standing by the bat rack. He walks slowly down the runway and goes to Scrappy's locker. When Scrappy looks up from the card game with an expectant smile, Narvel drops onto a stool beside him and begins to cry.

○ ○ ○

"You're right, Apples," E.T.A. says. "We *should* have talked about it." He looks to the group seated on the stools gathered around Scrappy's locker. "It's always a danger with this thing."

"I didn't mean that," says Apples. "I meant we should have talked with *Eddie* about it. We should have seen it coming with *him*."

"I really don't see how we could have," says E.T.A. "Eddie didn't seem any worse than the rest of us."

"But look at the kind of guy he was to begin with," Apples says. "It's like it was a longer drop for him to come down to where we were. We should have seen it."

"But look at Narvel," says E.T.A., an edge of impatience in his voice.

They all turn to Narvel, who frowns.

"You've been dropping the same kind of hints as Eddie all season, Narvel," E.T.A. explains.

Narvel's frown deepens.

"Well, you're still with us, aren't you? You were never serious about it, were you?"

"Hell yes, I was. I still am too."

"Jesus, Narv'," Scrappy blurts out, blinking nervously. "No. *No*. Me 'n' you gotta *talk* about this. Don't do it. Jist don't do it."

Narvel manages a smile. "Okay, Scrappy. I won't. Not for a while, anyway. I wanna see who wins the World Series."

Apples sighs. "He was always saying, 'Pick me up. Pick me up.' We should have seen it. E.T.A., *you*'d been talking to him. You should have seen it. We *all* should have seen it."

E.T.A. says nothing.

Scrappy says, "Anyone told Grammock yet?"

"He must know," says Apples. "The TV. No reporters."

"Jesus," Scrappy says angrily, looking down the aisle and scowling at the closed door to Grammock's office.

"What the hell was he thinking?" asks Narvel. "Was he going to keep us here all night? Even if we win today, we would have found out after the game."

"You know Grammock," says Buford. "One game at a time."

"The *real* question," says E.T.A., "is what we are going to do if the rain lets up."

Scrappy, still looking at Grammock's door, lets out a small, bitter laugh. "Ya' know, if ya' look at how Eddie arranged it, Grammock was right. I hate to admit it." He looks at E.T.A. "It was like Eddie couldn't take it no more, not even for two more days. I guess he *had* to do what he did, but he didn't want it to mess us up none. He probly didn't wanna be found till the Series was over. So maybe he *did* want us to play."

"Exactly," says E.T.A. "Now, then—"

"But I jist had another little thought," says Scrappy. "That way a thinkin' is good only so long as we didn't know

225

what he done. He probly didn't take his thinkin' no farther 'n that. An' now that we *do* know, hell, I don't see how we can play. It's jist plain impossible."

Apples nods. "He probably wouldn't have been found so quickly if it hadn't been for Tina. That narrowed the search."

They are silent. E.T.A. says, "Let's settle this. I vote we play."

Apples shakes his head. "We need time to absorb this. I don't really give a damn who wins right now."

"E.T.A.," says Scrappy, "you got any thoughts 'bout Eddie? You ain't said nothin' 'bout him."

E.T.A. gives him a close look. "What do you mean, exactly?"

"About why he done it. You spent a lotta time with him. I'm thinkin' about our last night in New York, an' how down he was the next day—you know, when we was havin' breakfast with Narvel's folks."

"And . . . ?"

"Well, you was with him the night before that, right? He give you any hint a what was comin'?"

"Are you saying I should have seen it?" E.T.A. says sharply. "Apples has already been kind enough to suggest that. You too now? Anybody else? Why don't you draw up a petition or something—"

"Take it easy, E.T.A.," says Scrappy. "I didn't mean nothin' a the kind."

"I'm sorry I said that, E.T.A.," says Apples. "It was out of line. We're all to blame."

"I was jist wonderin' what he mighta said that night," says Scrappy. "That's all."

"Well, I'll tell you, then, Scrappy. And you just see what you can do with it, since you seem to be running things here. He didn't say a thing. Nothing of consequence was said at all."

Scrappy looks at him a moment. "Well, that's that, I guess."

The door to Grammock's office bursts open and he bustles out, beaming like the sun. When the players see him, their faces go blank with desperate hope. Grammock looks as if he knows something. The reports about Eddie must be mistaken. Maybe Narvel's father got it wrong. Of course!

"Game's over," Grammock announces proudly. "First called game in World Series history. We won it, jist like that. Second happiest day a my fuckin' life. Tomorrow's gonna be my first happiest, if you boys do your job like you're supposed to."

Narvel rises slowly to his feet. Scrappy steps between them and glares at Grammock.

"You got no place here, Grammock," he says. "You better git your ass outta here while you still can."

A weak grin flutters at Grammock's lips. "Shee-it, boys," he drawls. Then, as his eyes move from player to player, his grin disappears and his eyes finally drop to the floor. He turns and walks to the exit.

○ ○ ○

"Hey, Apples. You ever do somethin' ya' know is right, but you still ain't able to say *why* it's right?"

Apples, seated on an ice chest, his long legs sprawled toward the campfire, says, "Sure, Scrappy. Sometimes."

"I'm thinkin' of right now. This here fishin' trip."

"What time is it, Frank?" Buford interjects.

"Six fifty-seven."

"What are you gonna say, Apples?" Scrappy asks. "To the reporters an' the rest of the guys."

Apples scoots the ice chest back a bit from the fire. "I don't know, Scrappy. I guess I'm going to say I wanted some time to think—about Eddie, and about lots of things. I'm going to say this is my way of being with Eddie. If he's going

227

to miss the end, I am too. If people don't understand that, it's just too bad."

"How 'bout you, Bufe?"

"I don't know, Scrappy," he says. "Ellie and me were talking about it this morning, right after the club announced they were going to go ahead with the game, and then when you called with your idea, it just seemed like the natural thing to do. Ellie's behind me all the way." He laughs. "In fact, she wanted to come with us."

"What's your reason, Narv'?"

Narvel smiles. "I was afraid you'd ask," he says. He tells them about the rebellious little trick he pulled in the dugout, and how he took his phone off the hook last night so that his mother couldn't bother him with her questions about where his father might be. He says that he doesn't know what got into him, but that he *does* know he is terrified of facing them.

"Speakin' of facin' people when we git back," says Scrappy, "think of Grammock. I'll bet his guts is oozin' out right about now."

"Seven o'clock," Frank announces. Involuntarily, they sigh.

"How 'bout you, Frank?" Scrappy asks. "Why are you here? Speak up, man. We miss you, kind of."

Frank grins and pokes a long stick at the fire. "Hell, I just wanted to be with you guys."

They look at Jaime, the sixth member of their truant party. He sits beside Frank, looking into the fire, his face glowing in its warmth. He has nothing to say. He has finally determined that something bad has happened to Eddie, but he knows of no connection between that and this trip. He thinks the World Series is over—that for some reason, perhaps a religious holiday he knows nothing about, they played a six-game Series to a tie and will just leave it at that.

"Where's the water supposed to be?" Narvel asks.

"I think it's somewhere over this hill in back of me," says Frank. "Does it matter?" he adds with a laugh.

Apples laughs too, but at something different. "I just figured out why Bubba didn't want to come," he says. "I just remembered a certain lady who he must think is now available to him."

Scrappy gasps. "Poor Jacqui." He shakes his head.

"Too bad about E.T.A.," says Apples. "I never figured him for a coward."

"Apples," says Scrappy, "*you* don't think our jobs are on the line, do you?"

Apples shakes his head. "I see big fines in our futures. That's all."

There is a pause. Narvel says, "Anybody else besides me regret our no-radio rule?"

They all agree that they do.

"There's one in the car," says Frank.

They all say no. No.

"Think the other guys can win it?" asks Narvel.

They discuss it. E.T.A., Bubba, and Grammock's much-despised bench—can they do it?

Apples jumps to his feet. "Well, Frank said it's game time. Let's relax. I'll throw out the first pitch." He opens the ice chest and tosses a can of beer to Narvel, who bobbles it and drops it at his feet. They boo him, and then they all laugh.

○ ○ ○

"Yeah. Grammock was there at Frank's house to meet us. He was staked out all mornin' on the porch. Started to give us a blisterin', but we hooted him down. He said he was gonna break up the club an' trade us all, he was so sick of us, but I jist told him to stick his tallywhacker up his twitchet."

Scrappy's guy laughs heartily. "You've become a real

hell-raiser, Scrappy. Is that when you found out who won the game?"

"No. I found that out earlier. I'll tell ya' about it. When I woke up, I thought I heard cheers, an' I popped my eyes open, but it was still dark, an' the noise I heard was jist crickets. I looked around an' seen that everyone else looked to be all humped up in their sleepin' bags, out for the count. I found my watch draped over the toe of one of my boots—five a.m., it says. I figure the game's gotta be over by now—either that, or they're in the thirty-fifth inning, with Grammock definitely runnin' low on substitutes.

"So I lay back down an' start thinkin' about the stadium, how cold an' empty it must be, an' I think about the field, picturin' papers an' trash blowin' acrost it in the breeze. Then I git to thinkin' 'bout the team, an' how everyone turned out. I think a Apples out there on the mound, an' how much better he is, all on accounta that nice new woman a his. I look into home plate 'n' see Narv' a-squattin' away, an' he ain't no better, far as I can tell, but he's a helluva guy, an' I got hopes for him yet. I go down the line—you know, in my mind—to first base, an' there's E.T.A., a guy who sure has been buzzin' a lot all season, but I can't see that he made any real progress. When ya' think 'bout his initials, it's kinda funny. He ain't *never* gonna arrive, far as I can tell. He spent a lotta time with Eddie, in the end, but it sure don't seem like he done him much good, considerin'. Then I'm on my way to second, only Bubba trips me an' rubs my face in the base path. That's Bubba—no better, no worse. He'll always be the same. Then there's Frank at third. He's tryin'. Honest, he's tryin'. He's still dangerous, a course—show him too much interest an' you can forget the rest a the day. But you can see him fightin' it. You can see the battle bein' fought right there on his face. It really is hard for the poor guy.

"Then, at short, there's me. Hell, you know all about me.

"Then there's the outfield. Good ol' Buford an' his twins.

230

Can't think a Bufe without thinkin' of his twins. In a way, he's kinda like Apples—jist plain lucky, 'cuz both of 'em was picked up by somethin' comin' into their lives from clean outta the blue. Still an' all, ya' make your own breaks, I guess. That's what Grammock always says, an it jist might be the only true thing he ever said too.

"Then there's Eddie in center. Well, my thoughts ain't too clear on Eddie. I figger anyone who ain't killed hisself already can't really understand what Eddie done with his life. Like on our way to the lake, when we drove by the exit off the highway that he musta took to git to the town where he dropped Tina off, an' to git to that field where he killed his-self, we all went silent an' didn't know *what* the hell to say. I still don't. I sure do feel sorry for that Tina, though. An' Jacqui too. I ain't no expert on the subject, but if ya' ask me, I think she loved him all along, only that's somethin' he could jist never see. Or maybe he could see it but it didn't mean nothin' to him.

"Well, then there's Jaime in right field. Ain't much to say 'bout Jaime. He's still a loner. Fact is, we woulda plumb forgot to take him with us if it hadn't a been for Frank. Seems like Frank's got a new friend there. They talked all the way to the lake—sort of. I guess Frank kinda carried the conversation, with Jaime jist laughin' now an' then, or throwin' in somethin' like 'Oh, mon,' like he says it, ya' know, 'Oh, mon,' or 'Sheet, mon,' an' then Frank'd come right back at him with the same point, an' with lots 'n' lots of examples to back it up too."

"It's time."

"Well, lemme answer your question, for Christ's sake."

His guy laughs. "You *are* a hell-raiser. No, I'm afraid it's time, Scrappy."

"Jist wait, now. So, I'm layin' there thinkin' 'bout the team, an' I git to itchin' 'bout the game. I think of Frank's car, an' how it's got a radio in it, so I crawl outta my sleepin' bag an' whip my clothes on fast, only when I git to the car, it's all locked up, an' I don't wanna wake Frank up for the keys. Then I remember seein' a bait shop 'bout a mile down the road, an' I git to thinkin' how there jist might be a newspaper stand there. I check my pockets for change, an' then I set out for it, stumblin' along the road in the dark. It's all clouded up, an' it starts to thunderin' in the distance, an' I think, Hell, I'm gonna git drenched sure an' there ain't gonna be no newspaper there neither. Then, as I'm walkin' along, I git to feelin' a little bit guilty 'bout the fishin' trip, not on accounta Grammock, not on your life, but on accounta how you could say we turned chicken at the end. You could say we was afraid a losin' the big one, afraid a losin' everything we'd gained in this hell of a season if we went an' lost that damned seventh game. Then I says to myself, 'Hell, Scrappy, look at it this way—you an' the guys jist managed to come up with one more way to handle this shit. How much can a poor guy be expected to take, after all?' I says to myself, 'Relax, Scrappy. Sometimes it's okay to go fishin'.'

"Then, up ahead in the road there, I see someone comin'. For a second, I think it's Grammock, ya' know, heftin' a tire iron or somethin' an' huntin' for me. But it turns out to be good ol' Apples, an' he's holdin' somethin' white, an' what he's holdin' turns out to be a newspaper. He'd beat me to it.

"Soon as he sees me, he goes all loose, like he does, ya' know, an' he starts to chucklin'. When I git close to him, he says, 'It's truer than it ever was, Scrappy. We don't deserve to win, but one way or 'nother we sure do.' Then he throws back his head, an' he jist fills that mean ol' dark sky with the sound of his laughin'.'"